I and Claudie

I and Claudie

Dillon Anderson

Foreword by A. C. Greene

Texas Tech University Press

I and Claudie is reproduced from a 1951 *An Atlantic Monthly Press Book,* Little, Brown and Company edition copy and is published as part of the special series Double Mountain Books—Classic Reissues of the American West.

The paper used in this book meets the minimum requirements of ANSI/NISO Z39.48-1992 (R1997). ♾

Cover design by Tamara Kruciak

Library of Congress Cataloging-in-Publication Data
Anderson, Dillon, 1906–1974.
I and Claudie / by Dillon Anderson ; new foreword by A.C. Greene.
p. cm. — (Double mountain books—classic reissues of the American West)
ISBN 0-89672-429-8 (paper : acid-free)
1. Texas—Social life and customs—Fiction. 2. Rogues and vagabonds—Texas—Fiction. 3. Male friendship—Texas—Fiction. 4. Humorous stories, American. I. Title. II. Series.

PS 3551.N34558 I15 2000
813'.54—dc21 99-055783

00 01 02 03 04 05 06 07 08 / 9 8 7 6 5 4 3 2 1

Texas Tech University Press
Box 41037
Lubbock, Texas 79409-1037 USA
1-800-832-4042
ttup@ttu.edu Http://www.ttup.ttu.edu

Foreword

I was seated recently at an outdoor cafe with Christopher, an archivist friend, discussing a dinner we had attended that included among its guests three notable Texas storytellers. One after another they provided personal experiences, each tale eliciting another, then another. It had been a hilarious evening, everyone reluctant to break up the gathering.

"What makes a good storyteller?" Chris asked, as we tried to consume our Texas pecan pie as decorously as possible. After affecting a moment of thought, I offered a theory, hoping not to sound pompous. "A good storyteller," I said, "never lets himself be the obvious winner." I quickly added, "It applies to a woman, too. I know a charming wife who can convulse you with laughter while she keeps a straight face relating her misadventures."

Although I hesitate to offer this as a maxim for daily life, it works well for literary storytelling. Take Dillon Anderson's *I and Claudie.* Clint Hightower, the I of the title, often rescues Claudie Hughes from his six-foot-six clumsy errors—but Claudie is not always wrong, and Clint is not always right.

Clint and Claudie, as you will discover, are a pair of rogues, genially outsmarting bankers, politicians, Texas oilmen, and other targets, all of whom are quite capable of taking care of themselves when it comes to chicanery. But about as often as they win, Clint and Claudie have to hightail it out of town, sometimes victims of their own cleverness, sometimes unable to overcome their softheartedness. They operate mainly in East Texas, after having had to leave New Orleans in a hurry. East Texas, in the oil boom atmosphere of the time, is tailor-made for their scams—or for them to get scammed themselves. They are rascals, but not avaricious rascals. Anderson, their creator, says of them, "The experiences of *I and Claudie* are in no sense autobiographical, but sometimes I am sorry they are not."

Dillon Anderson was a partner in the famed Houston firm of Baker-Botts, and lawyers are usually full of stories. He was a director of more corporations, clubs, and national associations than one book jacket can hold. He was almost elegant in his dress—when I met him he was wearing a tattersall vest with carefully coordinated coat, trousers, and tie. In horn-rimmed glasses, he had a scholarly look. Although his law career was highly successful, he seemed increasingly to enjoy his literary career, and one wishes he could have shucked some of his memberships and done more writing. Texas is a strong cultural background for his work: Clint and Claudie could scarcely have operated in equal fashion in another state.

Anderson came late to his literary life. Born 1906 in McKinney, he graduated from Yale Law School in 1929. He became a partner in Baker, Botts, Andrew and Shepherd in 1942. A colonel in World War II, Anderson began writing in 1943 after Edward Weeks, the longtime editor of *Atlantic Monthly* magazine, asked him to submit a story. Although the story was accepted, Weeks made Anderson rewrite it several times. The *I and Claudie* stories initially appeared in that magazine, where I encountered the first story in 1951.

I included *I and Claudie* in my 1998 book, *The 50+ Best Books on Texas* as well as in its earlier edition. There has been criticism that Texas, and chicanery, have changed since *I and Claudie* first appeared and that their adventures are no longer valid. This is nonsense. They may carry important corporate titles, wear different clothes and drive different cars—Clint and Claudie had a disreputable jalopy—but hustlers never change. The Texas confidence man may operate on a higher financial plane, juggling millions via stock schemes, cooked books, insider trading, and spurious lawsuits, but Clint and Claudie would be right at home today, wearing imported tailoring and driving Lincolns, secure in the knowledge that greedy hearts are unchanging.

Texas and the grifters may or may not have altered since the first publication of *I and Claudie,* but, sadly, we now have no Dillon Anderson to record their exploits for us with charming storytelling.

A. C. Greene
Salado, 1999

TO LENA

Contents

But for

Ted Weeks, Bobby Cutler and Dudley Cloud and their encouragement in the early stages of this book;

Ammi Cutter, who blew up big squalls several times when the voyage of Clint and Claudie was utterly becalmed;

The kind forbearance of my Mother and Father, who never quite approved of my characters;

The Michauxes, Wrays, Hutchesons and Blaffers, who gave thoughtful help in various ways;

The passenger trains, whereon, for the most part, the work was done;

and

Sergeant Maude Tomlinson, late of the U.S. Army, whose typing made it first readable;

I and Claudie would never have left New Orleans.

I
The Lavaliere

OUTSIDE Louis & Pierre's Restaurant the New Orleans night was damp and murky. The place inside was plumb empty, except for my table and one close by mine where a frizzly-haired little brunette with round black eyes and full wet lips was sitting very close to a big fellow with a long horse-type face and a heavy bass voice. The girl was smoking a cigarette in a very fancy way, and I watched her out of the corner of my eye. Each puff she handled with as much care and pride as if she'd been playing a very classical piece of music on a big harp.

From their glances my way it seemed they must have been talking about me. Then I saw the little brunette nudge her man a couple of times, and he spoke up and asked me, out loud, if I couldn't eat them pretzels without making so much noise. I didn't feel a bit like being pushed around, so I only looked down and gnawed away a little harder on a nice crisp pretzel. But when I looked up, the horse-faced fellow was standing by my table, while the girl looked sideways toward us with a light pout on her face.

"What's that you said?" he asked me, and I looked him up and down from head to foot. He was about six and a half feet tall, if he was anything, and he looked nearly that broad across the shoulders.

"Nothing at all," I answered, and he turned back to the

little brunette and spoke. "The man says he didn't say nothing, Pet."

At this she turned her pert little nose high in the air and looked the other direction in a very haughty way. That left the big fellow just standing there without much to say or do or anywhere much to go. After a few minutes of this, it seemed time for somebody to make a move, so I took another bite off my pretzel, looked up at him and said, "Excuse me, mister, but I don't believe I and you have met socially."

This made a big hit with the little brunette, and she laughed right out loud, but in the long run it was a bad thing. A look like bad-weather-on-the-way came across the big guy's face as he kept standing there, staring down at me. Pretty soon I'd had about all of this I could use, so I got up and said, in a low voice, "Run on back now and sit down, mister. You're away off base, but I don't think it's your fault."

It wasn't low enough, though; she heard me and spoke up hurtlike: "He says I'm to blame, honey. Are you going to take that?" Then he took a deep breath, bit down on his lower lip and swung on me. I dodged him, and it was a dandy thing that I did. I had been kicked once by a mule that wasn't much bigger than he was, and my joints were still a little loose from it. Off balance, he reeled and knocked my bottle of beer off the table. Then he came at me again, and I looked toward the waiter that had just come running through the swinging door from the kitchen. But he stopped too far away to do me any good and stood there like a man nailed to the floor. The big fellow swung once more, and I only partly dodged him this time, but as he moved in on me he stepped into my beer on the floor. He slipped and went down; his head caught the corner of my table, and he went out as cold as a frostbit cucumber.

The little brunette came in a run. She bent over him for a minute and pouted a little whimper; then she had me by the arm in a jiffy. She put her big, wide eyes on me and said she'd never seen such a clumsy lug in all her life as the big guy was. After checking again and seeing that the big guy was only a little stunned, she said she wanted to get out of there before the law came; she wondered if I would take her home. I couldn't see any percentage in staying around any longer, so I left with her.

It wasn't far, she said; and since the mist had let up, we walked. On the way she told me she was fed up with the big fellow anyway. She said his name was Claudie Hughes, and of all the dumb hicks she'd ever known, Claudie was the dumbest. She finished with, "I'm a lady that's really had enough of that country clown."

"I didn't get your name," I said.

"Evangeline La Farge; that's my stage name."

"I'm a man that can go for actresses," I told her.

Evangeline told me as we walked on that she lived with her aunt, Mrs. Blossom Nettle, and pretty soon we got there. It was a great big old three-story house with shutters and a lot of frilly ironwork around the windows, and before we went in the door Evangeline said she already liked me better than she did Claudie; couldn't I come in for a few minutes? I told her sure I could, so in we went.

The front hall was a little dark, but about halfway down it Evangeline opened a door, and the minute she did, I smelled the most beautiful perfume I'd ever smelled in all my life — strong too. The door opened into a parlor that was all lit up. It was elegant. Just inside there was a lion-skin rug with the lion's head still on it — sharp teeth showing and all. Big plushy chairs and sofas were all about. Two cut-glass vases on a round table were full of blue and yellow flowers. On the walls there were some calendars decorated with pink women wearing low-necked dresses and big hats, and one whole side of the parlor was hung in dark green curtains.

I was standing there by Evangeline, facing the lion's head and taking in the sight and the smell, when a tall gray-haired woman in a purple dress came from behind the curtains. She sized me up and said, "Come in, Evangeline; who's your handsome friend?" Just like that! I thought I had never seen such hospitality before anywhere in the whole South.

Evangeline turned to me and said, "You tell her," so I spoke right up: "Hightower is the name; Clint Hightower."

"You can call me Aunty Blossom, the same that Evangeline does," the lady in purple said with a big smile, and I noticed the wrinkles around her eyes and mouth all fitted in best when she smiled. She told me to sit right down, and when I sat, Evangeline did too. There by my side on the big plushy sofa.

Aunty Blossom pulled a green tassel at the end of a long cord that hung from the ceiling, and a heavy-set colored woman tiptoed into the room from behind the curtain and said, "Yes, ma'am."

"A little sherry, please, Anna Belle," Aunty Blossom said, and away the colored woman went and came back with little glasses on a big tray. As we drank the sherry, Aunty Blossom walked the floor and talked — very cordial talk, too. She started off by saying that she did not know anyone anywhere that was a better judge of human nature than she was. Then, Aunty Blossom went on to say that she'd taken a liking to me from the very first. Next she spoke of Evangeline; she thought Evangeline was getting prettier all the time and her personality was getting better too; she despised to see Evangeline going about with anything but first-class people.

I said I could see how she felt about that.

"I can tell a real gent from a phony before he ever leaves this room," she went on. "I don't mean just moneyed men either. Some of the biggest bums I've ever known threw money around like it grew on trees. Not that I mind money, you understand? I just don't let it turn my head, and clothes don't tell it all either."

I was awful glad when she said what she did about clothes because the New Orleans weather had been very disagreeable, and I'd slept in mine the past two nights.

Aunty Blossom drained her glass, walked over to the sofa where I was sitting by Evangeline, and said, "What's your line, Mr. Hightower?" She asked it fast.

"I'm an inventor," I told her.

"I knew it," she said. "I can tell a gentleman of class any time I see him." She nodded her head at Evangeline, then she turned to me and said: "Tell me what you've invented today, Mr. Hightower."

"Nothing today, Aunty Blossom. You see it takes a long time to invent something, and a longer time than that to get the patent to pending," I explained.

"Fact is," she went on, as she put one foot on the rung of a chair and leveled a very close look on me, "you haven't ever got one to pending yet, have you?"

"Not exactly," I admitted.

"Aren't you the fellow that's been barking up customers

down on Canal Street this past week for the B.A.B. Sightseeing Tours?" she asked.

"I'm the fellow," I stated.

"Excuse me," she said as she turned to go, "I've some little errands to run upstairs, so I'll leave you young people here to enjoy yourselves." I didn't much mind when she did go since she was beginning to sound a little sarcastic I thought.

Then a very strange thing took place. Aunty Blossom had no sooner gone behind the curtains than Evangeline put out her cigarette and threw both arms around my neck. Then she kissed me. Without saying a word, I mean. It went on and on, and when she quit I got up and reached for my hat. I'd sparked around with girls a good deal before, and I knew from the way Evangeline kissed me she had already put on too much mileage for the likes of Clint Hightower. I didn't have any doubt about it either.

"I've got to go, Evangeline; I just remembered something," I told her and left her standing there in the parlor beside the lion skin.

Something drew me, I hardly knew what, straight back to Louis & Pierre's, and when I got there I saw Claudie Hughes sitting at a table all by himself and still looking a little stunned. The lump on his temple where he'd hit the table was storm-cloud blue and as big as a goose egg. I walked over to where he was sitting and said: "I ain't mad at anybody. Let's I and you have a beer, Claudie."

He said he could use a drink, he guessed, but where did I get that wallop? I ordered two beers and a fresh batch of pretzels, and sort of offhandlike I said, "Oh, it's all a matter of balance. Have a pretzel, Claudie." Then Claudie said, "Where's my girl?"

"I took her home," I told him. "I was afraid the cops might come, and I knew you wouldn't want a sweet girl like that being driven off in any Black Maria."

A nice, friendly look drifted all the way down Claudie's long face. He said he was badly in love with Evangeline and the last thing he wanted to do was to get her into any trouble. Then he reached in his pocket and pulled out a tissue paper package and unwrapped it to show me what was inside. It was a big blood-red stone hooked onto a little gold chain about long enough to go around a woman's neck. Claudie grinned a shy, country grin and said, "Evangeline give it to me to prove that she loves me too. It was her grandma's lavaliere, when her grandma was a duchess back in Paris France."

I looked the lavaliere over. The little chain was already turning green in places, and from a quick glance at the stone I could tell that there was a better grade of glass in the bottles we were drinking beer out of. But I didn't have the heart to say anything except, "I'll bet you're real proud of that, brother."

He said, "I shore am," then he wrapped it back up.

"How long have you known this Evangeline?" I asked him, feeling my way.

"Nearly a month," he answered. "That's long enough before askin' her to marry, ain't it?"

"Yes," I told him. "I guess that's long enough. Have you got a job so you can keep her up?"

"No, but she's gonna help me get one," he said. "Purty soon too; I've 'bout run out of money."

Claudie bought the next round of beers and told me all about himself. He had a room over on Rampart Street, he said; he had been in town about a month; first time he'd ever been out of the Alabama wire grass country where he grew up. He'd heired a gold watch and five hundred dollars from a dead uncle; he'd given the watch to Evangeline and spent nearly all of the money courting her. His story put me in mind of the one about the prodigal son, and I thought about the awful cleaning he got before he came to himself and went back home.

After a while we cleared out of Louis & Pierre's, and Claudie told me good-by. "No hard feelings," he said. "No hard feelings," I told him; then I got him to give me the address on Rampart Street where he was staying, since by this time I had me a program all worked up.

Next morning I went to a Woolworth's store and bought some pink stationery and a dime's worth of the strongest perfume they had to sprinkle over it. Then I went to the post office and wrote Claudie a note in a fine, neat little backhand. It read:

> DEAR CLAUDIE:
> You horrible creature, getting into brawls with nice people in public places. If you ever come near me again, I will call the police. I mean it, you big, clumsy brute. Farewell forever.
>
> EVANGELINE

I mailed the letter and then went straight over to Aunty Blossom's house. Evangeline was there, but she was still asleep, so I had the colored woman wake her up and told her that if Claudie came around that day, she'd better run him off. Aunty Blossom came in and asked why, so I told her: "He's got a little touch of bubonic plague, and that's pretty catching, sister. He's also about broke."

As I walked away, I said to myself, "Clint," I said, "you

haven't put any money in the bank today, but maybe you have rung up a few extra stars for your crown."

2

It was nearly noon when I got around to the B.A.B. Sightseeing Tours stand and found they had hired somebody else to take my place. I told them what they could do with their corny job and went over on Conti Street to look in on Jules Rabinowitz, a friend of mine who was a seer. Jules gave the tea leaves a rundown on me for fifty cents — the same Persian Prophet reading that cost members of the ordinary public a dollar. He pointed out that a man with my brains needed an assistant. He also predicted a fine future for me in the west.

"You mean Texas, Jules?" I asked him.

"That's the way the leaves look to me," he answered.

A couple of nights later I drifted in to Louis & Pierre's, and there was Claudie. He was sitting over in a corner behind some green plants in blue pots, and he was low. His jaw hung down almost to the table, and his eyes looked like dried prunes. I went right over and said: "Howdy, Claudie. Let's I and you have some beer and pretzels."

First he acted as though I might have spoken in an unknown tongue; then he said, "I don't keer if I do or not," so I ordered the drinks.

"What the hell's the matter, Claudie?" I asked him. "You look a little bilious to me. Reckon you might need a course of strong medicine of some kind?"

He shook his head and said not unless it was strong enough to kill him.

"Come on, Claudie; come on," I told him. "It can't be that bad."

"It couldn't be no worse," he said as his lips trembled and his jaw looked like it might come unhinged. He took the pink letter out and showed it to me. The perfume was still so strong on it that I knew I'd got my money's worth. I read the letter with a straight face, then I said, "I wouldn't give up, Claudie; women don't always mean it when they say good-by. You better go and tell Evangeline you're sorry."

"I went by Evangeline's house and tried," Claudie allowed, "but she throwed a telephone book at me, and Aunty Blossom got out a butcher knife when I tried to argue. They didn't even give me a chance to give Evangeline back the lavaliere."

"Well," I admitted, "a woman with a butcher knife can do a lot of damage."

"I've 'bout ruined my whole life, I reckon; and it's all my fault," Claudie said and heaved a sigh that was like a cold night wind blowing through dead trees.

"Now you listen to me, Claudie," I said. "Did it ever occur to you that there are lots of full-grown people living all over this great big world — millions of people — and about half of them are women? That ought to be enough to keep a man from getting himself upset over any one woman."

If Claudie heard me, he didn't show it. He unwrapped the lavaliere, put it on the table and stared at it while he drank the beer. I ordered another round, then a third one, and finally Claudie's eyes at least began to look like something a body could see out of. I remembered what Jules Rabinowitz had told me about an assistant, so I said:

"How'd you like to go to work for me, Claudie? I've got an old Ford that will still run, and I'm about ready to travel."

"You haven't told me what you do," Claudie allowed.

"I have ideas," I explained. "I am the mental type, and I can use an assistant. What can you do?"

"I can farm, and I can sing bass," he said.

"Well," I told him, "you can take potluck with me if you want to."

"When do we leave?" was all the rest that he wanted to know.

The next morning when I went by the room on Rampart Street Claudie was ready. He had a big old wicker suitcase and a black umbrella. He wanted to buy some gasoline for the car, he said. I told him no, he needn't, but he said he'd feel better if I'd let him. I agreed, but when he went to pay the filling station man, it turned out Claudie was on his uppers; he didn't have enough money.

Claudie wanted to head straight for Texas. He started telling me about an uncle of his that went out there and got himself all prominent and involved in religion and politics.

"We'll go to Texas, Claudie," I told him as we drove north toward Baton Rouge. "But let's not get ourselves in any hurry about it. You see, I know quite a lot about it from tales I've heard ever since I was a little shaver. Out there it's a great deal like it was in the Old Testament stories. They haven't all learned to love new neighbors yet in Texas; they don't always turn the other cheek. By the way, what ever happened to that uncle of yours that went to Texas?"

"He got himself killed there," Claudie stated.

"That's what I mean," I said. "Now be quiet, Claudie, and give me a little time to think."

In Baton Rouge we didn't have it so good until a dog and pony show came to town. They had a she-kangaroo named Gloria that could box, and when they offered to pay ten dollars a round for anybody who could stay in the ring with her, I signed Claudie up. He stayed three rounds, but Gloria hit him so hard with her tail at the end of the third that his shoes flew off, and he quit. It was enough though, I calculated, to take his mind off of Evangeline for a while.

I figured it might help cure Claudie's broken heart when I got him in next with the theatrical set in Baton Rouge. There was a ballet company at the opera house there, and they took us on to carry spears in the shows and move scenery between the acts. They loved us, and the night the eunuch in *Scheherazade* got himself so drunk, we put those baggy pants on Claudie, and he played the part for an extra dollar. They couldn't pay us off at the end of the week's run in Baton Rouge, so we had to go on with them to Memphis and then to Chattanooga before we got our money. But we quit as soon as we got even with them, since Claudie said he did not wish to be any part of an outfit where the men were prettier than the women.

By this time the theater was in our blood, though, and we joined up next with a stock company in Atlanta. Claudie handled their wardrobe trunks, and I played spare parts. When we went with them to Mobile, I and Claudie carried out the dead Hamlet. That, I expect, was the best thing we ever did.

Later on, in Cincinnati, where we played *Uncle Tom's Cabin,* Claudie stood back of the stage and pulled the wire that lifted Little Eva up to heaven. Claudie used to cry when he did this part, and once I thought he was so good that I bragged on him. "A man is either born to the theater or not," I said. "You've got real talent, Claudie."

"Eva is short for Evangeline," Claudie answered.

The nearest I saw Claudie to cured from the blue funk that New Orleans woman gave him was early the next summer in Jackson, Mississippi, after a very rough winter when we had done a little of everything. I got him a job there taking the place of one of the Budweiser men who got sick. Claudie ate it up, driving those six big Clydesdale horses to the rubber-tired wagon full of beer in barrels.

But it seemed that nothing was ever going to make Claudie really happy. He was lugging a badly busted heart around, and every time he'd sit down and turn his mind loose, it would stray back to New Orleans and Evangeline La Farge. He still figured it was all his fault that he'd lost her. He'd take out the lavaliere and suffer over it until sometimes I'd nearly bust, I wanted so much to tell him the truth. But the right time to tell him didn't seem to come around, somehow.

After the regular Budweiser man got well we sold lightning rods for a while; then we drifted back down to Baton Rouge. We had pretty hard times there until I ran across my old friend Jules Rabinowitz, the Persian Prophet from New Orleans. Jules was in clover with a state-wide convention of schoolteachers going on, and I touched him for five dollars. But there was a mean sting that went with it; Jules told us that a while back the law had come to his place in New Orleans looking for me and Claudie — summonses and everything ready to serve on us, he said.

"What for, Jules? What have we done?" I asked him.

"The law didn't tell me that," he answered. "But there were three of them, and they didn't want to go away until they got a line on you two. Big mean-looking cops, too."

"What did you tell them?" I asked.

"I finally had to tell them you'd gone to Baton Rouge in order to get rid of them," he said.

"Claudie," I spoke to him as soon as we got out of Jules's earshot, "the time has now come for us to go to Texas."

3

We left Baton Rouge the next morning at daylight and headed west across Louisiana. As soon as we crossed into Texas at Orange the rain started, and it rained bucketfuls on us all the way to Beaumont. We got there about dark with no more money than we needed to get ourselves some hamburgers and a place to sleep down on Pearl Street.

Next morning I found a fellow that staked us to a bite of breakfast for Claudie's umbrella; then I went out scouting around to find something for Claudie to do. I figured I'd get him a job first, then I could find myself a position without having to do it under so much pressure. But it rained a frog strangler all day, and we drew a complete blank, except Claudie helped the man clean up the rooming house attic for one more night's lodging for us.

That night we were sitting on the cots in our room drinking some ice water Claudie had brought up when he said, "Clint, you don't look so good; you must be awful hungry. I seen a place across the street where they have fried fish and cornbread on a blue plate for a quarter."

"Don't mention such tnings, Claudie," I told him. "Of course I'm hungry, but you know we're plumb out of money."

"There's a pawnshop in this block," he said. "We could put the lavaliere in hock, and when we get us some jobs here, we can get it back."

We'd been in some pretty close places during the winter, but this was the first time he'd suggested this. I knew it was no time for Claudie to learn the truth about the lavaliere — on an empty stomach and all — so I said, "I don't believe I would."

It turned out, though, that nothing would satisfy Claudie but he should go and hock the lavaliere, and he wanted me to go along. He said he believed I could make a better trade.

"O.K.," I finally told him, "but it's a mistake, Claudie."

The fat pawnbroker with the bristly beard put a little glass up to his eye and took one fast look at the lavaliere before he threw it back on the counter and said, "French jewelry, huh? Go 'way before I call the cops." We both must have jumped when he mentioned the cops so soon after what Jules Rabinowitz had told us.

"What's the matter? What've we done?" Claudie asked him. Poor Claudie, I thought; here it comes.

"You would rob an old man?" the pawnbroker said. "This is trash; it is not worth one cent. Get out."

Claudie turned to me and said, "You talk to him, Clint. I can't do nothing with him."

"The man is right," I told Claudie. "It ain't no good. It's bogus." Then the time had come, I figured, to let him have it. "Claudie," I said, "you know I wouldn't lie to you — at least you ought to know I wouldn't. It was a good thing when you lost Evangeline. She was not a very sincere girl."

This straightened him up. He put fighting eyes on me, and I looked right back at him. It was as good a way to look as any, I figured, for a man that is about to get knocked down anyhow. But then Claudie looked down; he soaked up the whole idea without a word, and his big frame seemed to sag all over. He wrapped the lavaliere back up in the tissue paper, and we went out into the rain that was still pouring down on Pearl Street.

Next day the weather faired off, and I knew I'd find something. Hell, I had to; the ox was in the ditch. I put on the only good suit I had and went out and rustled around until I landed us jobs with a Mr. Exitonly who ran a high-class detective agency. He needed two plain-clothes men for a swell blowout that was being thrown that night by a big, rich oil man named Ellington Bozarth. I convinced Mr. Exitonly that I and Claudie had the experience to handle it. All we had to do to earn five dollars apiece was dress up, go to the party at the Beaumont Hotel and keep an eye on the guests' wraps and jewels.

"If anything happens, you can call the city police officers," Mr. Exitonly said. "They'll be right outside."

"We don't need 'em," I told him; but what he said bothered me some, since I knew we could not stand any truck with cops at this time. On the other hand, we'd had no food since breakfast the day before, and we had to eat, cops or no cops.

That night we went down and put on the dress suits Mr. Exitonly rented for us — white ties, white vests, silk lapels on frock coats built like claw hammers in the back. Claudie said he'd never expected to be dressed that well but once — when they put him in the casket. The shoes they had for

Claudie were much too little, but he fought his way into them somehow.

I tried to talk Mr. Exitonly into a little advance, but it wouldn't work; and I didn't think I ought to tell him we wanted it for food. It wouldn't have been dignified.

It was nearly ten o'clock when we got up to the ballroom at the Beaumont Hotel, but still nobody was there except a lot of hotel flunkies and Mr. Exitonly. He said we looked fine and told us where we were to stand. My place was by a potted palm near the entrance, and Claudie's place was at the far end of the room near the orchestra stand.

That ballroom was enough to make a man forget what a dingy, grubby world this one can be at times. It had everything: two big cut-glass chandeliers the size of cotton bales hanging from the ceiling; blue and red curtains with woven-in flowers along the walls; columns, big around as smokestacks, at each side of the room; and the floor all smooth, polished and shining. The whole layout was so damn classy that it almost made me feel like a tramp — dressed up as I was.

There was a scent in the air that smelled sweeter than the perfume back in Aunty Blossom's parlor, so I and Claudie followed it over to one side of the room where the curtains were. We pulled them apart to see what was behind, and Jehoshaphat! There was a sight! A table that looked half a block long was all covered with a white spread. Right in the middle of it was a goose all carved out of ice and as big as an ostrich. Waiters, wearing sprucier clothes than ours by a damn sight, were piling fancy food on a table — food in juicy little bites piled up on big plates; sea food and dry land food; food of all shapes and colors; foreign food and local food; several turkeys with slices of nothing but white meat cut off and piled up on the side of the plates. A fellow wearing a clean jacket and a tall white cap was pouring hot gravy over a knee-high roast. We had to leave that part of the ballroom to get any peace of mind at all.

At ten o'clock sharp the orchestra people — all eighteen of them — were in their places, tuning up their horns and fiddles. Then Mr. Exitonly came into the ballroom with a middle-aged fellow that looked very prosperous and well-fed. His hair was gray at the temples, and he had a very clean mustache that was gray too. Mr. Exitonly called us over and told us it was Mr. Ellington Bozarth, the man that was throwing the party; then he said it was about time we took our places. Claudie worked his way to the far end of the room by the orchestra, but by that time his feet must have been killing him. He walked like a man pulling a plow. I stepped back to my place, close by the entrance. Then Mr. Bozarth went to the door and said, "Come on in, honey," and she came in.

"No, Clint," I said to myself; "it can't be," but it was. I mean it was Evangeline La Farge, and now she was a blonde.

Before she could see me I ducked behind the potted palm and studied her. She looked fresh out of a bandbox. Her hair was done in rolls and curls piled on her head higher than the sliced turkey was on those plates. Her dress didn't start at her shoulders like women's dresses usually do — it started just in time. It was black and covered with glassy spangles that glittered as she walked like a million lightning bugs on a dark night. She had a diamond about the size of a domino in the ring on her left hand, and it twinkled and sparkled in the bright lights. She talked with a peculiar new accent; kept saying *ze* for "the" and *eet* for "it"; made me wonder where the hell Evangeline had been since I'd seen her last.

Then the guests started coming; guests with clean, well-scrubbed looks and dressed right to the hilt. Mr. Bozarth and Evangeline stood by the door, and the people marched by them. I could hear parts of what they were saying, and finally I got the whole pitch. Mr. Bozarth and Evangeline were pretty freshly married, and when he didn't call her "honey," he called her Yvette. She was from the French nobility, and that was why she had so much trouble speaking plain English. Mr. Bozarth had married her somewhere up in Canada, and the blowout was thrown so his Beaumont friends could meet his new wife.

As the room filled, somebody pulled the curtains back on both sides. Over on my left I saw that long table with the big ice goose and the mountain of grub. They'd put a lot more sweet-smelling victuals on it, though, since we'd seen it last. On the other side were two big bars with two bartenders at each one. The guests all went rushing over to the bars and left that food exposed there. The orchestra was playing for all it was worth, and pretty soon people started dancing. They danced and drank, and for what seemed a lot longer than it was, I and Claudie were the only ones that paid the food any mind at all. But there wasn't any way we could do anything but look; that was the awful part.

I stayed behind the palm all the time, but once when I leaned out to get a better view of the roast beef, Evangeline turned and saw me. When our eyes met, hers batted a couple of times and the leaders in her neck tightened up; then she set her jaw and turned away. Whatever it was I had done to her, I hadn't meant to, and I was almost sorry I had.

It must have been midnight or later, after all the guests

had come in, that Mr. Bozarth took Evangeline out on the floor to dance, and I lost them in the crowd. Not long after that I looked and saw that Claudie was gone from his stand by the orchestra. I looked everywhere for him, and I supposed he must have gone somewhere to give his feet a rest from those little shoes. Then I saw him. He was standing by the bar with a tall dark drink in his hand, watching the dancers. He turned the glass up and drained it at one swig. I knew he must have seen Evangeline, and I knew it wouldn't do for him to drink with no food to speak of in his system. I could see us getting fired without a nickel's pay, so I moved fast — but, as it turned out, it wasn't fast enough. By the time I got to the bar, Claudie was gone, and about this time I noticed that the orchestra had stopped playing. The people stopped dancing, and the drummer started beating his cymbals together. When all the noises had died down, the orchestra leader walked out on the floor and said, "Attention, everybody!" Then I saw that Claudie was right up there by him, and not five feet away Mr. Bozarth and Evangeline stood where they had been dancing when the music stopped.

The orchestra leader turned to Claudie and nodded, so everybody looked at him. Claudie took a deep breath and stood up straight like a man that is about ready to lead a lodge parade. He pulled the lavaliere out of his pocket, held it up between his thumb and big finger, and said, "Here's some jewelry that belongs to somebody."

He spoke in a brand-new voice for Claudie, and his words blotted out all the silence in the room. That lavaliere really looked like mud there in such a scrumptious ballroom with all the glitter and sparkle of bright lights and real diamonds everywhere. I moved a little so I could see Evangeline, and she couldn't have looked worse if she'd been Lot's wife, the day she got turned into salt. Claudie stood there and looked right at her until things got so quiet you could hear the auto horns honking outside on the street.

Claudie held her with his eyes; he was not about to let her go; nor could she escape. Finally, Evangeline slipped her hand from the crook of Mr. Bozarth's arm. She sidled away without looking at him and walked toward Claudie, and as she came up face to face with him, he seemed to get bigger while she shrank. Her lips that had looked so wet and juicy before now looked dry as the leaves of an old Bible. Claudie bowed and scraped; then he reached over her head and fastened the little chain around her neck. As he straightened back up, I thought Claudie was as fine a figure of a man as I'd ever seen.

The orchestra struck up a tune, and the dance went on as Evangeline hurried over to a door marked LADIES POWDER ROOM. Mr. Bozarth got me and Claudie together on one side and thanked us for being on the job. He pointed to the half-acre of grub on the long table and said: "There's a little boofay snack over there. Wouldn't you fellows care for some?"

"Mr. Bozarth," I said, "I would care for some."

"How about you?" he asked Claudie.

"He will too," I spoke for Claudie. "There isn't nothing bothering my assistant now that a nice boofay snack will not cure."

I I
The Receiver

IT WAS ONLY A COUPLE OF DAYS after I and Claudie got our pay for the plain-clothes job that we ran low on money again. The five dollars apiece that Mr. Exitonly had agreed to pay us would have gone a lot further if he hadn't deducted rent of three dollars apiece for the fine clothes we wore on the job. We were at Opal's Beaumont Star Café eating up the last of the Exitonly pay when I noticed that Claudie began to look awful blue and bothered about something. "Claudie," I said, "I never have run down the zodiac on you, but I believe you must have been born under a worry star."

"I can't help it, Clint," he answered. "Ever since Jules Rabinowitz told us the law was looking for us in New Orleans I've been aworrying. Reckon we ought to go back and give up?"

"Give up?" I asked. "What for? I can't remember doing anything in New Orleans that I'm downright ashamed of, Claudie. Another thing: we're in pretty good company in Texas. We've moved in a fine old Southern groove. According to what my grandma used to tell me there were family Bibles all over Alabama, Mississippi and Louisiana where the records were never made out on people after the part showing they were born. A lot of family lines ended back there with G. T."

"What's that mean?" Claudie wanted to know.

"That stands for 'gone to Texas'; it also stands for 'got in trouble,' and Grandma always said that it often meant both. But out here a lot of those same names are carved on statues in public parks and on courthouse lawns."

"Well," Claudie said — and I could tell he hadn't been following me at all — "I don't know why the law would be looking for us if we hadn't done nothing wrong."

"Claudie," I went on, "did you ever think about the good side of having the law after you?"

He said he sure hadn't, so I explained: "Well, it's like having a stout, strict conscience all geared up and working for you every day of your life; makes you think over every wicked thing you ever did and wonder which one was against the law; almost makes you wish you'd never done anything wrong in your whole life. It also gives you a good day-to-day reason for steering clear of the law. Don't you see, Claudie? It can be a dandy influence all around."

Claudie just sat there and tried to study these things out, as he poured another cup of coffee in his saucer and blew on it.

After breakfast we drove down to Anahuac, where I got Claudie a job in the oil fields. Then I found there was a fine murder case being tried in Liberty, so I went up there every day until it was over. At night I'd go back to Anahuac and tell Claudie all about it. Claudie said he'd always liked murder trials, and I told him this was a good one.

The fellow that was tried got ninety-nine years, and I figured he deserved every last one of them. After the jury brought in the verdict, the sheriff took the prisoner away, and in a few minutes the courtroom was nearly empty. The judge stayed on the bench, though, looking wise and tired;

and the clerk sat at his desk, moving papers back and forth as he studied them through his thick glasses. The bailiff stood over to one side, and I never let my eye get far off of him since he had a big silver star on his chest and a hog-leg pistol that hung all the way down to his knee. He was working on a big quid of tobacco, and from time to time he'd lean over to spit into a tall brass goboon there by the water cooler; then he'd turn and look back toward the courtroom as proud and relieved as if he had cast some kind of evil spirit out of his system.

I waited to see what would happen next, and then up stepped two strange lawyers that had been hanging around the courtroom all day looking mad at each other. One of them, a spry, spare little man with bushy gray hair and a wingbat collar, got up and told the judge that he wanted to make a civil motion. I eased up to the front row so I could hear better, as the judge leaned over and told the clerk to fetch him up the civil docket.

The judge said, "All right, Counsel, proceed. Case of *Schultz* v. *Schultz*. State your motion, Mr. Childress."

The little lawyer with the bushy hair got up and said: "Your Honor, this is a motion in which we pray for the appointment of a receiver. I represent Ferd Schultz, the plaintiff. You know Ferd; he's been living up north of town in the Trinity River bottoms all his life."

"I guess I ought to, Counsel," the judge said. "I've had a fishing camp on the river below the Schultz place ever since the year of the big drouth."

"All right," the lawyer went on, "you probably know too, Your Honor, that Ferd and his brother Ab Schultz have been partners in the hog business all this time."

"I suppose I do," the judge pointed out; "that's where I

get my spareribs and backbone every year at hog-killing time. But tell me about the case, Mr. Childress."

"Well, Judge, it's this way," the lawyer said. "Ferd and Ab never did get along together too well, but —"

"Mr. Childress," the judge cut in on him, "you are taking up the court's time with things the court knows better than you do. I've seen Ferd and Ab walking back and forth to town for years with Ferd about a hundred yards ahead. Everybody knows they've hardly spoken to each other since they grew up — but what's the case about?"

"Your Honor," Mr. Childress said, "I was just coming to that. As long as Ferd and Ab were both single men, things went along pretty well. But now Ab has gone and gotten married."

"You don't say," the judge allowed and leaned forward in his big black chair — "married who?"

"That's what I was coming to." Mr. Childress perked up at the judge's last question. "It all happened since you held court here last. Ab went and married that turkey woman that used to live by herself a little way up the river from the hog ranch; woman by the name of Gossett, who came to Liberty County from somewhere up in North Texas. You may not know of her."

The judge said he did not recollect that he did, and the lawyer went on: "Now here's what's happened. Since Ab married the turkey woman he wants to start raising turkeys on the hog ranch. Matter of fact, he's already gone and bought some with money that belongs to the partnership. Ferd will have no truck with turkeys on the place, but he finds that he now owns a half interest in some. But that's not all. Under the Community Law of Texas, Ab's wife is a partner with Ab in the profits of the business. Since Ab and

Ferd are partners, that sort of makes Ab's wife a partner with Ferd as well as with Ab. Now Ferd doesn't want any part of her or the turkeys."

"Where are Ferd and Ab?" the judge asked. "Bring them in the courtroom. Maybe we can straighten this thing out."

At this, the other lawyer — a much younger man with a heavy frown built into his face — got up and said, "Your Honor, I represent Ab Schultz. Ab wouldn't come and neither would Ferd. It would be dangerous for them both to be in the courtroom at one time. That's the one point where Mr. Childress agrees with me."

"Well, Mr. Willard, what is your reply to Mr. Childress's prayer for the appointment of a receiver?" the judge wanted to know from Ab's lawyer.

"It's this, Your Honor," Mr. Willard stated: "It is true that Ferd and Ab are partners. Ferd wants to raise hogs, and that's fine with Ab. Now Ab wants to raise turkeys, and he wants turkeys as much as Ferd wants hogs. Ab says why can't they both raise hogs and turkeys?"

"But what about the woman?" the judge asked. "You haven't mentioned her."

Lawyer Willard looked pretty uncomfortable at this and said, "Well, Judge, she's a newcomer, and I don't exactly represent her."

The judge said he didn't see any way out of the mess except the appointment of a receiver for the partnership, as provided in the Act of 1887, and unless he heard a good reason stated by Ab's lawyer, he was ready to grant Mr. Childress's prayer for relief. Mr. Willard stood there in front of the judge stammering and fidgeting and shuffling papers for a few minutes; then the judge banged his gavel and said: "Motion granted."

Mr. Willard sat down and Mr. Childress got up. "Your Honor," he said, "just one more thing — the receiver's job is going to be a little ticklish, I'm afraid."

"Any suggestions as to a receiver by either counsel?" the judge asked, but neither lawyer spoke. Finally Mr. Willard got to his feet, frowned, and said he didn't believe there was a man in Liberty County that would try it. It got very quiet in the courtroom; then I spoke up and said: "Judge, if you are looking for a receiver, I'll take the job."

They all three turned and looked at me the way an old-maid aunt of mine used to look at the younger members of the household. The bailiff looked too, and I looked right back at him.

The judge said, "Order in the court," and I spoke up again and said, "I want to be the receiver."

The judge said, "Stand up when you address the court. What are your qualifications?"

I stood up and said, "My name is Clint Hightower, and I know a lot about hogs and turkeys. I know something about people, too. Is that enough?"

It wasn't; but after I'd answered a lot more questions and told them about Claudie, the judge said it seemed like a good appointment; he wrote it in an order that said I was to run the business and report to him. Then he swore me in and said: "If you last until I hold court again here this fall, you can report to me in person; until then, just file your reports with the clerk here," the judge told me. I looked at the clerk, and he looked at me — very serious looks.

I figured since Mr. Childress was Ferd Schultz's lawyer and they had asked for the receiver, I ought to be able to get along with him and Ferd sort of automatically. Hell, I was the answer to the prayer in their motion. So I went over to Ab's lawyer, Mr. Willard, and said in a low voice, "I always sort of liked turkeys myself."

"That's good," Mr. Willard said; "of all the parties to this lawsuit, the turkeys might be the easiest to get along with. Those Schultzes are both meaner than river bottom hogs."

"I'll go up tomorrow to take over," I said. "What I want you to do, Mr. Willard, is write Ab a nice letter and tell him I love turkeys and he should work with me."

"He can't read," Mr. Willard said.

"How about his wife?" I asked. I was really boiling over with ideas.

"Matter of fact," he said, "she can read and write too." Then he wrote the letter addressed to Mr. and Mrs. Ab Schultz and gave it to me.

After lawyer Willard left the courtroom, I went over to Mr. Childress and told him how glad I was he had won himself a receiver. I added: "You could beat the bushes from one end of Texas to the other and you'd never find a better receiver, when it comes to getting along with hogs."

When I got back to our room at Anahuac about sundown, I found Claudie sitting on the bed reading a tomato can. First thing, he wanted to know about the jury's verdict in the murder case, and when I told him, he said he thought ninety-nine years was too long.

"Claudie," I said, "you're wrong about that, but leave us not argue. It wouldn't be fair since I heard the testimony. Now listen to me, because I've got some real news. We've got us a new job. You can quit the oil company first thing in the morning."

"What's that?" he asked. It was going a little too fast for him.

"Yes," I answered, "you are an assistant receiver, Claudie. We take over tomorrow."

"How'd you get the job?" he wanted to know.

"The judge at Liberty appointed me receiver, and I am appointing you assistant receiver right now," I told him and swore him in just like the judge had done to me.

"You don't sound to me like a man that is steering clear of the law, Clint," he said. "You musta forgot what Jules Rabinowitz told us."

"Clear of the criminal law, Claudie," I explained. "In Liberty, it's the civil docket they've got me written up in."

2

The next morning was a fine warm spring day, so I and Claudie drove up to Liberty and started early for the Schultz place. The road was fine for a little way; then it got worse and worse until the car got stuck in the red mud just before we made the last turn that led into the worst stretch of all, down in the river bottom. From there we went on foot, following a boggy lane cut through big water oaks that had Spanish moss hanging all over them like dirty whiskers.

We hadn't gone far beyond the turn when we were met by a pack of big brown and black hound dogs that came at us barking and snarling and showing their teeth. They looked lean and hungry and mad. It wasn't until Claudie picked up an old wagon end gate from the side of the road and batted one of the dogs into the ditch that they all went away and left us alone. Then we came to the house. We could tell it was Ab's place from the sign on the mailbox. Ferd Schultz lived about a quarter of a mile beyond Ab, they'd told us in Liberty.

Ab Schultz's house was half of a dog-run house. You could see where it had been cut in two, leaving only one side and half of the breezeway that had once run down the middle. Later we found that Ferd's house was the other half.

The yard was full of turkeys — a big old bronze gobbler with fiery red wattles strutting around the place; several hens feeding in the grass, and twenty or thirty poults that peep-peeped and darted around after crickets and grasshoppers in the Jimson weeds.

I told Claudie to let me handle the talking; then I went up and knocked on the door and yelled "Hello." The woman that came around the corner of the house didn't look at all like the turkey woman I had in my mind, but when I told her we were looking for Mr. and Mrs. Ab Schultz, she said in a nice, mannerly voice, "I am Mrs. Ab Schultz." I handed her the letter Mr. Willard had written about me and turkeys.

In spite of the mud on the boots she wore, the beads of sweat on her forehead and upper lip, and her faded blue gingham dress, she had a sweet, clean look about her. She was not a little woman, but I noticed as she read the letter that her wrists were small, and so were her hands. From the little wrinkles around her eyes, her iron-gray hair, and the blue pattern of veins on her hands, I judged her to be around forty-five or fifty.

She handed me back the letter and said, "Thank you, Mr. Hightower, that's a nice letter. You haven't introduced the other gentleman."

"Excuse me, ma'am," I said. "That's my assistant, Claudie Hughes. He is my hog specialist. I am a turkey man myself."

She looked up at Claudie and said, "How do you do, Mr. Hughes." Claudie fidgeted, looked down at the ground, scratched the back of his neck, and said, "Howdy do, ma'am." Mrs. Schultz's parlor-type manners were too much for him, and they were about to get me a little off balance, myself.

She asked us if we were thirsty, and we were, though I hadn't noticed it before. She drew a nice cool bucket of water from the well beside the house, and we drank our fill from a clean gourd dipper. Then she told us Ab had gone to the hog pen down in the pasture and showed us where the trail to the pasture began. "The pen is not over three quarters of a mile. Just follow the blazes on the trees," she told us.

"Before we go, ma'am," I said, "I want to be sure your husband will believe me when I tell him how much I love turkeys. It's in lawyer Willard's letter, but he says your husband can't read."

"That is true, gentlemen," she answered. "He is not able to read. But Ab is a good man, and if you tell him the truth, I am sure he will believe you."

"He is a lover of turkeys, too, ain't he, ma'am?" I asked. I figured it was as good a time as any to spar for an opening. She nodded and smiled and said, "He always told me he was, and I am certain that he is a truthful man."

"Thank you, ma'am," I told her; "we're going to get along fine, since I'm so fond of them too."

She gave me a funny look, and said, "Mr. Hightower, it seems to me that you are going out of your way to impress me with your sentiments about turkeys. Have you had this weakness long?"

"All my life, lady," I answered; I was coasting, I felt.

"Some people like children, some like chickens, others like dogs and cats, but me, I like turkeys. Don't you?"

She put a long, even look on me and said, "Mr. Hightower, they are an abomination to me; I wouldn't care if I never saw another turkey in all my life."

This rocked me some, and I could see that it fairly staggered Claudie. All I could manage to say was, "Well, you've sure got a passel of them around here, ma'am." She nodded and said that was true. Then she went ahead to say that she had had to deal with turkeys ever since she inherited the turkey ranch up the river and gave up her job in the Dallas library to go run it. She sold the ranch, she said, turkeys and all — and she sold it cheap — when she married Ab; but when he brought her home with him after the wedding, she found he had the Schultz place all littered up with another set of turkeys. Worse than all the other turkeys though, she went on to explain, was old Clarence, the gobbler. Clarence was familiar; he was impudent, and he was nosy. His bill was in everything about the place: the churn, the lard, the meat in the smokehouse and the victuals on the table if anyone left the kitchen door unlatched. He had never learned to keep his place. "See what I mean?" she asked. "Look at Clarence now." The old gobbler was standing there on one foot beside Claudie taking in everything that had been going on.

All during the courting days, she told us, Ab had told her how much he liked turkeys around a place, and she wanted him to be happy. "I love Ab," she finished, "and that's the only reason I am willing to tolerate these terrible turkeys in the yard. That goes particularly for old Clarence there."

"Mrs. Schultz," I said, "did it ever strike you that that was only courtin' talk on Ab's part? He may be putting up with these turkeys just because he thinks you like them."

"I hardly think so," she said. "Ab is a very genuine person. He wouldn't deceive me, I am sure."

I and Claudie thanked her and took off down the muddy trail. I told him to go along ahead and watch out for the blazes, since I wanted to walk along behind and think, without anything to take my mind off of my job.

We walked a long time before we came to a clearing in the woods ahead, and there we saw our man. Before he saw us, we watched him as he rode an old rusty-gray saddle mule back and forth along a barbed-wire fence that led from an empty pigpen down toward a muddy slough. He had a long-Tom single-barrel shotgun thrown across the saddle in front of him.

"I'll do the talking here too, Claudie," I said as we walked up to the man.

"Mr. Schultz?" I said.

"That's me," he answered as he swung down off of the mule, bringing the gun along with him. He was a stocky-built man of fifty or so with a square face and suspicious eyes. His boots were muddy, and his jumper and overalls were faded and dirty. He looked us over and said — not in a very kind way, either — "What do you want?"

"My name is Clint Hightower, and this is my assistant, Claudie Hughes," I said.

Mr. Schultz said, "Well, what do you want?"

I had been thinking all the way down the trail about what I was going to say to Mr. Schultz, but somehow it did not exactly come to me at the time, so I said, "I am the receiver."

"Uh-huh," he said.

Then I remembered. "Mr. Schultz," I said, "your lawyer, Mr. Willard, sent you a letter. I showed it to Mrs. Schultz.

It says that I am the receiver appointed by the judge, but I'm very partial to the turkey side of the lawsuit. You see, I'm a great lover of turkeys myself."

"Turkeys, huh? I'm glad to know that," he said.

"I thought you'd be," I told him; then I and Claudie both moved up closer to where Mr. Schultz was standing.

"How the hell did you get here?" he asked us, and he almost seemed to be out of sorts with us.

"We followed the trail Mrs. Schultz showed us," I explained.

"You must have took the wrong fork," he said. "I'm Ferd Schultz. I'm the hog side of the lawsuit."

3

It was easier to look at Claudie than it was to look at Mr. Schultz, so I looked at Claudie. He looked awful — worse, I figured, than he would look again until some time after he died. Then I turned to Mr. Schultz and said, "Mr. Schultz, you've got a mighty fine lawyer in Mr. Childress. He had the judge eating out of his hand yesterday."

Ferd Schultz did not say anything. He just stood there looking at us until I began to feel about the way Claudie looked. The air got so tight and heavy all around us that it almost seemed like things were taking a better turn when Ferd Schultz spoke up and said, "When are you bastards gonna get out of here?"

Claudie turned to leave, but I said, "Hold it, Claudie; we have not finished our business with Mr. Schultz yet." Then Mr. Schultz said, "Oh yes, by God, you have."

I couldn't see how anything I could do was going to make

things any worse, so I said: "It's not exactly my fault that we took the wrong fork, Mr. Schultz. My assistant, here, led the way and he must have geed somewhere back there when he should have hawed."

Ferd looked up at Claudie; then he looked back at me and said, "Get out before I use this gun."

"Mr. Schultz," I said, and I knew it was my last stab at staying, "I'm the receiver appointed by the court. I may not be a very good one, but I'm the only one there is. I've got to know one more thing before we go — Where are the hogs?"

The color started seeping up in Ferd's face until he was as red as a seed catalogue tomato around the eyes. He tightened his grip on the gun and said, "Ab's got most of them locked up."

"Where at?" I asked him.

"He fixed up an old pen over behind his house," Ferd said, and I saw the muscles around his jaw tighten up as he went on: "Sometime last night he drove all the hogs he could find over there and penned them up. I've rid this fence here by the old pen all day to stop any strays that head Ab's way."

"Where do the hogs belong?" I asked as fast as I could, to keep his mind off of the turkeys.

"Right in this here partnership pen," Ferd answered. "That's where we've allus kept the hogs."

"How far away from here is Ab's new pen?" I asked.

"Not over a quarter of a mile, I reckon," he said.

"No distance for a real hog caller, Mr. Schultz," I told him. "The assistant receiver here in charge of hogs is a bass singer from the part of Alabama where they learn to sing by calling hogs."

"But I told you Ab's got the hogs penned up," Ferd

Schultz pointed out. He was still mad, but I could see that I was taking a tuck in his dander.

"No trick at all for a real hog caller," I said. "If that pen's in no better shape than the partnership pen here, Claudie can call 'em right out of it. They'll break out for a good enough hog caller." Then I turned to Claudie and said, "Claudie, kindly call them hogs back where they belong."

Claudie looked like a new man. After balling us up the way he had when he took the wrong fork of the trail, he was ready to call those hogs through a barbed-wire fence if he had to. He unbuttoned his collar, hitched up his britches, took a deep breath and started with the slow, soft "Soo-soo — soo," like a river steamboat in the fog a long way off. It wasn't loud, but it was enough to take a hog's mind off of other things and set him wondering whether the call was meant for him. Knowing hogs as well as I did and having called a fair amount of them myself, I imagined I could see them stir and rustle about in the early restlessness of being called by a real expert.

Then as Claudie went on, the higher notes started to roll out — the "whoo, whoo-oo-oo pig, whoo pig," in full tones like a brass bugle that cuts through the muggy air and cleans out all other noises. Claudie's voice urged, it persuaded, it begged and it demanded the hogs to come on. Faster and louder and stronger it got until I knew no hog could hold out any longer. I could almost tell the very time they must have been breaking out of the pen.

After that Claudie tapered off. He held the last call — a long, sweet, mellow one — until it was hardly like a call at all; it was more like a song of thanks for listening. When he was through, Claudie sat down on a cypress stump, limp as a dishrag. His eyes were glassy and dry and his nose was bleeding. I turned to Ferd and said: "Mr. Schultz, there is a man that can call hogs."

Then they came; must have been fifty or sixty hogs, counting the runts in the litters and all. Ferd opened the gap that led to the partnership pen, and after they all went in Claudie helped him close it. Ferd got back on his horse, and though he still had hold of his gun, I knew he wasn't fixing any more to use it. For the first time that day he looked to me like a man that could smile. He glanced up at the sun and said it was about time for some chuck; wouldn't we like to come to his house and eat with him? He lived all alone, he went on to say and he didn't have much, but it wasn't far to go and he wanted us to have potluck with him. We took him right up.

When we got to Ferd's house, he went down to a little bayou close by to run a trotline and brought back several nice big catfish, the biggest about the size of one of Claudie's feet. Then he gave us some warm corn whiskey and a bucket of cool water to wash it down with. That made Ferd's fried catfish, beans and turnips taste a whole lot better; and when we'd eaten all he'd cooked up, he found us an apple apiece. Claudie was still so hungry that he ate the core and all.

Afterwards, we sat on a bench in the shady part of the yard and talked with Ferd. In a little while I picked my time and said, "Mr. Schultz, I believe we've got the hog part of this lawsuit in pretty good shape. All we've got left is the turkey part."

"It's that woman Ab married," Ferd said, and the color rose up in his face again. "If it wasn't for her, Ab wouldn't have gone and bought them damn turkeys."

"You mean he don't like them?" I asked.

"Hell, no," Ferd said as he lit a cigarette he'd made.

"From what the neighbors tell me that old gobbler, Clarence, is about to run him crazy. He'd get shut of 'em all mighty fast if he wasn't trying to please that woman he married."

Claudie started to say something, but I cut him off with a sharp look and thought hard for a minute or two while everything was quiet except for the raspy song of a locust close by. Then I leaned over to Ferd Schultz and said, looking him right in the eye, "Where do Ab's turkeys roost, Ferd?"

His face brightened up all over. I doubt if the prophet Elisha put any nicer look on them ravens than Ferd put on us. He stood up and stomped his cigarette out on the ground; then he said, "Let me get you fellers another little drink," and went into the house.

While he was gone I turned to Claudie and said: "That whole passel of turkeys ought to bring forty or fifty dollars on the market in Beaumont."

"How's that gonna do us any good?" he wanted to know. "They ain't ourn."

"Leave that to the receiver," I told him.

When Ferd came back with the jug, the three of us took good stiff swigs of the corn; and after we'd all had a second one, I was feeling right brotherly toward Ferd, so I set about to explain some of the law I'd learned when I got appointed receiver.

"Ferd," I said, "I heard Mr. Childress tell the judge the turkeys Ab bought belonged to the partnership. The judge agreed."

"No, by God, they — " Ferd started.

"Wait a minute," I cut in, "let me finish. You are a partner, too. If a partner can buy turkeys, a partner can sell them — or he can give them away." Then I quit talking so as to let that last part sink in.

"I was hoping you'd steal them turkeys from the roost," he said.

"Ferd," I stated, shaming him with a straight look, "you would not want us to do that. It wouldn't be right to steal them turkeys, but if one of the partners told us to take them, it might be some time tonight before I and Claudie could get by there to pick them off of the roost. You see, our car is stuck out on the Liberty road, and we've got to get some help to get it out."

"You've got help," he told us and he got up from the bench. "I'll hitch up a team of mules, and we'll go pull it out."

"We're in no hurry, Ferd," I said. "I think we might even have time for another swig of that corn. I and Claudie haven't got any more work to do until after dark. But you never did tell me where them turkeys roost."

"In Ab's barn," he answered. "It's a good hundred yards from the house."

"That's a nice, safe distance, Ferd," I said.

Late that afternoon, when we left Ferd Schultz's house in the wagon with him, the sun was slanting through the trees at a little cooler angle, or at least it seemed cooler on top of the rest of Ferd's jug of corn. We were not drunk, but we were not exactly sober either, and I kept noticing that the Spanish moss on the trees looked a lot cleaner and prettier than it had that morning.

When we passed Ab's house on the way to get our car unstuck, I put a close look on the place to size up the location of the barn, since I didn't remember seeing it at all that morning. Ferd told us you couldn't see it from where we were, but it was easy to reach from the road, if you turned off at a place where there was an old end gate propped against the fence.

"That must be the end gate I used on them dogs this morning," Claudie said; then I realized there was a big gap in my program. Those dogs were tough enough in broad open daylight; they could be fierce at night.

"What are we going to do about the dogs?" I asked out loud.

Ferd handed me a brown paper sack and said, "Feed 'em. Here's some bones and scraps that ought to do. I brought 'em along for Ab's dogs so they wouldn't make you no trouble."

There wasn't any moon that night, and by the time we'd got our car unstuck, it was pitch dark and the screech owls were tuning up for the night.

As Ferd Schultz drove off down the road in his wagon, I told Claudie I had our legal rights straightened out; all we had to do was exercise them. I said, "Claudie, we will take these turkeys strictly under the civil law. That's not the kind of law that things are against. The case of Schultz against Schultz is about over."

We waited a while until the spooky fuss made by those owls was beginning to get on Claudie's nerves; then we drove down the road and turned in toward Ab's barn through a gap in the fence by the old end gate. The dogs met us and I fed them Ferd's scraps and quieted them down before they'd barked much. When Claudie pulled up beside the barn, we could just see the shape of Ab's house through the trees. All the lights were out.

Once we found the turkeys, roosting in a lean-to by the side of the barn, it didn't take us long to get them in the car. A turkey that is half asleep in the dark is no match for a man with his wits about him in a roost, but they did let out some fairly noisy peeps and squawks as we piled them into the back of the car.

I was holding the turkeys down with both hands in the car and Claudie was bringing the last two from the roost, when a lantern showed up at the back of Ab's house and made for us fast.

"Claudie," I said, "let's get out of here. Here comes Ab Schultz."

"I didn't think — " Claudie started to say, but I cut him off, since it is never very good what Claudie thought, even when he is right. "Come on," I said, and he piled in the car with the last two turkeys under his arm.

The lantern was right on us when we started, but we got away, with Claudie and the two turkeys in the front seat, and me and the rest in the back. We headed for the gap, and we'd have made it easily if Claudie's turkeys in the front seat hadn't tried to get out of the car on his side. I saw wings and tails and feet all around Claudie's head for a minute; then we hit a big oak with an awful jolt. How we held onto all the turkeys in the jumble that followed, I don't know, but we did, and Claudie was backing away to pull on out when the lantern caught up with us. I was ready to hear Ab — as ready as I'd ever be — when the voice came from behind the lantern. But it wasn't Ab at all; it was Mrs. Schultz, speaking in her sweet Sunday school type of voice. "Gentlemen," she said, "you almost got away without old Clarence, the gobbler. Can't you make room for him?"

"Lady," I told her as she passed the old gobbler into the back seat with me, "room for Clarence is what we've got plenty of."

III
The Carnival

As THE FERRYBOAT eased out of the Bolivar slip, I and Claudie got out of our Ford and went forward to watch a school of porpoises playing ahead of us in Galveston Bay. It was a blistering July day, and the heat waves dancing on the water between us and Pelican Spit made the quarantine station there look like a bay scene painted on canvas that has come loose.

After we'd watched a long line of shell barges cross ahead of us, Claudie turned to me and said: "Clint, I never seen a finer turkey than old Clarence was, but are you sure that he was ours?"

"Of course he was ours," I told him. "After all, Clarence was only part of our pay for being receiver. Don't you worry about us getting into any trouble about them turkeys. I explained practically everything to the clerk of the court and the bailiff too." This seemed to satisfy Claudie, who had had his mind mostly on the porpoises anyhow.

From the Texas mainland to Galveston Island, the ferryboat took us no more than a couple of miles or so; but as we drove away from the slip into Galveston, it seemed that the distance might as well have been a lot farther. We had left the smoke and steam and dust of places where money was being made, and in no time at all we found ourselves breathing new whiffs of sen-sen, witch hazel, fresh popcorn, and all the other gaudy smells of places where money was being spent. This easy climate began to agree with us right away.

That afternoon when we were having beer and pretzels and hard-boiled eggs on Murdock's beach, I counted our money. "Look, Claudie," I said, "we are back down to eight dollars, and we would be worse off than that if we hadn't raffled off old Clarence at that Juneteenth picnic last week. Why don't you be plumb quiet awhile and let me do some thinking?"

Claudie, who hardly ever talks much anyhow when he eats, just went on chewing. With the last hard-boiled egg, I blotted up some mixed salt and pepper from the newspaper it was wrapped in, and right where the salt and pepper had been, I read:

BUSINESS OPPORTUNITIES

> Going concern operating from trailer house has opening for partner with an automobile.

It was signed "Professor E. Ludington Pye, Buccaneer Hotel, Galveston." I passed the paper over to Claudie, and he cut out the notice with his pocketknife. Then we saw that the Buccaneer Hotel was standing there right across the street.

I and Claudie bought shaves and shoeshines in the hotel barbershop, and marched up to the mail desk where a nice clean-looking lady clerk was polishing her fingernails. She said that Professor Pye did not exactly live at the hotel; he just used some of the facilities, including the mail department. She thought he might be along any time.

We waited, and pretty soon we saw a very fancy character come into the lobby. I could tell, though of course Claudie could not, that it was the Professor, the minute he walked in. The mail lady pointed us out to him and steered him over to us. I sized him up as he stated who he was. He was a thin-faced, thin-flanked fellow of around forty, with a sharp look about his face and head. His black hair was long and parted right in the middle. He wore shell-rimmed glasses which were hooked onto a long black ribbon that ran into a little sprocket of an affair pinned onto his lapel, and his coat and pants did not match. This two-tone effect impressed Claudie very much, but I thought from the first that the pants that went with his coat had simply worn out.

I showed him the ad and told him my name was Clint Hightower. He said, "Who is this big fellow who seems to be here with you, Mr. Hightower?"

"That is my associate, Claudie Hughes," I told him. There is a program all over the country of calling people who work for you "associates." It is supposed to make them work harder for the same pay.

"What is your proposition, Professor?" I asked him, not wishing to waste a lot of my time unless this citizen had something good.

"First," he said, "I want to know what your line of business is; what kind of experience have you had, Mr. Hightower?" He blew on his glasses and polished them with a silk handkerchief; then he tucked the handkerchief into his coat sleeve and looked at me through the lower part of his glasses.

"Well," I said, "I have tried not to limit myself."

"Can't you be more specific?"

"All right," I answered, "I have tended bar, I have sold fire extinguishers, patent medicines and lightning rods, and I have tuned pianos. Also, I am an actor. I have written, though I have not chiseled, tombstone epitaphs, and once, in Flomaton, Alabama, I cured a colored man that had fits. I have sold Jewel tea and trained Tennessee walking horses."

The Professor said, "But . . ."

I went on: "I can organize a union and I can call a square dance. I was a consulting statistician in the Department of Agriculture at one time. I can read the Morse code. I can play a mandolin, and I can preach a fair sermon from either the Old or the New Testament. I do not do manual labor. My friend Claudie here handles that for me and sings bass." Claudie cleared his throat.

"What," the Professor asked, after a little pause, "are your present engagements?"

"We can be had on the right basis, Professor Pye, but from the way you have been talking, a body might suppose that you had the automobile and we had the trailer. You're asking a lot of questions for a man who is nothing but stranded."

The Professor put out a lot of talk about offers he had from sedans, convertibles, station wagons, and such; but when I squeezed the water out of this talk, I found that he was just trying to make the best trade he could with us. He finally admitted that his wife — "a preacher's daughter at that," he said — had run off with his car the week before. She had gone back for good to her mother in New Orleans, Louisiana.

It was getting late in the afternoon when I and Claudie took the Professor in our Ford to a trailer camp down on the West Beach where we looked over his place of business. It was an old gray trailer house with two entrances; it was equipped with a coal-oil stove, two beds, a cot, and a little cage to hold the Professor's pet coon, Julius. On one side of the trailer house was painted a large outline of a human head, all divided into sections labeled PITY, KINDNESS, AMBITION, LOVE, RELIGION, HOPE, and several other worth-while topics. Under the head, in big red letters running the whole length of the trailer, the words PHRENOLOGIST INSIDE were painted. On the other side was a sketch of a camera on a tripod, with the words PHOTOGRAPHER INSIDE in big letters below.

"Which," I asked the Professor, "did Mrs. Pye do?"

The Professor had a way of not answering questions right off, and it was not until he had adjusted his glasses and fired up an underslung pipe that he said, "We alternated, Mr. Hightower, but I always preferred the chair of phrenology."

"What did you usually do?"

"Photography."

"Well," I said, "you can have your phrenology full time if we team up. I believe Claudie can handle the photography."

It was plain to me that once you let this fellow know that things were decided, you had him. By this time, his manners were along the "excuse me" line — a little like those of a funeral parlor attendant. As he sidled up to me to ask a question that I knew was coming, he said: "What would be your part?"

"Psychology," I said, looking over the trailer for enough space to spell it out.

When the Professor told us of his plan to leave in a day or two with a traveling carnival show, I agreed that I and Claudie would join up with him. The program was to follow the cotton-picking season north across the State of Texas.

The next day I painted my psychology sign on the rear of the trailer and went to the public library to check up on my new job.

2

Two days later we hooked the trailer onto our Ford and drove behind the red carnival trucks and cars to Richmond, Texas, where the rich, overflow land in the wide Brazos bottom had produced a bumper crop. The cotton gins were running twenty-four hours a day, and money was plentiful.

The first afternoon in Richmond we watched the carnival folks set up their concessions near a grove of oak and pecan trees on the riverbank. I was about to put the trailer right in the big middle of it all when we were told very harshly to get the hell out. That was how I first found out that the Professor was not with the carnival in the way I had thought — in fact, he wasn't with it at all except in a very loose way. He didn't even know the head man — a Mr. Flick, who owned some of the concessions and had an interest in all of the rest. It turned out that the Professor's plan had just been to mooch along on the carnival crowds by setting up the trailer as close as we could get to the carnival grounds.

We parked across the street from Mr. Flick's operations that first night, but we were so close to the show that we were getting as much of the bright lights as any of his concessions. After a little while Mr. Flick came over to speak to us. He was a smallish fellow with a big face and a loud voice, and he walked with a sway and a swagger, the way little guys often do, sort of making up that way for what was lacking in size. He had a very peculiar accent that I was never quite able to button down. He was wearing a double-breasted suit with wide lapels and padded shoulders. He talked without taking a black cigar holder out of his mouth, and he talked a great deal. He was going to sue us; he was going to enjoin us; he was going to have the sheriff of Fort Bend County after us; and as he talked, he kept taking a little comb out of his pocket and combing his hair. I never cared a little bit for a grown man who was always combing his hair.

I stood there waiting for the psychological moment to speak, while the Professor and Mr. Flick fussed and argued. It all boiled down to about this: Mr. Flick wanted us to go away or else give him a 25 per cent cut in our take. The Professor said he did not wish any entangling alliances with anybody's carnival. About this time Claudie came out of the trailer. Now Claudie is a very large citizen anywhere, and that night in the bright glare of the carnival lights he looked as big as a skinned mule. He wanted to know why somebody was going to call the sheriff of Fort Bend County.

"Claudie," I said, "Mr. Flick, here, is the one that wants to call in the sheriff."

"Why?" Claudie asked, and I'll have to admit that for a man that was getting more sheriff-shy by the day, Claudie didn't look very scared. He only looked mad.

"Well, it's this way," I explained, while Claudie stood there sort of hovering over Mr. Flick. "We do not care if some of our customers do business with Mr. Flick's carnival. But Mr. Flick, here, is sore at us because some of the carnival's customers might be doing business with us."

"Sore huh?" Claudie made it sound like one word.

"I am not bothered by this big oaf," Mr. Flick said, and here he made his mistake. Claudie, of course, didn't know what an oaf was; but Mr. Flick said it in the same way you would say some of the few things that Claudie will not let himself be called at all; so when Claudie saw how mad I was getting, he latched onto the scruff of Mr. Flick's neck with his right hand. With his left hand he caught Mr. Flick by the seat of his pants. Claudie lifted him right off the ground and started moving away fast with him, while Mr. Flick's arms and legs waved about in a very helpless way like a beetle's legs when he is turned over on his back. I stopped Claudie as soon as I could and sent him back into the trailer. It took the Professor and me quite a few minutes to quiet Mr. Flick down and stop him from talking about several very rough programs he had in mind for Claudie. Then I made my move. I said: "Tell you what we'll do, Mr. Flick; we'll give you 10 per cent of our take if you will let us set up this trailer anywhere we want in the carnival layout."

Mr. Flick argued a little, but he was going to agree. When he did, the Professor said he wanted his side of the trailer right in front of the Ferris wheel, so that the first thing the riders would see as they came down would be his PHRENOLOGY sign. Then I told Mr. Flick that he should put the merry-go-round on Claudie's side of the trailer.

"Hell," Mr. Flick said, "I can't build the carnival around your trailer."

"Mr. Flick," I answered, "don't make me have to explain that to Claudie."

"Well, all right," he said, "but which concession do you want to support your psychology racket?" and he sounded a little sarcastic, I thought.

"I'll take the Tunnel of Love," I said. "Not the front where they buy tickets and start out on their ride. I want the rear where the riders pop out into the open after the first half of the ride and before they go back into the tunnel for the return trip. In that minute of daylight in the middle of the ride I want them to see my PSYCHOLOGY sign."

It was on this very sound basis that we joined the carnival.

3

Our business in the trailer prospered almost from the very first. Claudie learned to work the Professor's camera a lot sooner than I expected. The Professor helped pose the customers, and Claudie got so good that he could develop a finished print of a family group in about the same length of time that it took the Professor to explain to someone in the group that he possessed the most amazing bumps on his head that the Professor had seen in his lifelong study of phrenology. We hardly ever let a customer get away until he had been given the full course. Then we pooled our take, gave Mr. Flick about 10 per cent, and divided the rest three ways.

Cotton was bringing nearly thirty cents a pound that year, and the Professor found many chances to turn up unexpected talents in men and women and children. He saw in the most unlikely prospects such ordinary futures as writing poetry, serving in the legislature, or teaching school. He saw heads of future generals, admirals, ranchers, governors, and even a few Texas Rangers among the members of the families of these farmers who only came around in the first place to get their pictures taken. One child's head showed that he could even write a whole Sears, Roebuck catalogue if he set his mind to it, and the Professor took three dollars from a farmer for finding enough bumps on his son's head to make him Secretary of Agriculture when he grew up. A cabinet member is as easy to discover this way, the Professor pointed out, as a cabinet maker is.

Most people preferred photography or phrenology at first, so it usually took some selling to get them into my department; also, it turned out that the couples on the Tunnel of Love hardly ever unlooked each other as they rounded the bend near the trailer. But there was a better tone, as a rule, to the customers who came to me on their own hook. I was the only one in the trailer who gave them a chance to express themselves, since you do not talk while you are having your picture made; nor did the Professor listen to them while he was feeling the bumps on their heads. I picked up many a two-dollar payment simply by paying close mind to what they said and telling them how sorry I felt about it. Naturally, most of my customers were women.

After a week in Richmond, we started working our way up the Brazos Valley, following the peak of the cotton-picking season as it moved north in the bottom land along this Texas Nile.

When we got to Waco late in September, Mr. Flick made a deal to set the carnival up for a two-week stand in the old Cotton Palace Exposition Grounds. Our customers here stood in line on three sides of the trailer.

It was in Waco that Claudie got in a crap game with the bearded lady and her brother-in-law and lost nearly all the money he had made. I was never so disgusted with Claudie in my life. I spoke to him about trusting people he did not know any better than he knew these people, but he said that it had not seemed to him like real money; it had been so easy to make.

"You country hick," I said. "You trout head. Your mind has not improved a bit since you left the Alabama wiregrass country where you came from. The trouble with you is that you cannot get used to money that has not been dug out of the ground with a hoe and a plow."

Claudie just looked down at a place where he was rolling a little pebble around with the toe of his shoe, and I went on: "In this work we are relieving these country people of their cash without having to do any manual labor, and it's too much for you. You just can't stand it."

"Don't your conscience ever eat on you for taking their money?" Claudie asked.

"No," I told him, "it certainly does not; it might even be that the fun they have at the carnival is worth more to them than the money they spend on it."

"Well," Claudie said, as he walked away toward the freak shows, "I had a whole lot of fun in that crap game."

4

We left the Brazos at Waco and went on to Fort Worth where we found a stand in the north part of town near the stockyards.

The first afternoon we were there, I was sitting in the trailer listening to a champion rodeo rider that the Professor had brought in. He had picked up some bumps on his head by being thrown from bucking horses, and this fact had naturally upset the Professor's study. The champion was talking about his troubles with a girl he'd been two-timing, and I was listening to about every third word as I sat there looking over his shoulder at the couples going by on the Tunnel of Love.

Then it dawned on me that I was not hearing him at all.

One of the two-seater cars had come out in the open from the Tunnel and swung around for the return trip, and there was only one person in it. She was the prettiest redheaded woman I had ever seen in my whole life, and she was looking right down at our trailer all the time she was in sight.

I said something to the champion about the tangled web we weave when first we practice to deceive, and let it go at that. When I finally got him to leave, I could see the beautiful redhead coming my way from the exit of the Tunnel of Love.

By the time she reached the trailer house, I was as wide-awake as I had been for weeks. She was tall, slender in the waist, and right willowy in the way she walked; but in front and behind she was billowy, too, in ways that the plain cut of her gingham dress did not begin to hide. She almost passed by, but after she had taken one full look at the trailer house, she came to the entrance where I was sitting. She was as pretty as a lilac bush in full bloom.

I asked her to come in, and for some reason my hands and feet began to feel bigger and heavier. All at once I felt sorry that I could not do a death-defying, tightrope act before we got down to psychology. She said, as she sighed and sat down, that she knew she had come to the right place. She had a way of meeting my look with her wide, greenish-gray eyes; and instead of looking down or away, as most women will do, she would hold on until I found myself looking away first.

"Madam," I said, studying her strong, well-shaped hands and the plain band on her ring finger, "please tell me how I can help you. The charge will be two dollars."

She did not look away until she said: "I have been missing my man in many ways. Do you think you can help me?"

With this, something inside my chest vibrated like the other end of an arrow does when the bull's-eye has been hit.

"Here," I said, "is your two dollars back, lady. This one is on the house."

"But I haven't given you two dollars yet," she said; and there I sat, holding out my two one-dollar bills and feeling as numb and tingly as I do in cold weather, or when I hear "Mighty Lak a Rose" played on a violin cello. She continued: "I am a lonely woman, and with winter coming on I know I am going to miss that man more than ever."

"How far away is this man of yours?" I asked her in such a brittle voice that it sounded like somebody else. I was hoping he might be in Siberia or Fort Leavenworth, Kansas.

She hesitated, a kind of peculiar smile flitted across her face, and she said: "Right now he is in the front part of the trailer with his hands all over some big brunette's head."

"Mrs. Pye," I said, getting up from my seat after a few slack minutes, "this is where a word must be said to the id."

"The what?"

"The id," I explained.

"Sit down," she said, as she leaned across the table toward me. "Tell me some more."

I could not tell whether I had my heart in it any more or not; but going on, as she looked at me, was easier than trying to figure out what I might do instead. So I went on: "To a psychologist, when you want to do something, that is your id; when you know you should not do it, that is your superego; when you decide to do it anyway, that is your ego."

"When you do not do it," Mrs. Pye cut in without looking away, "that is sometimes your own fault."

"Your psychology begins, Mrs. Pye," I replied, "right where mine leaves off. You must know that my id ran off to the woods with yours as soon as you came in. Don't you think we'd better head them off?"

Then, before she answered, I swung back into the routine I had picked up in the library in Galveston. "You may follow the id when you shouldn't, and you may get by with it; you may fool everybody else; you may never get caught; still you do not win."

"Why?" she asked, and her long, roan eyelashes were steady above the even look in her eyes. She was winning the argument all right.

"Because," I went on, "you spend the rest of your life dodging the punishment that you know is coming to you for going against the rules. Your subconscious is always on your trail; it is a lot like the Northwest Mounted Police. Every noise in the night — every hoot owl, every tree frog, and every loud clap of thunder — all these are threats of punishment. That is the guilt complex, and it was discovered in Topeka, Kansas, where it is easier to get psychoanalyzed than it is to get a bone set or a tooth filled."

Mrs. Pye said: "Do you mean they have discovered in Kansas that 'the wicked flee when no man pursueth'?"

"Ma'am?" I said. Then I looked outside, and there was the Professor coming around the trailer with Julius, the coon, on his shoulder. As he came in, I said in a too loud voice: "That will be two dollars, please."

The Professor drew in a quick breath, gulped, dropped Julius and finally said, "Eula!"

Mrs. Pye said, "Oh, Exeter!"

I said to myself, "That answers one question. Now I know what the 'E' stands for in E. Ludington Pye."

The Professor kissed her; then they kissed each other, and

I could tell that they were both in dead earnest. Mrs. Pye then opened a little paper sack and took out some persimmons she had brought along for Julius, and I saw that here was a real reunion. I stepped out of the trailer into the glare of the carnival lights; they were bright against the purple dusk settling along the high ground over to the east of the Fort Worth stockyards.

When the Professor and Mrs. Pye came out a few minutes later, they said that they wished to drive into Fort Worth right away to talk things over. I offered to handle any cases that might come up in the Professor's department that night, and this seemed to please them both very much. When Claudie came out, I called him over to one side and took some pains to explain to him what was going on. He grinned and said he was awful glad to see what a nice thing had happened to the Professor.

Mrs. Pye cried a little and told us that she had sold the Pye automobile and spent nearly all of the money on some sick relatives. She cried some more, and then she admitted that she had put most of the money on some very slow ones at the Fair Grounds Race Track in New Orleans. I could see that this was the guilt complex. We all stood there looking at each other and somehow nobody could think of anything to say; then Mrs. Pye said to the Professor, "Wouldn't it be just like old times, Exeter, if we only had a car to go into town?"

I said, "Why don't you take our car?"

This made them both very happy, and they were about to leave when Claudie went over to the car and took his gray fox tail off the radiator cap. Then he allowed as how he hoped there were no race tracks in Fort Worth.

"Don't mind my friend here," I said to them. "He wants

you to go in the car, I am sure." Then I turned to Claudie and said, "Don't you, Claudie?"

While I was still looking at him, Claudie said: "Yes, I guess I do." Then, when I turned to look at Mrs. Pye again, Claudie said: "But not very much."

Mrs. Pye smiled a nice, big, elegant smile at Claudie and said: "There is one more thing, though, we ought to have your title papers on the car, just in case we get a parking ticket or something."

While I was looking for the papers, Claudie fumbled around a while, then he said, "Can't you all get in touch with us if you need the papers?"

Claudie does not understand law points like this at all, so I said: "Please don't pay him any mind; he is only the ox that treadeth out the corn. Here are the keys and here's the registration."

Then Claudie remarked, "Maybe you ought to leave us the papers on the trailer, Professor Pye. We might be spoke to by the law for overparking before you all get back."

The Professor did not hesitate; he gave me the title papers on the trailer, and they left. I don't believe I will ever forget the contented expression on the face of Julius the coon, looking back out of our car as the Professor and Mrs. Pye drove away toward the Fort Worth viaduct.

I turned to Claudie and instructed him about his manners. I pointed out to him that he did not begin to understand female psychology. I could tell that he was doing his best to follow me, but it has always been hard to keep Claudie's mind on one thing very long. When I had finished, he said: "The right tire on this trailer is flat."

"You better fix it the first thing in the morning," I told him.

"I'll have to wait until the Professor comes back," Claudie said. "The jack is in the car."

About two weeks later, I and Claudie were sitting in the trailer discussing our past and our future. We still had a flat tire, since we had not seen anything of the Professor or Mrs. Pye or the car. It had been raining for two days, and we saw no signs of the rain letting up. We were breathing smells there near the Fort Worth stockyards that were strictly different from the holiday scents in Galveston. The carnival had pulled out the day before, and we were very lonesome in the trailer. Claudie's face was so long that he could have eaten oats out of the bottom of a churn. For a long time I and Claudie sat there looking out at the vacant block where all the lights had sparkled and all the laughing people had milled around while the carnival was there.

"Claudie," I finally remarked, "after the carnival has gone away is a bad time to be at the place where the carnival was. Where all those people were happy and gay around the Kewpie dolls with pink and purple feathers, there are only empty popcorn bags and puddles of water. Down where you see those guy wires, they stood in line for a chance to chuck lopsided baseballs at the rag dolls, and . . ."

"But nobody ever hit enough dolls to win the gold watch and chain," Claudie put in.

"Please," I said, "I have not finished. . . . Over there to the left, where that blonde in pink tights wrestled with the boa constrictor, you can't see anything but the rear end of a vacant garage. The glitter is gone with the carnival. The echoes of the steam calliope don't ring out any more against that row of billboards, and the Tunnel of Love has gone to Oklahoma. It's getting so dull and quiet around here, Claudie, that I wish to get the hell out right away."

"How?" Claudie asked in his dumb, vacant way.

"Now, Claudie," I cautioned him, "you almost brought up that subject that we agreed not to discuss any more." I and Claudie had agreed that we would not talk any more about our car or Mrs. Pye and the Professor, or even Julius the coon.

That night we turned in fairly early, as there was nothing else to do and the rain kept pouring down, and pretty soon I heard snoring. It was coarse and heavy against the high, keen whine of the wind that blew through the loose weather stripping on top of the trailer. I stayed awake for a long time, since somebody had to do some thinking about the subject which I and Claudie had agreed not to discuss.

The next morning Claudie had bacon and eggs ready on the coal-oil stove when he came to wake me up. He brought me my coffee, already saucered and blown. The weather was nice and clear, and a fresh norther was blowing. In the middle of my second cup of coffee, I stopped and said, "Claudie, I have a real plan for us."

"Good. What is it?" Claudie wanted to know.

"We need a partner with an automobile. We have only a trailer. Where is the ad that we answered in Galveston?"

Claudie produced it and did not say a word.

"Here is a dollar. Take it into town and get it run in the *Fort Worth Star-Telegram*," I said.

Claudie grinned and said: "I already did." Then he showed me the classified section of the paper for the day before; and, sure enough, there it was. It read just exactly like the one we had read in Galveston, except Claudie had got the heading a little mixed up. It was headed: "Psychologist Wanted."

I V
Turtles Galore

A MAN that has had his automobile run off with, like a man that has had his wife run off with, is apt to look around next and take stock of what all he's got left.

"It could have been a dern sight worse," I explained to Claudie that fall in Forth Worth while he was fixing the flat tire on the trailer house. "Suppose when Professor E. Ludington Pye stole our car he had not left his nice warm trailer with us. Winter's coming on, you know."

Claudie grunted a blurred "uh-huh" as he spit on the inner tube and looked for a bubble to rise up where the leaky place was. Then he allowed as how he'd like to put the Texas Rangers on Professor Pye's trail to see if they couldn't get us our car back.

"Claudie," I said, "are you forgetting that I and you are not having any truck with the law? Remember the law is looking for us, and I don't wish to make it any easier for them than we have to."

"I guess you're right," he answered, as he peeled the back off of the cold patch for the inner tube.

"Another thing," I told him, "we've still got just about enough money left to take in the Dallas Fair. It's the biggest one in the whole State of Texas, it will be a lot of fun, and it will improve our minds, too. No telling what we might turn up at the Dallas Fair."

"If we turn up anything that ain't for free, we can't afford it," he said. "We're awful low on money."

"Well, Claudie," I went on, "it's a good thing one of us is as wide-awake as I am. At that, the Dallas Fair almost got by us. Here in Fort Worth you can learn all about things as far away as China, Russia or El Paso quicker'n you can hear a whisper about the Dallas Fair. I just happened to be shrewd enough to pick the news up yesterday from a fellow at the fire we went to."

The next morning we went down early to the depot and caught the train to Dallas. I planned it so we could ride the fast T & P passenger train that had come all the way from California — the Sunshine Special. We bought the cheapest round-trip ticket to Dallas they had, but we plushed it clear to Dallas by eating breakfast all the way over.

Claudie was a caution, sitting there in the elegant dining car with all those swells — women looking over the bill of fare with glasses held up to their eyes on long silver handles; gray-haired men wearing neat, sharp-trimmed mustaches; and well-scrubbed, starchy-looking kids with spoiled, pouty expressions on their faces. It almost seemed to make Claudie dizzy to be in such classy company, and all the way to Dallas he was ordering waiters around, calling them "sir," and drinking coffee with his little finger sticking straight out in the air. I had explained to him that it was not a sound program to try to drink his coffee out of the saucer on the train.

In Dallas we caught a streetcar by the depot and rode out to the Fair Park entrance on Exposition Avenue. It was a beautiful entrance, too, with a lot of flags flying on top of big gates made out of brick and stone.

I and Claudie were just before going right in to the fair grounds when, all of a sudden, an idea struck me just like a ton of bricks. It was terrific; the sort of thing that would never happen to Claudie in a hundred years, since he is no part of an idea man.

"Claudie," I said, as he stood there and watched the crowd pouring through the fair gate, "hold everything. We might find our car yet. Kindly look across the street at all them concessions *outside* the Fair Park." Claudie looked, and I went on, "Remember that time in Richmond, Texas, when we were with the carnival? Where was Professor Pye? I'll tell you where. He was mooching on the carnival crowds there by setting up his show *outside* the carnival grounds so he wouldn't have to pay to be a part of the show."

Claudie still was not getting it. The whole size of my idea was missing him, so I explained, "Now listen, Claudie. If the Professor and Mrs. Pye came to Dallas in our car, you know they couldn't stay away from the Dallas Fair. And if they came to the fair, where would he be most likely to go into business? Let's look these *outside* places over."

Claudie showed, in the way he looked, that he was very proud of the way my mind was working; he said I almost sounded like a detective, and while I hadn't thought of it in this way before, I could tell that there was a lot to what he said.

"Thank you, Claudie," I said; "thank you very much."

By this time we were walking down the street, looking the outside concessions over. One had pennants, china plates and satin pillows with DALLAS FAIR printed on them; there were several hamburger stands, and all kinds of cold drink places. Then we came to the turtle place, and there she was!

I mean it was the lovely Mrs. Pye with the bright red hair, wide-apart eyes and slender waist. She was there in a little booth that opened up on the street, and she looked so pretty that I felt as slugged in the pit of my stomach over her soft slender sweetness as I had been the time I'd first seen her; the day she rounded the bend in the Tunnel of Love.

Professor E. Ludington Pye was not in sight anywhere, but the sign said GENUINE PYE HAND-PAINTED TURTLES — 25 CENTS and there Mrs. Pye stood, surrounded by hand-painted turtles galore — dozens and dozens of little turtles, all spread in even rows on big boards, and each one in a box with an isinglass top so you could see the flowers painted on his back.

I and Claudie just stood watching her in her pale yellow smock while she painted a red flower on one of the turtles. She was so busy that she didn't see us at all as we walked up. She had a round board hung over her left arm, and on this board she'd daub paint with a long brush; then she'd back off and eye the turtle from several angles before she'd add a little touch here and there.

"A woman artist at work is a fine sight," I whispered to Claudie as some other people drifted up to watch what was going on, and all the time Mrs. Pye went right on without paying us any mind at all. Then the other people wandered on off without offering to buy a turtle, and Claudie spoke up in a very coarse way, saying, "We want our car. You can have the trailer back."

It was about as impolite a thing as I have ever heard — particularly from a guy that had been calling waiters "sir" on the train not much over an hour before. And it flustered Mrs. Pye aplenty. Her pretty face turned pale, but it only made her big eyes brighter and her hair redder; redder, I thought, than all the little berries in the woods after the first frost.

"Never mind, Mrs. Pye," I said; then I spoke to Claudie and told him to leave the rest to me.

"We were going to bring the car back. Exeter will tell you so himself," she said. "You aren't going to call the law, are you?"

I knew, of course, that I and Claudie could not afford to call in any law, with the law already trying to find us, so I said, "That would probably be the last thing we would do, Mrs. Pye." At this she looked at me so sweet and thankful that I turned to Claudie and said, "Wouldn't it, Claudie?"

Claudie's only answer was to look down at the sidewalk and shake his head, but he had a very stubborn look on his face. About this time Mrs. Pye said we'd have to excuse her for a minute, and while she went next door to the painted pillow booth, I took Claudie to task about the way he'd been speaking to Mrs. Pye. He repented a little, I thought.

Mrs. Pye came right back, as I was hoping she would, and pretty soon a little boy with a handful of balloons and some Cracker Jack popcorn came along with his mother in tow. Mrs. Pye sold one of the hand-painted turtles for a quarter.

"That looks like a bargain to me," I said as the balloons moved on. "Have you painted all these here turtles yourself, Mrs. Pye?"

"Not exactly," she answered, and I noticed the color was coming back to her face. "I keep the one here on the counter as a sort of demonstration. Aren't they pretty turtles?"

"Prettiest turtles I ever saw anywhere," I told her, not taking my eyes off of her eyes. "How many of them have you got here in all?"

"Over a thousand," she said. "The rest of them are in this big box down here under the counter." As she said it, another lady — this time with two little girls — came by and bought a couple of turtles. I could see that business was good.

I went into some fast figuring in my mind — a thousand turtles at two bits apiece; two hundred and fifty dollars. I could bark them to the crowds and put Claudie into the painting act. We could raise the price to thirty-five cents — three hundred and fifty dollars for a thousand turtles. While I was thinking, I saw our old car parked across the street, and I felt downright ashamed of it. Missing the car the way we had after Professor Pye ran off with it, I'd almost forgotten what bad shape it was in; but I could see it was the worst run-down automobile on the street there in front of the Dallas Fair. It needed a coat of paint about as bad as a car could. The tires were worn through until you could see several layers of fabric underneath. Some of the glass was broken out of the windows; all the fenders but one were dented, and it was plumb gone. Seeing the car made me remember, too, about the bad miss in the motor that we'd never been able to get shut of.

The day was a brisk, chilly one in late October, and with colder weather due, I realized I wasn't exactly crazy about giving up the nice warm trailer house the Professor and Mrs. Pye had left with us in Fort Worth. This was how I came by my second big idea of the day: maybe we could make a trade with the Pyes. But before I could open up the subject, Claudie spoke again. What he blurted out was, "We was scared you and the Professor wasn't gonna come back with our car."

"But — " Mrs. Pye started to say; then Claudie, still mad, went on, "Stealing is agin the law."

At this I had to take over again. I said: "We're not going

to put the law on the Professor — if you all do the right thing, that is."

"You are a fair man, Mr. Hightower," she said; and as she did, she put a very nice long look on me. I just stood there soaking it up and feeling bubbles way down inside of me until a man and his wife came along with four kids and bought four turtles. After they'd gone on, I continued with Mrs. Pye: "Do you suppose you and the Professor would want to keep the car and let us have the trailer? We'd let you, if you'd throw all these turtles in to boot."

"But these hand-painted turtles are worth twenty-five cents apiece," she argued; and at this point — just when I was in the big middle of a trade — Claudie tried to butt in and say something.

"No, Claudie; not now," I told him. When I am on a trade, I cannot stand it for anybody to interrupt, particularly Claudie.

But all the time I was working out the terms of the deal with that pretty Mrs. Pye, Claudie kept on trying to get a word in here and there. It would have been enough to pester hell out of a weaker character than I am, but I went right ahead because I could see that the longer it took to agree, the more money it was costing us. At that, Mrs. Pye sold three more turtles and put the money in her purse before we finally shook hands on the deal. It was exactly the same proposition I'd offered her in the beginning, and her hand felt strong and soft in mine when we shook.

We both wanted to bind the trade right away, so Mrs. Pye reached in her purse and pulled out the registration papers on our car. She reminded me that when we'd let the Professor have the papers that day in Fort Worth, I hadn't signed them. She had a fountain pen, so I signed the papers right there in the turtle booth with Claudie as a witness, and Mrs. Pye put them back in her purse. Then I said, "Mrs. Pye, how about the registration papers on the trailer house? It's ours now."

By this time she was selling another turtle, and Claudie pulled me off to one side. I said, "All right, all right; what's it all about, Claudie?" I knew I wouldn't have any peace of mind until I let him have his say.

"It's about the people that's been buying them turtles. They are all coming out from behind the next booth — the one with the silk DALLAS FAIR pillows," was what Claudie had been trying all that time to tell me. Then Claudie turned to Mrs. Pye and said, "That last quarter is ourn."

Mrs. Pye smiled a very sweet, ladylike smile and said, "Why, sure," as she gave the quarter to my coarse friend, Claudie.

2

It turned out that we could not get the papers on the trailer house signed right there, since they were made out in the name of Professor E. Ludington Pye and wife, Eula Pye. The Professor, she said, was not around that morning. His concession was inside the fairgrounds, way over at the far end. He was working, Mrs. Pye told us, in the booth where they guess how much you weigh, and if they miss, your exact weight is on the house.

"That is no problem at all," I explained. "We will leave Claudie here to sell the turtles while we go and find Professor Pye."

"It costs a dollar apiece to get in the fairgrounds," Mrs. Pye said.

"Think nothing of it," I answered. "Let's go in your car, Mrs. Pye."

I don't believe I had seen Mrs. Pye look half as pretty before as she did when she blushed a little, looked down and said, "Very well, Clint."

"Claudie," I found myself almost yelling at him, "kindly watch after the turtles while we are gone." His mouth flew open, and he looked like some great big animal caught in a little trap; then I turned to Mrs. Pye and said, "Let's go, Eula."

It gave me a very peculiar feeling to be in the car that had been mine and Claudie's — but this time alongside that sweet Eula Pye of the big gray-green eyes that looked level at me when she talked. Eula had on a little green sweater that was buttoned down the front, and the sleeves ended above her elbows. Her arms looked soft and slender. She had a way of holding her head high as she looked my way, and the easy angle of her chin against her smooth white throat was enough to drive all the cars and trailers and hand-painted turtles in the world out of a man's mind.

As we pulled away from the curb, I knew that we would go straight into the big fair entrance with the brick towers and flags flying; I knew we would drive across the fairgrounds through all the crowds to the place where the Professor would be guessing people's weights; I knew he would sign the papers on the trailer house back in Fort Worth, and that would give me and Claudie good legal title to it; then I would drive Eula Pye back to the turtle place, and it would be all over. As I say, I knew all these things in my mind; but, somehow, I did not give a damn that morning whether those things were true or not. They were in the future, and I wasn't bothered any more about the future than I was about the past which was all over. The future, I always say — even if it's the very near future — is not happening, and what you think it holds may never take place. Right now a man does not live yesterday; he does not live tomorrow, right now. He lives right now, and that is all at any one time.

As we took our place in the line of cars before the entrance to the Dallas Fair, I found myself wishing that old car had been some kind of a low-hung black automobile like a Stutz Bearcat, with big tires and silver exhaust pipes coming straight out from the hood — a car with a roaring motor that would shoot us off somewhere at a hundred miles an hour to a soft grassy place alongside a blue ocean with big, rough, foamy waves splashing hard against jagged rocks. At such a rate of speed on the way to a place like that, the very same wind that would blow against my face would also blow through Eula's bright sorrel hair, and if wind was meant for any better use in this crummy world, I couldn't figure it out for the life of me.

It cost a dollar for me to go into the fairgrounds, a dollar for Eula, and for the car it cost another fifty cents that Eula had not spoken of before. That took nearly all the cash I had, but I handed the money to the man at the gate in the same careless way that you'd throw away an old razor blade.

We drove straight ahead into the fairgrounds; then all hell broke loose.

The first sign of trouble came from the motorcycle cops. About a dozen of them exploded from our left and swung alongside the car and in front of us. They all blew their whistles and waved us down. As I stopped, I thought of all the sins I'd committed since I was a little shaver back in Alabama; I thought of Jules Rabinowitz, too, and what he'd said about the law looking for me and Claudie. I thought about those turkeys we'd taken off the roost in Liberty, and I thought about Claudie sitting back there on Exposition Avenue with all those turtles — and in no trouble.

I looked at Eula and saw what all that commotion was doing to her. Seeing a scared woman is the only thing I know that tightens up a man's liver and lights more than seeing one cry, and this time I felt all my insides tangled up into the kind of big, hard knot that nobody but a sailor or an Eagle Scout could ever undo. The guns those cops had on looked like they'd weigh forty pounds apiece. I could not blame Eula one bit for the question she asked me. It was: "What the hell is this you've got me into, Clint? Is this car hot?"

Notice that she was still calling me Clint, though. I didn't think of an answer, but I could tell that pretty soon something had to give somewhere. The way it did was for a band to start playing. It was off to our right, and it was loud too — sharp, brassy horn noises, squeaky piccolo peeps, and the heavy bumps of big drums. I looked, and there was the biggest, best-dressed band I'd ever seen — bright red pants, gold-braided blue coats with pincushions on the shoulders, and big fuzzy caps like the ones worn in England by those guys that guard the King himself. They were playing "Onward, Christian Soldiers," and from the way it all made me feel, I might as well have been a waterboy in the forces of the Old Scratch.

When the band finally played itself out on the piece, I could still hear the drums, or the motorcycles or my pulse pounding my my ears, I couldn't tell which. I noticed the motorcycle cops were forming themselves in a line that led from the car to a sidewalk across the street on our left. They all stood straight and stiff, with their chests stuck out in front; then a bugle blew *tata-ta-tata-ta-ta-taa,* and the cop that was standing nearest the car saluted us and said: "The Honorable Mayor of the City of Dallas wishes a word with you."

I looked down the line of cops, and there came the Mayor — a nice, friendly-looking little gray-haired man, dressed within an inch of his life, and wearing a big white flower in the buttonhole of his coat. He walked up to the car, and two other citizens — not cops — walked along behind him.

"Greetings," the Mayor said to Eula and me.

"The same to you," I answered, but Eula did not say a word. The next thing I knew, the Mayor was shaking hands with us, and then one of the citizens behind him handed him a key as big as a barrel stave. The Mayor bowed and gave it to me, while people rushed up from all sides and started taking pictures with flashlights. The Mayor said: "Congratulations! Yours is the millionth car to attend the Texas State Fair this year. I am happy to present you with the key to the exposition grounds."

I figured it was pretty late to be giving a man a key after he'd spent about all the money he had to get into the place — unless, that is, it was a key that would be sure to get him back out; but all I could think to say was, "Much obliged."

Then the band broke into another loud marching song. We were holding up traffic as far as I could see on Exposition Avenue, and we had all those cops and the Mayor of Dallas on our side. Hearing that good music filling the air and seeing hundreds of people gathering around to gawk at us, I knew there was plenty of honor to share with Eula, so I looked over at her and smiled. She smiled right back and said something nice, but I couldn't hear it for the beautiful music. Then I thought of Claudie standing back there in the middle of all those hand-painted turtles, and what went through my mind was, "If that big ugly bastard could only see me now!"

3

The Mayor went on with the ceremony as soon as the band stopped playing. He asked us to get out of the car so he could present the President of the Dallas Fair Association to us. Then he presented the Directors and some other stiff, dignified citizens wearing stovepipe hats and patent-leather shoes. The Mayor spoke through a loud-speaker and said it was the first year since the fair started that a million cars had been through the gates. All the people cheered, and the band let off another loud brassy blast. I never felt so much like running for office before or since.

All the excitement and speeches brought more and more color to Eula Pye's cheeks. She'd had a lot to begin with, and being so happy over the celebration and the honor of it, she made the other women standing around there look as plain and flat as so much skimmed milk.

Next, the Mayor asked everybody to be quiet, then he spoke again over the loud-speaker and said he wanted to introduce another prominent citizen to us, Mr. Biggerstaff, the President of the Dallas Automobile Repairmen's Association.

Mr. Biggerstaff was a pint-sized fellow, pale-blue-eyed and bald as a nest egg. Through the loud-speaker he said:

"It gives me pleasure to greet the millionth car to the Dallas Fair this year. To the owners, with the compliments of the Dallas Automobile Repairmen's Association, go these certificates. Here is one good for four new tires and tubes to go on your car; this one is good for fender and body repair of all kinds — whatever your car needs; here is a certificate for motor tune-up and another one to overhaul the rest of the car; this big certificate here will get you a complete paint job, also free; here's another one that will give you six months' complimentary supply of gasoline and oil, good at all Southwest Oil Company filling stations in the whole State of Texas."

There were some more certificates, but that was all I heard. I could see in my mind a picture of the car when all those things had been done to it free. Then Mr. Biggerstaff was through, and he was handing me a sheaf of certificates.

"Thank you, Mr. Biggerstaff," I said. "These all go to the little lady here on my right," and I handed them to Eula Pye. I could tell that she was very happy, and so was I.

The Mayor then said it was time to break it up and let the other folks in the Fair Park; the ceremony had held up traffic long enough. He pointed out the million and oneth car that was just back of ours — a big green sedan full of people — and said some real nice things about them, too. Then he told us to take the key along and do anything we wanted. With it we could go anywhere or ride anything in the whole exposition grounds, and it wouldn't cost us a cent. "Your money is no good today at the Dallas Fair," was the way he ended the speech.

From then until 'long about sundown was the nicest day that I'd ever spent — up to that time, I mean. I don't remember much about all the places we went, the free food we had to eat, the different flavors of pop we drank, or even some of the things we rode. The key got us in free everywhere, and we didn't miss much of the fair that day, but when it was over, the fair part of it was a blur. About all I remembered at the end was Eula and how at the Dallas Fair she was having the fun that she'd been meant to have all of her life, but hadn't. I do remember the House of Mirrors, where a man could see forty or fifty reflections of himself and the person with him at the time. It was hard for me to leave such a place, with scads of views of Eula and me, when I knew that after that day and from then on out there would not be even one more sight of us together.

All that afternoon nearly everything that happened would seem funny. I never laughed so much in my life before, and Eula vowed she hadn't either. The things I say are sometimes pretty funny any day in the week, but this time I was really going good, and everything I'd say, Eula would throw her red head back and laugh so that all her nice, even teeth showed. "You're a card, Clint," she said over and over that afternoon at the Dallas Fair.

I never did exactly forget about Claudie that day, nor the Professor either; but they were so far back in my mind that I might as well have. It was almost like a sweet dream, when you know damn well there's something dull and dreary you're going back to when you wake up; but you never quite pin down in your mind what it is.

I guess I'd come about as near to forgetting all about the Professor as I had all day when we turned up late in the afternoon at the Acme Amusement Emporium. It was a big, barny place, but with bright lights all inside; and there were dozens of things in there where you could have fun — marble machines, fortunetelling booths that told your future on a card for a nickel in the slot, penny peep shows of Hawaiian dancers, showcases where you could pick up knives or cigarette cases or candy with a little derrick worked by a lever from the outside, a shooting gallery, and various other things.

One of the other things we saw in the Emporium was Professor E. Ludington Pye's weight-guessing booth. He was standing by the scales with his horn-rimmed glasses pinched on his nose and the long black ribbon sagging from them to his coat lapel. He was studying the size and shape of a heavy-set countrywoman that waited for her weight to be guessed. Just about the time I saw him, he saw me; and when he did, he left the big countrywoman flat-footed and ran toward the back end of the Emporium.

"Look, Eula," I said. "There goes the Professor." She started running after him, yelling, "Oh, Exeter; it's all right. Come on back."

But it didn't do a bit of good. He ran through the swinging doors under the sign that said GENTS WASHROOM, and Eula stopped some distance short of where he'd gone in.

"I can't imagine what's got into Exeter," she said.

It did not seem to be a nice thing to go in and leave Eula alone, but it seemed better than for us to hang around outside waiting for him, so I went in and got him. I brought him out, and he was shaking all over like a wet puppy, until we explained to him that the law was not in on things at all. "Yet," I said.

When Eula told the Professor about our trade, and he saw for sure that he could keep out of trouble by simply signing the registration papers on the trailer house, he signed in a hurry, blubbering a little as he did, about how he had been aiming all along to bring our car back to Fort Worth. He was still in pretty bad shape from the scare he'd had, and he didn't seem to gather himself together until Eula showed him the Dallas Automobile Repairmen's Association certificates and explained to him what they were good for.

I could tell it was about time for me to leave, and, since I'm no hand at dragging out good-bys anyhow, I took the papers on the trailer and said, "Good-by, Professor." I spoke the way you'd speak to a waiter that has just brought you a second bad egg.

When I turned to tell Eula good-by, she was not standing there any more. She was walking away toward the weight-guessing booth. Her bright red head was held high, and in her straight, firm walk I coud see that she was having to make herself do what she was doing. I knew that I would not see Eula Pye again, and that was the best way for it to be; but I knew, too, that all hell, high water and wild Indians could never take away from us the day that we had had together at the Dallas Fair.

Outside the Emporium it was just getting dusk. A three-quarter moon, as slick and shiny as a fresh-peeled onion, was hanging over the fairgrounds. A little put-put came along pulling a long line of trailers full of people, and the sign on it said, TO FAIR PARK ENTRANCE — 5 CENTS. I found, though, that I did not have five cents in my pocket, so I walked toward the big gates on very tired feet. This was the first I'd noticed it though.

It turned out to be a long way, and my feet got to bothering me more as I went along, so I stopped after a bit and sat on the curb near a lamppost to give them a little breather. I saw a colored folder there and picked it up to read while I rested. The folder told a lot of facts about the Dallas Fair, and on the back it had a calendar of all the big doings from the first day to the last. Here was a good chance, I figured, to see how many days of the fair we had left to get a thousand turtles sold.

By the time I got back to the turtle stand outside the gates my feet were really killing me. They'd got ten times worse, it seemed to me, in the last half mile I walked. There wasn't an electric light in the booth, but Claudie had dug up a lantern from somewhere, and in the sickly lantern light his face had the hue of thin yellow whey.

"How's business, Claudie?" I asked him, as cheerful as a man can be with both feet throbbing like drums in bands sound.

"I ain't sold nary a turtle all day, and several of 'em has died," he answered.

"You've had all your worry for nothing," I said. "It don't make a whit of difference. This is the last day of the fair anyway."

V
The Auction

NORTH FORT WORTH is a nice enough place when you are not downwind from those stockyards, but all that winter we spent there it seemed to me that the Dolly Dimple Trailer Court was located a little downwind from them, no matter where the wind blew.

I and Claudie stayed on at the trailer court though, long after spring broke, and there were several reasons. We still did not have a car to pull our trailer house; that was one. Another was that Claudie had a job at the stockyards that helped us pay for groceries and stuff while I thought a lot about several things I might invent and broadened my contacts here and there. The other reason we stayed was that a Mrs. Spilt owned the Dolly Dimple Trailer Court, and she was claiming some sort of lien on our trailer house for what we owed her.

One Saturday in late May, Claudie didn't come straight from work after he got paid off; in fact he didn't get back to the trailer house until after I went to sleep that night. The next morning I slept late, the way I always do on Sundays, and Claudie had the whole trailer house full of coffee and bacon smells when I woke up. As he brought me my breakfast I said, "Claudie, you can quit your job at the stockyards now. I've got us a brand-new line."

That seemed to scare him some, as it always does when a change is brewing. He knows I have a very active mind, and he's never sure that he'll be able to keep pace with it. "Kindly step out of the trailer house and look what I've got painted on the side," I told him.

He went outside, and when he came back he was grinning like a mule with briers in his teeth.

"The sign says: COLONEL CLINT HIGHTOWER, AUCTIONEER," Claudie announced. "Looks like you've been promoted, Clint."

"In Texas," I explained, "if you are an auctioneer, you are a colonel. It's sort of automatic."

"I didn't even know you was a auctioneer," Claudie said.

"Well, I certainly am," I told him.

"Since when?" he wanted to know.

"Since I got hired yesterday to run a big auction."

"By who?"

"By a college man named Earl Stutter."

"A real college man?" he asked.

"Sure he is; he is a student in Grubb's Vocational College over at Arlington. When he came in to Fort Worth to find an auctioneer, I found him. Hurry up now and get this trailer cleaned up inside because that college man will be along before noon to hook on and pull us out to the place where I'm going to do the auction."

"What about that money we owe Mrs. Spilt?" Claudie wanted to know.

"I've got that figured out, too," I told him. "Your last pay check will just about cover it, Claudie."

He looked down and started twisting a button on the front of his shirt. That was when I learned about the Ouija board. Claudie had gone by a place near the stockyards for a beer and a game of dominoes after work, and before he'd made it to bed he'd gone and spent about all the money he had left on the Ouija board. But it was the classiest one I'd ever seen, and I hardly blamed him for buying it. It had some real frilly decorations painted around the *Yes* and the *No* at opposite ends of the board. The letters of the alphabet were blue, and the figures through nine were green. The zero was canary-bird yellow.

I managed to square things with Mrs. Spilt just before she called in a policeman, but it took about everything I and Claudie could rake and scrape out of the trailer to do it. In fact, if Mrs. Spilt had only known how shy of policemen we'd become, she might have wrecked my career as auctioneer right then and there.

It was nearly noon that Sunday morning when Earl Stutter came for us in an old touring car. He was a very large young citizen of twenty or twenty-one, and he had a nice, polite set of college manners, including a handshake that nearly knocked me down. Earl was not wearing a hat, and his hair was cut so short that it looked like oat stubble. He had a big, long jaw, and he was smoking a heavy black pipe that I figured a lighter-built jaw wouldn't have handled.

While Claudie was getting our trailer house ready to roll, I showed Earl Stutter the big auctioneer sign I'd painted across the side of it the day before, but I didn't let him get close enough to see that the paint was still wet. I could tell he was mighty proud to know me because he offered to shake hands again. I braced myself, and as we shook I said, "I don't believe you told me what it was you wanted auctioned off, Earl."

"Livestock, Colonel Hightower — some cattle, horses, pigs, and sheep at Papa's farm over close to McKinney," he told me.

"I specialize in livestock," I explained. "Claudie here, my assistant, is good at handling animals too. He's even had stockyard experience."

Pretty soon Claudie had the trailer house hooked on behind Earl's car, so we pulled out. I and Claudie rode back in the trailer so he could keep things from jostling about too much and I could practice auctioneering.

All the way to McKinney I practiced on Claudie. I auctioned off everything we had left in the trailer house to him. Then I said: "Claudie, now let's suppose this old lantern here is a nice young Poland China shoat, and you are the crowd at Mr. Stutter's farm."

"I s'pose so," Claudie allowed, but it was pretty hard for him to follow me.

"All right, gentlemen," I opened up in a loud voice, "what am I bid on this fine animal? Look at him! What a dandy pig! What a frame for pork! Look how broad he is across the hindquarters! Look what hams he'll have when he fills out! Think of the chitlins and cracklings, the souse, and the sausage he'll make! The backbone, the pork chops, and the ribs! I've auctioned off pigs from one end of this great state to the other, gentlemen, but if I've ever seen a finer prospect for real hog meat than this one, my name is not Colonel Clint Hightower. Man and boy, I've never seen the like of this one. What a shoat! What am I bid? — How am I doing, Claudie?"

"A lantern is a lantern," Claudie said. That will show you how much help Claudie is along any line where a man would need to have brains.

But I went on: "Another thing, gentlemen — time flies. Here it is spring already. Summer is right on us. Fall will be here in no time; then the first norther; cold weather!

Hog-killing time. Hog meat! This here shoat is as bright and wide awake a one as I've ever seen. He won't have to be slopped half as often as the ordinary pig, and I'll tell you why. Look what a keen eye he's got; he'll make his way; he'll find acorns; he'll find spoiled fruit in the orchard; and by winter it will all be turned into pork. Why gentlemen, you are buying a machine that Henry Ford couldn't make for a million dollars; a machine that will turn scraps and slop and garbage into sweet pork by the time winter gets here. What am I bid, gentlemen? — Goddamit, Claudie, what am I bid?"

"About a dollar, I expect," was all I got from Claudie, who is a clod.

"Thirteen dollars is the bid by the gentleman back there in the blue jumper. Thank you, sir! You can tell a real shoat when you see one. Thirteen dollars! Going at thirteen — thirteen I'm bid. Gentlemen, you wouldn't want to steal this fine shoat, would you? Who'll make it fourteen? — Are you done? — all through? — going, going — are you through? — Who'll make it thirteen-fifty?"

By this time I had a full head of steam and I was roaring; then I looked outside and noticed that we were parked in front of a filling station in McKinney. I didn't know how long we'd been there, but I could see that quite a good crowd was gathering around us.

"Just warming up," I told Earl Stutter when he came back and looked in the trailer. He didn't seem to understand what had been going on any better than Claudie had.

"By the way, Earl," I asked him, "how much farther is it to the farm?"

"About thirteen miles, Colonel," he said.

2

As we went on from McKinney, I sat up in the car with Earl while Claudie rode back in the trailer alone, and Earl told me a lot about himself and his folks. He had a large vocabulary of words, as college men often do; his talk was full of such things as "apropos," "necessarily," and "quaint," but he didn't get as much said as a lot of people who are much plainer in their talk.

"Why are you all having the auction?" I asked him. I figured I might as well know.

"Mamma and Papa are going to send me up North to finish my education, and the auction will raise the money," he said.

"Why is it, Earl," I asked him, "that you wish to get more education? Sounds to me like you have taken on a hell of a lot already."

"Mamma has always wanted me to become a college professor," he answered. "I'll need a Master's degree to do that."

"What'll you be teaching, Earl?" I asked.

"Vocational agriculture," Earl announced.

"What does your old man think about that?" I asked him, but before he could answer we passed a very pretty girl standing by a yellow pickup that was parked facing us on the far side of the road.

"Hold it, Earl," I told him. "Hold it. Do you see what I see?" Earl put on the brakes and stopped.

"Yes," Earl said in a kind of slow, strained way. "It's Fanny Lou Dilworth; she seems to have a flat tire."

He backed up until we were next to the yellow pickup, and we saw that it was filled with fresh garden sass — big handsome heaps of green onions, radishes, beets, mustard greens and turnips. Vegetables scarcely ever grow in the garden as pretty as they look in the seed catalogues, and hardly any girls grow as smooth and even in person as Sears and Roebuck show them. But we saw enough right before our eyes to give a man new faith in the catalogues.

Fanny Lou had the prettiest lines I ever saw, except maybe in the corset cover ads. Her hair was silky black, and her eyes were the same clean blue as the early morning sky after a quick shower. There were a few freckles on her nose, but no man in his right mind would have wanted a single one of them removed. She stood with her hands on her hips and there was plenty of room — but not too much — for each hand.

Earl said, "Hello, Fanny Lou," and she said, "Hello there, Earl"; then they both looked away from each other. Damnedest thing I ever saw. Earl would hardly glance her way at all, I could hardly keep from it, and Claudie just stood there looking like a little boy that sees a stained-glass angel in a big church window.

I said, "Can't we help, lady?" and she said, half crying, to Earl, "My jack is broke. If I don't get to McKinney with these vegetables today, I won't win the spring garden prize; the judging starts in the morning — Who are these people?"

"Auctioneers," Earl told her, and Claudie's face brightened up the way it does when he sings bass.

"Lady," I said, "do you have some cold patches for the inner tube?"

She said she thought she did, and in a minute she had produced a can of them from under the front seat of the pickup. Earl got a jack from his car. I told Claudie to fix the tire as fast as he knew how, and he went right to work.

There was still a thin skim of ice in the air between Fanny Lou and Earl, and I watched him as he kept fumbling around without looking at her. He had the same kind of look on his face that I saw once in a fellow with a stiff neck at a balloon ascension in Rome, Georgia. Fanny Lou talked some, though, to Earl, and I could tell from what was said that they had been in high school together in McKinney.

Claudie had her flat tire fixed in no time at all, and she went on toward McKinney in a very fine frame of mind. I thought the red apples in her cheeks and her wide smile were good pay for what we did. Her teeth were white and even.

As we drove along I said, "Earl, why don't you try your vocabulary on that corn-fed angel back there in the yellow pickup? She's the prettiest, healthiest-looking thing I have seen in the whole State of Texas."

"She sure has improved since high school days," he said, "but Mamma never did like her much."

"She ain't supposed to, you big lug," I said. "That's your department." I don't think I would have called Earl a big lug if it had not been that Claudie was back there in the trailer, and he was a bigger lug than Earl was.

"Another thing, Earl," I went on, "you acted mighty funny while Claudie was fixing that tire. You and Fanny Lou must have been sweethearts at one time or another."

"How'd you know it?" Earl wanted to know.

"It was just in the air," I told him. "What busted it up?"

"She stayed on the farm when I went away to college. She did not care for a higher education."

"Earl," I said, "did it ever strike you that in college you might just be learning some more words to call the things you already knew about before you went?"

"I never thought of it in exactly that way," he said, lighting his pipe. Then he opened the throttle one more notch.

"And that Fanny Lou Dilworth might be learning more in her garden than you are learning in college?" I went on. "And getting prettier all the time."

"Her outward appearance certainly has improved," Earl said, and he drove on without another word until we came to the Stutter farm.

3

Wholesome is a word I never studied in college or anywhere else, and I have not done many of the things or gone to many of the places that would teach a man all that it can mean; but the clean, tidy look about a well-kept farmhouse early of a Sunday afternoon just about fills the wholesome bill with me. Everything spick-and-span and well scrubbed; people still dressed in their Sunday-go-to-meetin' clothes, and the womenfolks wearing clean aprons over their good dresses until the Sunday dinner dishes are washed and put away.

That's the way we found the Stutter household, when we got there along about two o'clock and parked our trailer house in the shade of a sycamore tree down by the well. Earl took us up to the house and nothing would do but we should sit right down and have some cold fried chicken, warmed-over biscuits, okra and buttermilk.

We saw where Earl got that underslung jaw as soon as we met Mrs. Stutter, and we could tell more about it still when they introduced us to her mother, Granny Singleton, since jaws have a way of showing up more on older people's faces.

Mr. Stutter was a polite, soft-voiced man of fifty-five, maybe sixty. His hair was gray, but his eyebrows were black. He had kindly brown eyes like you see in people who are very religious, but in a solemn, quiet way.

Those ladies really took on over Earl, and little dabs of it seemed to spill over on us, since we had come along with him. They were real proud of Earl for finding an auctioneer, and they were so dadgummed nice to me and Claudie that it made me feel the way I sometimes do when I dream I am in church somewhere with no clothes on.

After we'd eaten our fill, Mrs. Stutter and her mother asked Earl to come into the parlor and tell them about how things were at college. As they went in, Mrs. Stutter said, "Colonel Hightower, we'll leave you men with Mr. Stutter so you can talk business. The auction is set for Tuesday, the day after tomorrow."

I and Claudie and Mr. Stutter went out to the front stoop and sat in rockers that were shaded from the afternoon sun by a big black walnut tree. First we talked about my pay for the auction, and I told Mr. Stutter I believed I would charge 10 per cent of the total take. He said, "Fine, Colonel; whatever's customary." Then we talked about the weather that had been fair, the crops that needed rain, and the stock on the place. Mr. Stutter allowed as how livestock you had raised could be a lot of company on a farm. Claudie had been laying off to say something ever since we got there, and with fewer people around he finally spoke up. What he said was: "We shore do like it here, Mr. Stutter."

"This is good country," Mr. Stutter admitted. It was

plain that he wanted to say more, but he was going to do it in his own time.

In a little while Claudie asked, "How long have y'awl lived here?"

Mr. Stutter said: "All my life. My pappy came here as a boy in an early day — right after the Osages killed off all of his family but him. He came from Bois d'Arc over in the Red River Valley, about forty miles from here; they call the place Bonham now.

"Pappy was one of the old settlers that took up this country when the land was new. They outfought the Indians and the Mexicans and the hurrah grass to put it in cultivation. They made it produce, and it took good care of them. Then the others came in: the wagon-yard keepers, the junk dealers and the tombstone salesmen; the saloonkeepers, the pawnbrokers, and the jewelers; the lawyers, the bankers, and the insurance agents. These latecomers built up the towns, and that's where they all live, but they own most of this country now."

"You don't say!" Claudie chimed in.

"That's the way it is," Mr. Stutter went on. "See that farm out there to the west — the one with the yellow barn? That's the old Overstreet place, but it don't belong to that family any more. The Overstreet boys have all gone off to work for the government or the chain stores. The place is owned now by a hardware drummer's widow, and she rents it to some colored people who don't keep it up. Same thing is true all around me. An Indian from Oklahoma rents the farm on the east of me, and if I don't watch that Indian like a hawk, he'll let the east gap down in the spring so his cattle can eat my young corn. The only real neighbor I've got left is Crusoe Dilworth."

"Fanny Lou Dilworth's old man?" I asked.

"He's her pappy," Mr. Stutter answered. He had such a kind, earnest look as he talked that it put me in mind of something I'd heard once in Sunday school: that God writes on people's faces what kind of folks they are. I knew Mr. Stutter must be the right kind.

Mr. Stutter sat there, silent for a while as the shadows got longer; then he went on: "I hate to think of this place in the hands of renters, but it looks like I'm going to be the last owner to live on it. Earl's mother and grandmother don't want him to stay here; they want him to go off and teach school somewhere."

"What a shame it is for a man so well built for farm work to be going off to college, learning ways to avoid it," I said.

"They're afraid he'll come back to the farm and marry Fanny Lou Dilworth," Mr. Stutter said. "She's only a farm girl but she sure does know how to make things grow."

"Don't you reckon Earl might change his mind and come back to the farm?" I asked him.

"I don't rightly know, Colonel," Mr. Stutter answered. "The boy is gettin' so well educated that I can't hardly talk to him any more." That was all he had to say, but I could tell it helped his feelings to get these things said.

4

The next day was Monday and, first thing, I explained that it was no part of my work to fool with the stock; my assistant, Claudie, handled such details. I only auctioned them off when the time came. Mr. Stutter and Claudie spent all morning cutting out the stock to be auctioned off on

Tuesday. They decided to put the ones that would be sold in the south pen below the barn.

While Mrs. Stutter and Granny Singleton filled the clothesline with wash that soon fluttered in the wind, I sat on the front porch and thought for a while; then I went looking for Earl. I located him in the parlor studying a McKinney High School yearbook. I couldn't help seeing over his shoulder that the book was opened at a page with the picture of a pretty face on it. "McKinney High Queen" it said at the top of the page, and the girl was Fanny Lou Dilworth. When Earl saw me standing there, he got up in a hurry and closed the book. He was very red in the face. I did not think of anything to say to Earl, and he seemed to be at a loss too, so we shook hands, and I went back out on the porch. When it comes to college manners, I can hold my own with the best of them.

At noontime Claudie told me they had been having a very slow time with the stock. First, Mr. Stutter had picked several calves, an old bay mare named Babe, and a span of gray mules to go into the south pen; he told Claudie he couldn't see how he could spare a single one of his milk cows, his pigs or his sheep. Then Mr. Stutter decided he wanted to keep the old mare, one of the mules, and all the calves but one that had a white eye. Later he took the other mule back and put an old brood sow in the south pen with the calf, and that was all the stock they had picked for the auction by noon.

By night it was all changed again, so Claudie said. They hadn't put, and left, anything in the south pen but a blind goat, two lambs, a turkey gobbler, a boar shoat that was the runt of the litter, a Jersey cow that was dry, and a thirty-one-year-old saddle mule that was getting a little stringhalted.

"It sure was sad," Claudie told me. "Them animals are like members of Mr. Stutter's family. He called 'em all by name and told the ones we left in the south pen good-by."

"That's too bad, Claudie," I said, "but the women are hell-bent on this auction, and we can sure use that 10 per cent."

"I druther be back in the stockyard job," Claudie answered.

"Come on, Claudie," I told him. "Don't get chicken-hearted about the stock. We've got us a job to do tomorrow."

That night after supper we all sat in the parlor for a while and talked. I stated that after a day of rest and meditation I felt I would be in good voice for the auction. Mrs. Stutter spoke of how proud it made her to think of Earl with two college degrees teaching higher subjects of some kind, and Granny Singleton chimed in that she was mighty proud too; Earl was the only person in her family to get one degree, much less two. Mrs. Stutter mentioned getting a teacher's certificate after two years at the Denton Normal, but Granny Singleton pointed out that she had run off and married Mr. Stutter before she ever got a chance to use it.

Then the talk got very draggy until it about petered out; everything that was said was something that had been said before, and I could tell that everybody was thinking, let's break it up, but how? Somebody would have thought up a way too, and the Stutter visit would have had a different end, if Granny Singleton hadn't gone and brought us back hot steaming cups of sassafras tea.

All this time Mr. Stutter had nothing to say, and Earl just sat there with his eyes on a corner of the carpet but looking like a man does when he sees something a long ways off. I noticed he kept pulling an ear lobe with one hand while he operated that heavy black pipe with the other. He was putting out big clouds of strong smoke.

I sat and thought about how broke we were, and Claudie out of a job too; how many things we needed to buy, and how far we could go on the money we'd make out of the auction; then I thought about Mr. Stutter and the way he felt about his land and his livestock — how he'd sweated all day over the stock he'd be willing to let go to educate that big, overgrown, pipe-smoking farm boy. I could just see Earl sitting up somewhere in a college all grown over with vines, while he talked about vocational agriculture when he should have been raising crops. I thought, too, about that pretty Fanny Lou of the light blue eyes and freckles; the farm girl that plainly was stuck on Earl, and the way she could make things grow from the soil. Then all of a sudden it came to me quick as a flicker. "Hell, Clint," I said to myself, "you can't let this auction come off. All the parts are here but the auction is the wrong recipe. Besides, all you and Claudie would get out of the auction would be only money anyway."

5

"Claudie," I said, "suppose you run down to the trailer house and fetch along that nice Ouija board we brought from Fort Worth. It's the best one I ever saw."

When he came back with it, the ladies insisted that I and Claudie take the first turn, so we sat in chairs facing each other with the board on our laps. We put our hands on the little heart-shaped pointer with felt-bottom legs and slid it around on the board to see how it would work. Everything was new and a little sticky, but there was nothing wrong with the board that a dash of talcum powder didn't fix. Just to warm it up, we asked first how company was treated at the Stutter place. From the place marked *Start,* the little pointer slid to *F,* then to *I,* then to *N,* and Claudie took his hands off.

"Put your big, ugly, cotton-picking hands back, Claudie," I said. "This board ain't through answering our question." He did, and the pointer slid over to the "E" and stopped.

"F-i-n-e, fine," I told them. "This here board is in tune with the stars."

Then the ladies wanted Mr. Stutter to try the board and he sat down with Claudie. They asked about the garden; would the vegetable crop be good? The little pointer went right over to the planets and comets on the *Yes* side of the board. Earl, who had been quiet all this time, spoke up and said he thought the board must be right; it appeared to be a good year for vegetables. Granny Singleton and Mrs. Stutter smiled and pulled up their chairs. It was plain that with the ladies our goose was hanging high — high, that is, for a goose that would be cooked within an hour.

Next I took a turn with Granny Singleton. We both touched the pointer with our fingers, but she said she couldn't think up a very good question right then. I figured it was time to make my move, so I said, "Well, I've got one that's been bothering me a lot today."

"What is it?" Mrs. Stutter wanted to know.

"It's about the auction tomorrow," I answered. "An auction, you see, is a lot like catching fish. All the signs have to be just right. I make it a rule not to auction off anything if the signs are wrong. You see, I've got my reputation at stake in every auction."

"Well, I declare," Granny Singleton put in.

"Take the moon," I went on. "I've seen many an auction ruined — other auctioneers' jobs, I mean — just like I've seen many a fishing trip spoiled, by the wrong kind of moon. I've been wondering if the moon is right for this auction."

But Granny was too fast for me. By the time I'd said it, and before I could even look down, the little pointer slid over to the *Yes*. Then Granny Singleton looked up at me and smiled the same sweet, innocent smile that you see in some of the art work on Mother's Day greeting cards. I wasn't licked, though.

"Then," I explained, "there's the zodiac. The signs of the zodiac have to be right. Let's see what the Ouija board says about that." I was braced and ready for Granny this time, but before we could get the little pointer back to the starting place, Mrs. Stutter got up and said there was an almanac in the kitchen that ought to have the answer to any question about the zodiac. When she came back with the almanac we looked under the month of May, but I pointed out in a hurry that it didn't say anything at all about auctions, and that sent us right back to the Ouija board for the answer. Mrs. Stutter said — a little peevishly too — that she wondered when her turn with the board was coming, and from the set of her jaw as she asked it, I figured she knew.

"Excuse me, ma'am," I said, as I got up, since I could tell she had me. "Why don't you and Claudie try it next?" Claudie was a long shot, but he looked like the only one; and as he sat down with Mrs. Stutter, I tried to catch his eye. It wasn't any use though; he was so parlor scared that he never even looked my way at all.

"What I'm afraid of, folks," I stated, "is that the signs of the zodiac are not right for auctioning off those nice stock down in the south pen. Listen to me, Claudie — the south pen. Maybe the Ouija board will tell us if they are right."

Long before this question had had time to soak in through Claudie's thick skull, I saw the leaders in Mrs. Stutter's wrists tighten up. The little pointer shot over to the *Yes* so fast that it nearly flew right out from under Claudie's hand.

"Well, Claudie," I said, and I wished I could have said it with a bumblebee stinger, "that takes care of the zodiac."

The ladies looked at each other and nodded. Claudie looked like a man with the sun in his eyes, and Earl sat and smoked away at his big pipe. I studied Earl a little and said to myself, "There sits the last chance them stock have."

I pointed out that Earl was the only one that hadn't tried the Ouija board, and Mr. Stutter said sure enough, Earl hadn't had his turn. Earl said he didn't believe in Ouija boards, except for strictly amusement purposes, but he would play the game with his father if somebody had a question. Granny Singleton stated she thought it would be a pity if they didn't; then Mr. Stutter and Earl sat down with the board.

Nobody asked me to, but nobody told me not to, so I put the question. I asked in a nice easy voice: "Is there a prettier girl in Collin County than Fanny Lou Dilworth?" The board did not waste any time. The pointer slid right over to the thunderclouds where the *No* was painted, and Earl looked up at Mr. Stutter as bashful as a collie pup that's been caught sucking eggs.

"Wouldn't Fannie Lou make a lovely wife?" I asked in a hurry, feeling like the home team had the ball.

The board said *Yes* fast.

Mrs. Stutter then said that was enough on that subject;

she wanted to work the board with Earl, and her jaw stood out like an elbow when she said it. As Earl and his mother sat head-to-head with the Ouija board on their laps, I couldn't help noticing how close a match his jaw seemed for hers. They'd no sooner sat than Mr. Stutter said he had a question; would they mind getting the board's answer? There was a new glint in his eyes, I thought, and he went on without waiting; "I've been wondering," Mr. Stutter said, "whether Earl was cut out to be a schoolteacher anyhow."

That did it. On Mr. Stutter's question that Ouija board froze. I had seen Ouija boards in my time that were balky; I had seen them hesitate before; I even saw one give the wrong answer once; but never had I seen a Ouija board stumped as bad as that one was. The air began to feel blinky, and Granny Singleton finally said maybe they ought to start all over again and repeat the question a little louder. Mr. Stutter asked it again, and again nothing happened, except that after a long, tight wait, the pointer slid up to the *Q* and stuck. Granny Singleton and Earl then tried the board on the same question, but they got nowhere at all; the board was on dead center again.

Pretty soon Mr. Stutter started yawning. He walked around the room looking at the calendars and mottoes on the walls. Then Earl got up and said: "Apropos of nothing, I think I want to go find out who won the Collin County spring garden prize."

"Why Earl," his mother said, "it's after eight o'clock. What do you care about the gardening prize, and wherever would you go to find out?"

"They will know down at the Dilworths' who won," Earl said. "Fanny Lou was in the contest. I think I'll just drive down to the Dilworths'; it isn't far." Earl left, and Mr. Stutter went through the door into the back part of the house.

I wish to state that I have been in some very quiet places in my time, I've been in graveyards late at night, and I've felt the stagnant silence of caves down under the ground, but I never before ran into so much quiet as took place after Earl left. The ladies sat there rocking and looking at me and Claudie. Their mouths were drawn in tighter than you can draw in the top of a Duke's Mixture tobacco sack, unless you wish to break the string. A little of this seemed to last a good while, and after a bit I and Claudie got up and left.

We went down and sat on the grass beside the trailer house for a long time, talking and watching the stars and the lightning bugs. Claudie said he was afraid he hadn't got his money's worth in the Ouija board. "Dumbest board I ever seen," he allowed.

"That's a better board than you think, Claudie," I told him. "It's a wise board that knows when to quit."

"Anyhow," he said, "I hated to see it balk that way."

"I wouldn't bother about it though," I said, "because Earl is somewhere with Fanny Lou now and from here on I expect Mother Nature has got a Ouija board skinned all hollow."

After this, Claudie thought and thought, and things got so quiet that I must have dozed off there on the grass, because the next thing I knew Claudie was shaking me.

"What's been going on?" I asked, still a little drowsy. Then I saw Earl and Fanny Lou standing there beside Claudie in the dim light of our lantern. They said the Justice of the Peace had refused to marry them without two witnesses.

"Earl," I said, "you could beat the bushes from one end of Texas to the other, and you'd never find two better witnesses than I and Claudie. But first, we'll have to wait until Claudie can go and let them stock of Mr. Stutter's out of the South pen."

V I

Never Start a Rumor

THE FOLLOWING MORNING, long about daylight, Claudie reminded me that all we'd got out of the auction was the lift that Earl Stutter gave our trailer house late the night before.

"Claudie," I said, as I got up and put on my shoes, "you are never at your best early in the morning. Didn't you agree with me that we'd worn our welcome mighty thin with those Stutter ladies?"

"We shore had," he allowed.

"Well," I went on, "here we are, several miles down the road from the Stutter place."

"Also," Claudie said, "we're low on food; we're nearly broke, and the right tire on this here trailer is near about flat."

"You only see the dark side of things," I told him. "Suppose I hadn't found out that the place where we are now belongs to the Widow Wiley? Suppose I hadn't learned that she had a tender heart?"

By this time it was broad daylight, and we could see that our trailer house was parked in the middle of a willow grove a hundred steps or so from the house place. A well of cool, sweet water wasn't more than ten steps away on one side, and there was a nice, quiet, new windmill to lift it for us. About the same distance in the other direction was the prettiest garden this side of what Eden must have been — full of all kinds of green garden sass growing. Beyond the garden a red barn was joined onto the cow lot by a *bois d'arc* hedge, and between the barn and the house there was a big apple and peach orchard. The air was full of all the green, growing smells of good rich land in the late spring. Underfoot in the willow grove a mat of Bermuda grass grew ankle deep, and, as the sun came up, the dew sparkled on the fresh green blades like real show window diamonds. A mockingbird in a big cottonwood tree not far away was tuning up for the day.

"Here," I remarked to Claudie, "are the makings of real hospitality. Personally, I think real well of faith, hope and charity, all three, but I believe I like hospitality even better; it is more apt to stick to your ribs. And I do not know a better brand of hospitality than the one found in the southern part of the United States — except, of course, the brand you find right here in the northern part of the State of Texas."

All Claudie had to offer was: "Guess we're gonna like it here if the chiggers don't eat us up."

"Claudie," I said, "that's the trouble with you. All a big red apple means to you is that there might be a worm in it. Go get me a big spoonful of that sulphur in the green alum can and then take one yourself. A chigger won't eat on a man that's got a little sulphur in his system."

"It's asfiddity for chiggers," Claudie said.

"All right, Claudie," I told him, "there you go, disputin' my word again. You take the asafetida, and I'll take the sulphur. By night we'll see whether they know anything about chigger cures back where you came from."

The sun hadn't been up but a few minutes when we

heard the screen door slam at the house. Then we saw her; not the Widow Wiley — she couldn't have been — but the girl who was to change the whole course of our lives for the next day or so anyway; and, since a man can live only one day of his life at a time, the next day or so was what counted.

I could tell that she had not seen us as she sauntered along through the orchard toward us carrying two milk pails and whistling a song by the name of "Can't You Hear Me Callin', Caroline?" There are people who will tell you that whistling is not a womanly thing to do, but they never heard that girl whistle. She made the peach blossoms look prettier and the early morning colors in the sky brighter. The mockingbird in the cottonwood tree could tell he was licked; he dried right up and flew away. When she wasn't more than ten steps away, she looked up and saw us for the first time. She stopped in her tracks, dropped the milk pails, and broke off in the middle of a long high note from "Caroline." I could see a lot of white around the blue in her wide-open eyes, and she looked so sweet and pure and scared that I felt like a cocker burr growing in a garden of roses. She couldn't have been over nineteen, and as she stood there in her plain, short-sleeved, yellow dress, I thought that if the good Lord did this much for all women, it would close all the beauty parlors in Texas and drive the Neiman-Marcus store to the wall. Her black hair looked as soft and smooth as a kitten's.

"Be quiet, Claudie," I whispered. "It will be all I can do to handle this myself."

As I took off my hat, I said, "Good morning, miss," and I was as polite as a Japanese undertaker. "We are looking for the Widow Wiley."

Then I saw an older woman coming down the path behind Miss Peaches and Cream. She was shaped a good deal like the younger one, only heavier. She came up and looked at us. There was no hospitality in her eyes.

"Who are you men?" she wanted to know. "And what is that thing down there in the grove?"

"Are you the Widow Wiley?" I asked.

"I am," she said, as if she had been proud of it.

"My name is Clint Hightower, and this is Claudie Hughes," I explained. "He works for me. We live in that trailer house down there in the grove, and we hope you will let us stay here until we can get a lift into Dallas."

As I talked, I studied the Widow Wiley. She looked to be forty-five or fifty, but she wasn't a bit gray. Her hair was done up in a little knot on top, but there were a number of wisps and strands that had been missed. They were dangling and floating around her temples. She had a sweet, motherly face with a lot of pink and red in her cheeks, and her eyes were a sort of tired-out blue.

"How on earth — " she started, but I knew I'd better pick up the lead again.

"You must need some help on a nice big place like this. There is hardly anything we can't do."

"But I don't know what kind of people you are. You might be escaped convicts," she answered. She went too far here; it was the opening I'd been sparring for.

"Madam, you have hurt me, and you have hurt my friend Claudie. He is more sensitive than I am," I told her. "They shave convicts' heads, you know. Can't you see that we have plenty of hair?" I turned to Claudie and told him to take off his hat. Neither one of us had had a haircut in some weeks.

"I don't want to hurt you," she said. "I just want you to leave. My daughter Emma and I live here alone, and we are afraid of prowlers."

I turned and spoke to Claudie: "We have asked for bread, and she has given us a stone." Then I looked at the Widow Wiley and said, "We do not have a car to pull our trailer house, but we are handy and we are honest."

"You don't have bad faces," she said, as she looked at Emma. Then Emma whispered something to the Widow Wiley. I looked at Claudie, and he looked down at the ground, and when I looked back at the Widow Wiley, she was shaking her head.

"Madam," I said, "would you ladies like some help with the milking?" In all my life I'd never seen anybody turn down help when it came to breaking a mule or milking a cow. "In fact," I went on, "we'll be glad to take over the milking this morning, and we hope you'll give us a bite of breakfast."

"All right," the Widow Wiley answered, as I took both milk pails from Emma and gave them to Claudie, "but be careful with the little Jersey; her left front teat is a mite sore."

The Widow Wiley walked and Emma floated along beside her toward the house. As Claudie milked the cows, I spoke to him about Emma.

"Claudie," I said, "kindly do not get any ideas about that Emma. Be careful how you look at her." Then I went down to the trailer house to shave and change my shirt before breakfast.

2

When I and Claudie carried the milk up to the house, the cats met us at the back porch — four or five big yellow ones and a litter of mottled kittens. I gave them some milk in a pie pan that was close by, just so the Widow and Emma could see how kind we were to animals. I'm not a man, though, that ever cared a lot about cats generally.

The Widow Wiley came out on the porch and strained the milk. Then they gave us breakfast at a table in the kitchen — big stacks of flapjacks, sausages and hot coffee. Claudie ate so much I was right ashamed of him. As I ate I bragged on the Widow's cows, her orchard, her cats, her cooking and her hospitality; and after Emma went in to the front of the house to clean things up, the Widow got into a real talking mood herself. She was like a lot of people in Texas; if they don't like you, they'll run you away. When they begin to like you, they will share their food and their story with you right off. She told us about herself and about her folks, and I and Claudie listened as we ate. A lot of hospitality works out about like that.

The Widow Wiley's people were among the earliest settlers in the country, she said. Her grandfather Elisha Corn had been a famous Indian fighter, and this was the place he had settled on. Her father, Elijah Corn, had put the whole farm into cultivation, and it was from him that she inherited it before she married Clem Wiley from White Elephant. They had no children for several years after they were married, then their only daughter, Emma, had come along, and Clem died when Emma was a little thing in pigtails.

In the eighteen years since her husband's death, the Widow Wiley had been going into debt nearly every year, she said. First it was the tombstone for Clem's grave. He'd always wanted a big one, and a big one he had, towering out there in the Walnut Grove Cemetery above all the others. The next year the barn had burned with less than half as much insurance on it as the new one had cost. Then there had been a crop failure the year Emma finished high school, and things had gone from bad to worse in a money way ever since.

"If this place hadn't been a homestead, they'd have taken it long ago," the Widow Wiley said; then this fine, sweet lady sighed so big that it was enough to cut a man all to pieces inside. The tears were right on the brim of her eyes, and I saw Claudie was so touched that he nearly stopped eating.

"Who do you owe all this money to?" I asked.

"I don't know what his name is; he calls himself George Texas. He came to McKinney about ten years ago from somewhere in Southern Europe. He bought bones and rags around here for years, but he's a big man now."

"How much do you owe him?" Claudie asked. Claudie has no sense at all about what questions not to ask. But this didn't seem to bother the Widow Wiley.

"Fifteen hundred dollars," she said.

"And interest?" I asked her.

"No, that includes the interest," she stated, as she got up and started clearing the dishes away.

About this time Emma came back into the kitchen to help with the dishes. She looked so clean and fresh and sweet that somehow it made me want to get up from there and beat the tar out of Claudie, big as he was. Emma had changed her dress to one that had some little flower designs on it. She needn't have, though; her own designs were enough. She had combed her hair away from her forehead, showing a little cowlick there above her right temple. I have seen camellias in full bloom that were not half as pretty as that cowlick.

After breakfast I told the Widow that I could see a number of things around the place that needed a man's touch. I explained that I would be glad to have Claudie fix these things up under my direction, and while I sat in the rocking chair on the front porch, Claudie got busy. He knocked some dents out of the Widow's coal scuttle, fixed a broken hinge on the storm cellar door, nailed up some loose planks in the smokehouse, and doctored a Dominecker rooster that had the limberneck.

Along about eleven o'clock Emma came out on the front porch with a little kitten in her arms. I got up and offered her my chair; but she blushed and said no, she would sit on the step. I noticed she had changed dresses again. She sat there stroking the kitten and looking out toward the front gate where Claudie was working on the latch. When he saw her, he started hammering away twice as fast.

We talked about the weather that day, which was warm; we talked about the way it had been, and then I predicted the way I believed it would be. I told her I thought she had an awful nice kitten there, and she said its name was Grace. We talked about the lilacs and the hollyhocks in the yard and the honeysuckle vine that curtained one end of the porch. Then we played two games of croquet in the front yard. Emma had looked prettier than a bowl of fresh fruit sitting there on the porch with her cat, but she was ten times as lovely when she moved about. It brought more color to her cheeks, too, when she exercised. She won both games.

The Widow Wiley called Emma, and as she walked back toward the house with me she asked, without smiling, "Does Claudie have to do all the work?"

"He works with his hands," I told her. "I do the thinking."

"Do you just think up things for him to do?"

"Emma," I said, "you don't do me justice," but I was afraid, as I said it, that she did.

3

When the Widow Wiley came out around noontime with some ham sandwiches, green apple pie, and clabber, I told her I had been thinking about how I could help her get out of debt. I stated that I believed her problem was right in my line.

"What is your line, Mr. Hightower?" the Widow asked, with Emma standing in the front door listening.

"There is hardly anything that is not in my line," I told her. "Hardly anything, that is, except I have always steered strictly clear of politics, smuggling, and all kinds of manual labor. A man can usually avoid these things, madam, and still find plenty of leeway for his natural gifts. It is only when he does the same thing over and over that his talents begin to wither and his spirits to fester up."

"The Lord would bless you if you helped me get out of debt," she said. It sounded genuine, like the Beatitudes my grandmother used to read me from the Bible when I was a little shaver back in Alabama.

"Madam," I went on, "how much land do you have here?"

"A hundred and sixty acres," she answered.

"Have you ever leased it for oil?" As I asked her this question, I glanced at Claudie and saw he was hard-hit with the size of my idea; he was batting his eyes like a bullfrog in a hailstorm.

"Never did," the Widow said. "Twelve or fifteen years ago they drilled a well a mile or so south of here and got everybody all excited — but they only struck granite. They said then that the whole north end of the county was condemned for oil." It would have been enough to discourage most of the people I know, but there was Emma standing there in the door, looking more and more like an angel, and the ideas were flashing across my mind like forked lightning.

"Mrs. Wiley," I said, "excuse me, but how long ago did you say George Texas came to McKinney?"

"Only about ten years ago," she said. "Why?"

"I just wondered," I told her; then I turned to Claudie and said: "Run down to the trailer, Claudie, and get me the blank oil and gas lease we found in that filling station in Fort Worth. It's in my raincoat pocket." While he was gone, I sat there alone on the porch and thought a lot more. When Claudie came back with the paper, I went in the house where the Widow Wiley was churning while Emma put the dishes away. I asked the Widow how much she wanted for an oil and gas lease on her place.

"I can't take any money," she said. "We don't have oil and gas. I tell you, it's granite underneath." This made me real proud of the Widow; she would not take advantage of us.

"Honesty is the best policy," I told her and nodded at Emma. "But look, Mrs. Wiley, you do not have to take any money from us. If you'll sign the lease, I'll try to sell it for you. Then you wouldn't be doing anything wrong."

"Would that be fair?" Emma asked me, but I could see that the Widow Wiley had a tempted look in her eyes.

"It would be fair if somebody didn't believe what they said about the granite," I argued. "Did anybody see the granite? Another thing: They didn't strike granite on this place, did they?"

"No, you're right there," the Widow said and paused; then she said: "I'll have to think it over. Something about it seems almost deceitful."

"Madam," I said, "my time is pretty valuable. We may have to leave any day. Sign this here lease, and we'll split with you whatever we sell it for."

You don't often get a woman convinced with pure reason and facts, but the Widow Wiley was no ordinary woman, and this last point shook her. She took Emma into the next room for a few minutes, and when they came back they had on their bonnets.

I and Claudie and the Widow Wiley and Emma drove down the road in the Widow's old Dodge sedan to the office of the Justice of the Peace. I made the lease out to me, and when the Widow had signed it, the Justice put his acknowledgment on it for free and served us all cool drinks of sarsaparilla.

That night we went to the trailer about dark, and Claudie, whose mind just about peters out at sundown anyway, went right to sleep. I lay awake and thought a long time about Emma and the oil business, but when I had finished, I still couldn't go to sleep somehow. I finally had to wake

Claudie up to get him to help me find the asafetida before I could ever get settled for the night.

The next day Claudie had milked the cows and gathered enough garden sass before breakfast to fill the back end of the Wiley sedan. Emma and the Widow agreed for us to take the vegetables to the market in McKinney. I explained to them that we would look into the oil business some more while we were in town.

Just as we were driving out of the front gate, I spoke to Claudie and said: "Claudie, you had better run back to the trailer and get our cash — I mean the money you've got sewed in your overcoat lining."

"Ain't but four dollars and a half left, and you always said it was for a rainy day," Claudie argued.

"It is for a rainy day," I told him. "A lot of people who don't know any better have the wrong idea about rainy days. Did you ever hear of the manna it rained on the Israelites, Claudie? Now hurry along." He went.

As we drove across the East Fork bridge on the McKinney road, Claudie spoke up. I knew it was going to be about the money, since Claudie had been quiet for twenty minutes, trying to think of how to bring up such a delicate subject. "What are we going to do with the money, Clint?"

"Well," I explained, "we've got to put that oil and gas lease on the County Records, for one thing. That will cost us about a dollar, I expect."

Claudie dug out a dollar and handed it to me. I didn't much mind him being so close about the money because it was his part of what he had made in Fort Worth, anyhow. "Then," I went on, "there is the matter of revenue stamps. You probably never heard of them, did you?"

"Not except on store-bought whiskey."

"Well," I explained, "for every thousand dollars that you pay for land, the law says you've got to put at least a dollar's worth of revenue stamps on the deed."

"Who told you that?" Claudie wanted to know.

"Claudie," I answered, "you have to depend on me for a number of things. It just happens that one of the contacts I made in Fort Worth was a notary public. He was a very smart man. He told me about stamps for a part of what you pay for deeds. It's the same for oil and gas leases."

"Well," said Claudie, "we didn't pay nothing for the lease, so we don't have to buy no stamps."

"That's where you are wrong, Claudie. It says that you have to put on *at least* a dollar's worth for each thousand dollars you pay. The law don't limit a man on how many stamps he can buy. You can put on as many more as you want to. Also, it helps support the government. Those stamps might be pretty cheap at a dollar apiece. I think I'll buy about two dollars' worth."

Claudie handed me the two dollars. It was easier for him than trying any harder to understand about the revenue laws. Then I asked him for another dollar to take care of miscellaneous expenses. This was the hardest part to explain, as it often is with miscellaneous expenses.

After a little while Claudie said: "That only leaves me four bits; were you plumb out of money, Clint?"

"No," I told him. "I've got a couple of dollars or so for some personal things I might need."

4

In McKinney I went to the post office and bought two dollars' worth of stamps. I put them on the lease and canceled them with my initials just like the man said at the revenue window. Then I went over to the County Clerk's office on the second floor of the Courthouse where they record papers. All this time Claudie was down at the wagon yard selling the vegetables.

The girl on duty in the Clerk's office was standing over by a window at the far end of the counter. She was laughing and rolling her big brown eyes at three overgrown young fellows who were standing around smoking cigarettes and shoving each other every time anything was said — the same way boys of that age always act around a girl in the spring of the year if they don't have any work to do. I waited a few minutes, trying to catch the brunette's eye, and finally I said in a loud voice: "I want to record an oil and gas lease on the Widow Wiley's farm over in the northeast part of the county. Who tends to that?"

The girl looked up and said, "I do." Then I went over and handed her the lease, holding it topside up where the signature, the acknowledgment, and the revenue stamps would all show. Her friends at first pretended not to be looking over my shoulder, but this did not last, and after a few minutes we were all looking at the lease together. After they'd all had plenty of time to look it over, I paid a dollar to the girl and went out. The boys left too, talking together a lot faster than they had to the girl.

After I left the Courthouse, I walked over to the barbershop on the south side of the square to get me a shave. There were several customers there, but the last chair in the back was open. A barber with a long, keen nose and glassy eyes took me. When he had a hot towel all over my face, except for a little island around my nose, he said in a half-whisper: "You're the fellow that recorded the lease, ain't you?"

"Ummhumm," I told him through the towel.

"Which one of the oil companies are you leasing for?" he asked me after a few minutes.

I didn't answer him right off, since the razor was working very close between my lips and my nose by this time, and he asked me again.

"I didn't even say I was leasing for a company," I told him.

"You don't have to," the barber said. "Nobody but the major companies pay prices like that."

"You must know," I said.

Then he asked me again, "Which major is it?"

"I don't think it is standard practice to tell, is it?" I didn't ask it in a way that called for an answer. I just let it soak in. When it did, he dropped his razor to the floor; then, after he picked it up, he put the towel back over my face. But I could see out, and I watched him go up and start whispering to the barber on the front chair.

I paid for my shave, and while the porter was brushing me off, the glassy-eyed barber came over to me. I tipped him a dime and he said, "I hope you all strike a gusher."

"Well," I told him, "sometimes it's a gusher, sometimes a dry hole. It's all in the day's work."

As I stepped out to the street, feeling with my hand how smooth a barbershop shave makes a man's chin feel, I met Claudie, and he was really in a dither. "Oil," he said, between deep breaths, "Standard Oil — Standard Oil Company on the Widow Wiley's place. Everybody is talking oil. Have you heard anything about it, Clint?"

"That's a hell of a question to be asking a man as he comes out of a barbershop," I said. "Gather yourself together, Claudie; you're pretty excited. Go on back to the car and wait for me there. Just act serious and mysterious if you can; don't say nothing to nobody."

5

I walked around the square and passed a lot of people on the sidewalk. They were gathering in little knots, and they talked and nodded at each other much faster than was natural. They'd be looking away from me as I walked toward them, but as soon as I passed, I'd turn and look and they'd all be staring at me. Some folks will tell you that nothing in the world ferments like hops and malt, but they don't know a thing about an oil scare in Texas.

I kept on walking until I reached the big store with the red front where a sign spread clear across the entrance read: GEORGE TEXAS — HARDWARE, NOTIONS, STATIONERY AND LOANS.

I walked in and saw that there were no other customers around. People were all out on the streets talking about oil. A tall, pale stringy-haired citizen with a big Adam's apple was clerking in the store. As I looked over the counters, he said, "Was there something for you?"

"Yes," I said, "I'll just look around the stationery here until I find it."

About this time I saw a big man get up from his desk in the rear and come forward. He walked like a man would walk in his own store. That would be George Texas, I said to myself as I studied his heavy face and buggy eyes. I noticed his hair grew down close to his eyebrows, and his chin was blue like a man's chin is when he has just come from a barbershop.

"Otho," the man with the blue chin said to the clerk, "you can go on back to your inventory; I'll wait on Mr. Hightower." Then he turned and said that he was George Texas, the proprietor of the store. I could tell from the hungry look on his well-fed face that there wasn't anything the barber knew that George Texas didn't know too. I nodded to him; then I kept on looking around until I came to a stop by the counter with pencils, erasers, and fountain pens on it. There wasn't a thing in sight that sold for an even sum of money. Everything was nine cents, or ninety-eight cents, or a dollar nineteen, and so on.

"What is the price," I asked George Texas, "of the best fountain pen in the house?"

"Here you are," he answered, as he handed me one with a gold-looking point and smiled at me like you've seen people smile at well-heeled old relatives. "The price is ninety-eight cents."

I tried the fountain pen out on an envelope he handed me, and it worked all right. While I was doing this, I said out loud to myself, "In my business people have to sign their names in ink." Then I turned to him and said, "I'll take it," and I handed him the last one of Claudie's dollar bills — the one for miscellaneous expenses. "Just keep the change," I told George Texas.

When I took the fountain pen and started to walk out, George Texas followed me to the door. He wanted to give me a bottle of blue ink to go with it, and I let him. Just as

I was pushing the store door open to leave, George Texas said to me in a low, confidential tone of voice: "Can you step back to the rear of the store with me?"

"Sorry," I told him, "but I'm a busy man, and I haven't got much time. Let's have it right here."

He looked towards Otho, who was going through some motions with his hands while his eyes were on us; then George Texas said in a hoarse whisper: "Will you take twenty-two hundred dollars for the Wiley lease?"

"That won't touch it, Mr. Texas," I said, but I stood right at the door and added: "Besides, I'm afraid it wouldn't be right."

"Course it would," he argued. "It's in your name, ain't it?"

"Yes," I said, "it's in my name all right."

"Twenty-three hundred?" He said it like an auctioneer says it just after he had said "Going, going," and before he says "gone."

Then I let him have it. "I said it wouldn't be right if I sold it," I told him, and I looked at him in the way I always felt Moses must have looked at Aaron when he came down from the mountain and caught him worshiping before the golden calf. But I didn't quite get out of the door.

"Hokay," George Texas said and started toward the rear of the store.

"Tell you what I'll do," I wheeled and said as I let the door close again. "I'll take twenty-five hundred dollars in cash, but I can't fool around about it. Time is important to me."

"You've sold it." George Texas almost snapped it out. He went on back to a big black safe by his desk and got out a brown envelope. He counted twenty-five hundred dollars in tens and twenties, and we went straight over to the Courthouse. We had to push our way through the crowd in front of the store. I put my name on an assignment and acknowledged it before the Clerk; then George Texas said he was going to record it. "Oh no," I said, "not until you have put the revenue stamps on it. That will cost you two dollars and a half. I'll go with you to the Post Office, where they sell them."

We went over and got the stamps, and I showed George Texas how to cancel them with his initials; then we went back and got the girl with big brown eyes to record the paper.

After George Texas paid his dollar for the registration, I turned to him and said: "Now let's have the Widow Wiley's note — it's fifteen hundred dollars, I believe." Back to the store we went and up to the big black safe, but right there George balked on me.

"Hold it," George said. "Just a minute; this is too fast for me."

"Fast, huh?" I said. "Is there anything wrong with this money? It's the same money I got from you. Ain't it legal tender?" I knew all about legal tender from that smart notary public in Fort Worth.

George said the money was good, all right, but he was not sure what all was happening to him.

"I'm paying off the Widow Wiley's note," I said, "and I want you to mark 'Paid in full' on it — now. I am tendering you the money."

That did it. As George Texas got the note out, he walled his eyes like a suckling calf does when he is pulled away from the cow by his ears. I held fifteen hundred dollars' worth of the money in my hand until he wrote "Paid in full" on the back of the note and gave it to me. Then I went back to the car, where Claudie was waiting for me.

"Claudie," I said, "I and you are about due for a nice cold drink. Let's go into the drugstore across the street, and I'll set 'em up to you."

While I had an egg malted milk and Claudie had a banana split with cherries, I told him about our trade. I even told him how all the oil excitement got started, and he seemed to understand it pretty well. I showed him the Widow Wiley's canceled note, but I didn't let him see the bills. I have never been a man to flash large bills around in a public place. Claudie seemed so stunned by it all that he had very little to say as he gnawed away on the banana split.

"What the hell's wrong with you, Claudie?" I finally asked him. "Aren't you glad for the Widow Wiley? Aren't you glad about us? What do you think about it all?"

"I was just thinking," Claudie said through a sliver of banana he was scooping in, "how silly we'd feel if they ever struck oil on the Widow Wiley's place. George Texas would be the one to get rich."

"There you go again, Claudie," I said. "Still looking for a worm in every apple."

By this time a large number of other people had come to the soda fountain; they were gawking at us, ordering cold drinks of one sort or another and talking. All through their talk we could hear the word "oil" spoken over and over. They spoke of places like Ranger, Spindletop, Borger and other oil towns until it was enough to get on a man's nerves. Other words like Cadillac limousines, private swimming pools, porterhouse steaks, and French champagne kept dropping out of their conversation.

"Let's get the hell out of here, Claudie," I told him. So I went over and paid the cashier for our drinks and bought me and Claudie a couple of ten-cent cigars. As we walked out into the street, I remarked to Claudie that after buying the cigars I was down to no smaller change than a ten-dollar bill.

"It could be worse," Claudie said. "Let's us go on back to the Widow Wiley's."

"In a little while," I answered. "But first, I think I'll go back over to George Texas's place and trade him this blue ink for some that's green. You take this canceled note and hold on to it. I'll see you at the car after a little bit."

We were over halfway back to the Widow Wiley's farm when Claudie spoke up. "Clint," he said, "they ain't anything we need worse than a car to pull our trailer, is they?"

"I don't know, Claudie," I said. "A car is a lot of expense and all. If we had a car, we'd have six tires to go flat instead of just the two that we've got on the trailer."

"I'm the one that fixes the tires," Claudie said. "I wouldn't mind."

"Claudie," I told him, "don't it make you happy when you think of how relieved the Widow Wiley is going to be when we give her back her note, marked 'Paid in full'? She's out of debt."

"Sure does," Claudie answered, "but not as happy as a new car would make me."

"Haven't you got any sentiment at all, Claudie?"

" 'Course I have, Clint," Claudie told me. "But it's pretty hard, and it's gittin' harder, to hitchhike with a trailer house."

"You must not be thinking of how much it costs to get

the valves ground on a car. That's awful expensive," I told him.

"I believe I could grind the valves if we had a car," Claudie said. "Let's take that thousand dollars and buy us a car tomorrow."

"Claudie," I said, "there is something I have to tell you about that thousand dollars. We don't exactly have it any more."

"We don't what?" Claudie asked, and he looked a little chalky around the gills.

"You see, it's this way," I explained. "We bought back a part interest in that lease from George Texas when I went back to swap him the blue ink for green."

"How much did we pay him?"

"Nine hundred and eighty-nine dollars," I told him. "George Texas is a sucker for an uneven sum of money."

After a bit Claudie said: "I can't figure how we've got but eleven dollars left." His jaw was sagging like a gate with a broken hinge.

"Right," I told him, "and here it is. Put it back in your overcoat lining." I handed him a ten and a one.

"What part of the lease did you buy back?" Claudie wanted to know.

"Well," I said, "George Texas is a hard trader. At first he didn't want to give up any part of it. I finally got a one per cent interest — a full one per cent."

Claudie looked all worn out. It was too much for him to try to understand percentages, so I said: "Buck up, Claudie. Try to look at the bright side of things. You've got more money for a rainy day. The Widow Wiley is not in debt any more, the government is about four dollars better off, and we are not in any trouble. Nobody is hurt; not even George Texas. We didn't do anything to him that he didn't do to us — and then some."

"Looks like everybody got something out of that deal but you, Clint," he said. "What do you want?"

"Well," I told him, "before we leave the Widow Wiley's, I might want to show Emma the Widow's note marked 'Paid in full.' "

VII
The Windmill Fixers

I AM A MAN that can move fast when I'm on the trail of something really good, and this will show you what I mean: It was on a Saturday that the Widow Wiley and Emma gave our trailer house a tow to Dallas and left us in the park; on Sunday I met Angus Pratt at a band concert in Dallas, and by Monday I and Claudie were on our way again. Then, while the trailer swung and swayed along behind the big green cattle truck, was the first real chance I'd had to explain to Claudie about our new specialty.

"Claudie," I said, "there is more of nearly everything in Texas than any other state in the Union, and this goes for windmills too. Also, you will find more wind in Texas to turn these windmills, more trouble in locating water for them to lift, and more space that needs watering."

Up ahead in the cattle truck, Backlash, the fat little colored driver, sloped for Waco. He had our dollar and the nearly full bottle of vanilla extract we had given him for the lift. He was driving so fast that the wind screamed and whined about the eaves of the trailer house like she-panthers at midnight. Backlash was due in Waco before dark, and the sun wasn't over three quarters of an hour high.

"Another thing to bear in mind, Claudie," I went on —

"even the best windmill is apt to get out of whack now and then."

"Windmills or no windmills, I don't like the way that boy is driving up there." Claudie was sitting on the trailer floor holding the coal-oil stove, the lantern and the coffee-pot in his lap so they wouldn't jostle about.

"Well," I told him, as I braced my folding chair against the rear door, "it's hard to be choosy when you've got to hitchhike for a trailer house. Now don't get me off my subject again, please."

"What's that?" he wanted to know.

"Our specialty," I said. "We're going to be windmill fixers."

"But we don't know nothing about windmills," he argued.

"Not yet," I admitted, "but listen to me, Claudie: we've wandered all over Texas, we've dabbled in this and we've dabbled in that; we've been specializing in other people's business, but so far I've been finding better jobs for us than we can hold."

"We've sure been fired from some nice jobs," Claudie admitted.

"That's what I'm trying to tell you," I went on. "We need a specialty, and I've got it all planned."

"Uh-huh," was all I got from Claudie.

"Now I'm going to tell you about it," I said. "While you were wasting your time yesterday in Dallas at that pin ball arcade, I talked to a man who is a real windmill expert—fellow by the name of Angus Pratt. Look what he gave me: a picture folder put out by a Waco concern. It shows all the parts of a windmill and exactly how they work."

I let Claudie see the folder; then I explained it to him

as best I could, and as he seemed to understand it fairly well, I went on: "They can teach you there in Waco how to fix windmills. A two weeks' course. That's where Angus Pratt learned about windmills. I and you will sign up there for a little higher education tomorrow."

Claudie nodded his head, but the look on his face was vacant, like that of a man playing music by ear. I told him I was afraid he was never meant to be anything but a hewer of wood and a drawer of water.

About this time two police officers came roaring alongside us on motorcycles, and Claudie started swallowing and running his hand around under his collar. He actually looked at me like he figured I must have planned to get us arrested. With the Louisiana law after us anyway, and here we were getting arrested, I suppose I must have given Claudie about the same kind of a look as Backlash slammed on the brakes and brought us to a very rough stop.

The biggest officer — the big one with two guns on his hips and a forked scar on his cheek — said to us in a very harsh way: "What the hell kind of contraption is this? Where is your permit?"

Backlash dug out his permit, but of course it did not cover our trailer house or any part of it. The officer looked us up and down; then he said, "You will all have to come with me to the Justice of the Peace."

"Officer," I said, and I knew this had to be good, "you look like a fair-minded man to me. This truck and these cattle belong to a nice man in Waco, Texas. He is a very honest man; he is very prominent in the cattle business; also he is without malice aforethought." The officer listened.

The other officer came up and said, "I think he is about to outtalk you, Elmo."

Elmo gave the other officer a very bilious look and said, "Just who the hell is making this arrest?"

"So far, nobody is," the other officer said, and he said it in a very haughty way.

Then I made my move. "Elmo," I said, "I think you are a fine type of officer. Tell you what: If you'll let Backlash pull us off this road, nobody will be violating the law any more. Let's all let Backlash take this truck full of cattle on to Waco."

Elmo then said in a loud voice that we'd better get that damn trailer off the highways of the State of Texas before somebody got into trouble. He spat on the side of the road and looked hard at the other officer. As Backlash pulled us into a green pasture by the side of the road, I noticed that the sign on the mailbox said E. C. Wigginbotham.

We unhooked the trailer under the shade of some pecan trees, while the motorcycles sputtered off toward Dallas. Backlash left, fast, in the other direction; then I and Claudie looked things over. We were about a hundred yards from a big white farmhouse surrounded by some cedar and hackberry trees, a red barn, a silo and a tall windmill. I pointed out to Claudie that the windmill was running at a fast clip in the brisk June breeze.

Claudie had no sooner scotched the wheels and leveled up the trailer then we heard dogs barking. Then we saw a whole pack of them spilling out from behind a long lilac hedge by the big house. They came bouncing our way, and along behind them came a big square-shouldered man carrying a double-barreled shotgun over his shoulder.

He walked up to the trailer house, shushed the dogs, and said in a very sarcastic way: "You fellers seem to be making yourselves pretty well at home." He was about nineteen hands high, and he looked even bigger than that, carrying the gun and all. He had a big black bushy mustache. His eyes were bright blue, and he had a way of squinting them like a man who has spent his forty-odd years in a high wind.

I took off my hat and said: "Mr. Wigginbotham, right now we do not exactly have any way to get out of here."

"Well," he told us, "you'd better figger a way to get out. You are trespassers, and I don't want the sun to go down on you here." At that, I looked out toward the west, and there was the sun, not over an hour high.

"Mr. Wigginbotham," I said to him as I looked up toward the house place, "I don't like the way that windmill of yours sounds. Ever have any trouble with it?"

"Some," he said, but he didn't say it like a man who counted on having any more.

"Listen to it," I went on as I cupped my hand over my ear. "Hear that *calung-capluk, calung-capluk?* Sounds to me like there's something loose somewhere."

"What do you know about windmills?" Mr. Wigginbotham asked me. He was drawing a mighty fine bead on me with both eyes, but he'd quit talking about trespassing.

"We're windmill fixers," I told him, and I held his eye to be sure he didn't look at Claudie. "You'd better let us check it over in the morning, first thing. An ounce of prevention is worth a pound of cure."

"There is something to that, all right," Mr. Wigginbotham allowed, then I went on: "My name is Clint Hightower. I and my assistant here, Claudie, will have that machine singing like a new one before noon tomorrow. It won't cost you a penny."

Mr. Wigginbotham agreed to let us take a look at the windmill the next morning.

2

Even a trespasser has certain rights in Texas if he hasn't been run off by sundown, and a share in the chuck is one of them. We had a nice supper that night with the folks at the big house. Mrs. Wigginbotham was a fine cook; she served us hot biscuits, fried chicken and cream gravy, three or four kinds of garden sass, and wild plum jelly. It all smelled so good and looked so good that Claudie didn't even close his eyes when Mr. Wigginbotham said Grace before we ate.

Mrs. Wigginbotham was not much bigger than a bar of soap, but she ran things around that house. She was the law and the prophets, and she was prompted from time to time by her old-maid sister Lula, who lived with them. Miss Lula and the Missus, as Mr. Wigginbotham called them, had little black snapping buckshot eyes, soft fair skin, and dark straight hair. They both had very small hands, too, but with big knuckles.

The ladies were pretty nice to us; nicer, in fact, than Mr. Wigginbotham was. From something in the air, I had a hunch that if he'd liked us more, they'd have liked us less. As we were eating, I noticed, too, that Miss Lula was putting a right agreeable eye on Claudie from time to time.

After supper the ladies went back into the kitchen to do the dishes. I and Claudie went out on the front veranda, where we sat with Mr. Wigginbotham in some big wicker chairs by the honeysuckle vines. We looked out over the long row of hollyhocks that nodded between us and the low ridge of blue hills in the west, and it was awful quiet, except for the regular *calung-capluk* of the windmill and the homey sound of clean pots and pans being put away in the kitchen.

After a bit I said, "Mr. Wigginbotham, it's nearly dark. I think I and Claudie will go on down to the trailer house and turn in."

"No," he said, "when the Missus and Miss Lula get the dishes done, we'll have the music."

"Music?" Claudie asked, and cleared his throat.

"Yes, Miss Lula has a talent for music," Mr. Wigginbotham answered. He said it in the same way you'd speak of someone having the bots. "We have music every night of the world." In the half-dark I thought Mr. Wigginbotham looked older than he had before.

"You all must like music an awful lot," I said.

"I listen to it an awful lot," he allowed. "Tonight you can help me with that."

"We can do better than that," I told him. "Claudie, here, can sing bass."

"He don't have to," Mr. Wigginbotham answered. "I just wanted some company with the listenin'."

About this time Mrs. Wigginbotham came to the front door and said: "All right, Elbert, we've finished the dishes. You can bring the men on in."

When we started into the parlor, the Missus handed the coal-oil lamp to Mr. Wigginbotham, and he put it in the holder on the wall; then he turned the reflector around to where it put the best light on the organ.

It was a beautiful brown organ, as big as some I've seen in churches. It had a dozen or more stops above the keyboard; and along the top, as well as along the sides, it had frilly carved wood decorations. The name of the company that made it was printed right on the front of the organ, but in such fancy letters a man couldn't even read it. I noticed that there were real sacred pictures on the parlor walls — Jesus and Joseph and some other people with long beards, that must have been prophets or scribes or Pharisees, anyway. There were some good mottoes, too. One, in a silver frame over the organ, said, "Music Hath Charms," in sloping gold letters.

While Miss Lula pumped away at the organ and knocked off a few chords to warm it up, Mrs. Wigginbotham sat close by in a big chair that had red plush on it as deep as it is on seats in trains. I and Claudie sat where we were told, on a green sofa with a hard bottom, and Mr. Wigginbotham went over to a rocking chair by a window on the far side of the room from the organ.

Then Miss Lula turned on her talent. She played and sang a number of the old favorite hymns, like "Rock of Ages," "Beulah Land," and "Old Rugged Cross"; next some songs about nice places a long way off, such as "My Old Kentucky Home," "Blue Ridge Mountains of Virginia," and "Little Gray Home in the West." Toward the end, she rang in a few numbers about long-ago love: "Down by the Old Mill Stream," "Silver Threads Among the Gold," and "Moonlight and Roses." She veered her target toward Claudie, I thought, when she sang one called "Comin' Through the Rye."

It was all better than average as such music goes, and I liked it pretty well since I like even ordinary music more than no music at all. Miss Lula had a sweet, silky voice up in the higher notes that women sing, but on the low ones it had a way of bogging down into a blur as a duck call sometimes does when the reed gets wet.

The music had been going on for over an hour when I

looked over at Mr. Wigginbotham. His eyes were plumb glassy; he was gazing out of the window, and he looked, for all the world, like a man who had just gone clear across the country in a covered wagon. Then he looked like a man learning he'd have to go all the way back when Claudie asked Miss Lula if she could play "Mother Machree." Claudie said he wanted to sing it.

Now Claudie sings a fine brand of country bass, and after he'd finished with "Mother Machree," he did a duet with Miss Lula. She pulled out the *vox humana* stop, and they sang the one that begins, "Mine eyes have seen the glory of the coming of the Lord," while Claudie stood there by the organ and turned the sheets of the music. Miss Lula must have been ten or twelve years older than Claudie, but the way they looked at each other when they sang together was enough to put a man's teeth on edge. I noticed Mr. Wigginbotham was pulling the left end of his mustache down to his mouth. He seemed to be biting it.

After a while it was over. I could tell that the ladies were pretty much taken with Claudie, and he was more taken with himself than I liked to see. When this happens he is likely to talk himself into such deep water that I have to bail him out, but this time he didn't exactly. He only said, "There's a bad note in that organ."

"The organ does need tuning," Miss Lula said as she smiled at Claudie.

"Claudie, here, can fix it; he was a piano tuner before he started windmill fixing," I stated.

At this Mr. Wigginbotham got up and said it was time to wash his feet and go to bed, so I told them all that Claudie would tune the organ as soon as we got through with the windmill; then we went back to the trailer.

As we walked away from the Wigginbotham house I said, "Claudie, remember — the windmill comes first. I don't want you to touch that organ until we are through with the windmill."

"Wait a minute," he said. "You are the one that wants to fix the windmill."

"I'm only the one that had the idea," I answered. "You shouldn't expect me to do all the thinking and the work too. Now please don't try to start an argument, Claudie."

"No," Claudie went on, "I ain't tryin' to start no argument, but who's gonna go up on that damn windmill tower?"

"Claudie," I said, "you are too trying to start an argument. You know it makes me dizzy to climb up on high places."

3

The next morning, after breakfast, Mr. Wigginbotham went off early to the cotton field and I and Claudie went out to the windmill. There was a thirty- or forty-mile gale blowing, and I could tell it was going to take about everything Claudie had to stay on the tower long enough to make any showing at all, even if we got the windmill stopped. We found a lever on one leg of the tower that was very hard to work, but when we finally worked it, the windmill sang to a slow stop.

Claudie was balky as an old mule about going on the tower, even after I found him a monkey wrench and a pair of pliers. It was only when I pointed out that the ladies were watching him from the back porch that he gritted his teeth and started up the ladder. It made me right nervous to see that big lug picking his way along on the little bitty ladder, but as soon as he got to the platform up there, I felt better about things. I stood there looking up at him until I almost got a crick in my neck. I told him to check everything.

When Claudie came down, he said everything looked all right to him, but he had taken a little bolt out of a place where it didn't seem to belong and had put it into a place where it fitted better. We worked the lever, and the windmill started again with a loud whine. I told him I thought it sounded smoother, but he said he didn't notice any difference. "Leave that part to me," I said; "it's still running, ain't it?"

"Yes, it's running all right," he answered, "but it ain't pumping near as much water as it was."

We took a bucket of cold, fresh water up to the house and found that the Missus and Miss Lula were waiting for us on the back porch. They said the windmill had not been so quiet in years. They gave us some gingerbread with hard sauce on it; then Claudie, carried away with things going so good, said he was ready to start work on the organ. But when we went into the parlor, the ladies said we should sit down and rest up a bit from our windmill work. They showed us the family album and a big leather-backed Bible with everything Jesus said printed in red; then they showed us some stereopticon views. Just when we got to the one of Mount Etna in eruption, there was a worse racket outside than a volcano erupting against a tin roof. The noise was so loud that it started the dogs to howling and the guineas to chattering, and as we all ran out of the house, a peacock a mile or so away let out a long, high scream.

It was the windmill, all right. It was in an awful shape, and right there before our eyes it was getting worse. The vane and the blades were all winding themselves up and batting together, until finally all the machinery up there stopped completely. That windmill was tied in knots, and some big, bent pieces kept springing loose up there and falling around the yard, while I and Claudie and the ladies stood off at a safe distance and watched.

Mr. Wigginbotham came from the cotton field in a lope; he swore a little and said some things that really stung our professional pride. "What have you bastards done to my windmill?" was what he kept wanting to know.

"Calm yourself, Mr. Wigginbotham," I said. A soft answer like that is supposed to turn away the flame of wrath, but this only seemed to turn it up. The veins stood out on his forehead like fishing worms on the bottom of a can, and he kept opening and closing his mouth without saying a word.

Then I went on: "I knew it was loose somewhere; I knew something like this was bound to happen from the way that machine sounded last night."

"You've ruined it," he said.

"Oh, no," I told him. "It just broke down before we could locate the trouble."

Just then a big metal brace of some kind sprung loose from the windmill and landed on the smokehouse roof; it bounced twice and fell to the ground, not ten feet away from where we were standing.

"You've ruined it," Mr. Wigginbotham said again, and I decided it was best just to let the matter drop there.

"Elbert — " The Missus started to say something, but Mr. Wigginbotham paid her no mind.

"The stock — " he said as he stood there looking at what was left of the windmill — "how are the stock going to get water?"

I thought he moved into much easier territory for me with this question, so I said: "I and my associate, Claudie, will take care of that. Leave it to us, Mr. Wigginbotham. How many head are there?"

"Thirteen cows, eight mares and a span of mules," he said.

I looked at Claudie, and he looked down toward the silo; then I said, "Claudie, maybe you'd better start drawing water right away. It's a warm, windy day, and the stock will be getting pretty thirsty."

"No you don't," Mr. Wigginbotham said to me, and I could see that, when you got away from the house where the Missus ruled the roost, Mr. Wigginbotham knew how to take charge. "You're the fellow that didn't like the way my windmill sounded last night. Well, I didn't like the way it sounded a few minutes ago. You can draw the water." He had the same look on his face he'd had the day before when he had the shotgun on his shoulder. He stood there looking at me as the stock started coming from the pasture toward the empty water tank beneath the windmill. Finally he said, "The rope and the bucket are there by the well," and as he turned to walk up toward the house I said, "Yes, sir." He took Claudie with him.

A camel is supposed to be able to drink enough water to last him for several weeks, and I'd always thought no other animal in the world could match a camel in this way, but I'd never before drawn water with a small bucket for thirteen cows, and nine of them fresh. For a man who has no liking for manual labor of any kind, drawing a lot of water is a very aggravating thing. Just when I'd begun to hold my own with the cows, and they had quit bawling, the horses and mules came along. They were hot and thirsty, too. Then along came three big red brood sows with their litters — a part of the job that Mr. Wigginbotham hadn't even mentioned. They weren't any part of my trade, but they were there, and they were thirsty.

Along about noon the cattle grazed off, and I was just getting a little ahead of the other stock when the water bucket sprung a leak. At first it was just a small leak, but it soon got so bad that I wasn't able to get the bucket up more than half full from the well. I didn't see another bucket around anywhere, and, since Mr. Wigginbotham was still up there on the back porch watching me, I didn't think it was a good time to quit to go look for a bucket. Then the cattle came back for more water, and I couldn't help thinking what soft jobs those Israelites had in Egypt; they only had to make bricks without straw.

It must have been one or two o'clock when the stock all wandered off again, and I tried to stand up straight for a little rest. I couldn't do it. Long, keen, galloping pains arched up from my hips and looped across my shoulder blades. I found it was almost easier to draw another bucket than to quit and straighten up — but not quite. I just stood there, bent over the well casing, panting like a collie pup in the noonday sun.

After a bit the Missus and Miss Lula came down to the well and brought some cheese and crackers and a mug of cold buttermilk. While I ate, they told me Mr. Wigginbotham was still in a pretty ugly frame of mind. They said he had been trying ever since the windmill went out to get a telephone call through to a man in Dallas. He was trying to reach a fellow named Pratt there who could come out and fix the windmill, they said. He couldn't get Mr. Pratt on the phone, and this had made him a whole lot madder than he had been before.

"Angus Pratt?" I asked.

"Yes, that's his name," the Missus said. "How'd you know?"

"In the windmill business I know the right people," I told them. Then I asked them what had happened to Claudie. They said he was tuning the organ; he had told them he thought he would have it in tune by the time they got back from town.

"You're not leaving?" I asked as I felt a cold sweat pop out on my forehead and between my shoulder blades.

"Yes," Miss Lula said, "we're going to drive in to Midlothian to the meeting of the Missionary Society." They left in the old sedan, and as I stood there by the well I couldn't help thinking I'd like to be one of those missionaries so the ladies could send me off to a cannibal island somewhere.

It must have been an hour later that I saw Mr. Wigginbotham leave the house and go off toward the barn. I figured he must have got his call through to Angus Pratt, and I knew that time was working against us from then on. So I went up to the house to see how Claudie was getting along.

From the back porch I called him, but nobody answered. I looked and saw Mr. Wigginbotham hitching up a team of mules down at the barn, so I went on in the house to find out what had happened to Claudie. The ox was in the ditch, and I couldn't see how anything I might do could make matters any worse. Claudie wasn't there, but when I went into the parlor I could see him through the front window. He was fooling around the trailer house.

I had to try the organ. I tried the low notes first, with the stops in; and when nothing happened, I pulled out all the stops and pumped away for all I was worth. Nothing happened again. I tried the high notes and the middle notes, and I pumped until those pains started arching up into my shoulders again the way they had at the well. All I got was one little guff, like the noise a cow's foot will make when she pulls it out of a boggy place. That organ was deader'n a doornail. "Well, Clint," I said to myself, "there goes the ball game. It serves you right for depending on that big, ugly lug, Claudie, for anything but manual labor and singing bass."

Just then the telephone rang — two longs, a short, and a long. I answered it, and sure enough it was the Dallas call. Mrs. Pratt was on the line, and she said she had a message for Mr. Wigginbotham.

"I'll take it," I stated. "I work here."

"Tell Mr. Wigginbotham that Mr. Pratt is on his way. He'll be there in an hour," she said.

I hung up, ran out the front door and went down to the trailer house. Claudie was there, leaning up against the trailer door, cool as a cucumber. The expression on his face was as simple as a notch on a stick.

"Claudie, you clumsy cluck," I yelled at him. "What the hell have you done to the organ? How are we going to get out of here? What are we going to do when Mr. Wigginbotham learns you've ruined the organ too? What are we going to do when Mr. Pratt gets here? He's a real windmill fixer."

Claudie was so mixed up that he couldn't say a word.

The trouble he had caused didn't seem to be dawning on him at all.

"I can't answer all them questions at once," he said. Then I looked back toward the barn, and there came Mr. Wigginbotham in a wagon. Two mules were pulling it, and they came toward the trailer in a fast trot. As they pulled up even with us, Mr. Wigginbotham jumped out, and I asked him in a nice polite way what it was he had in mind doing.

"I'm going to pull your trailer down the road toward old man Nate Pinkney's place. He needs a couple of good field hands. I can't use you here." He had some chains and bailing wire, and with almost no help from Claudie and none at all from me he fastened the trailer house on behind the wagon.

I began to feel a little left out of things so I said: "Mr. Wigginbotham, while you were hitching up those mules, a phone call came for you from Dallas. They said Angus Pratt was on his way. He's a windmill man."

"That's good," he said without looking away from what he was doing. "I need a windmill man."

I said, "Mr. Pratt is a good one," but I don't think Mr. Wigginbotham heard me, since he was back in the wagon by this time. He spoke to the mules, and they went off so fast that I and Claudie had to run to catch the trailer house. We got in just as Mr. Wigginbotham turned south on the highway. He popped the whip at the mules, and they went down the road in a full gallop.

As we jostled along the road behind Mr. Wigginbotham's wagon, the sun was low and dark red in the west. While it slid from behind a lead-colored cloud bank into the gray dusk, I watched a long north-bound freight train pass about a mile away — edging along betwixt us and the sunset. The train whistle sounded lonesome and restless, and it did what a train whistle often does: makes a man wonder if things aren't a lot prettier and easier where the train is going than they are where the train is whistling. I looked at Claudie and thought of all the misery and bother he had caused me since sundown the day before. He looked down at the floor, and, as I sat there, I wondered how much longer a man with my talents could put up with him.

"It's a good thing," I remarked, "that we are getting out of here before the Missus and Miss Lula learn what you did to that organ."

"That's the way Mr. Wigginbotham feels about it, too," Claudie answered.

"Does he know about the organ?" I asked.

"He ought to, Clint," Claudie said. "He told me he wanted me to give it exactly the same treatment I had gave the windmill."

VIII
Carlsbad's Cavern

In some ways Claudie is a lot like a goose that wakes up in a brand-new world every morning of his life. I mean it; especially when the day before has been a big one, like that first Monday in June — Trades' Day at the old Waco jockey yard.

This will show you what I mean: We had about finished breakfast on Tuesday, the very next day, when I spoke to Claudie about maybe taking a trip to California, and he looked a little puzzled and said, "How?"

"Please bear in mind, Claudie," I told him, "I made a lot of trades yesterday, and when I got through that little Indian moved into our trailer house, and we drove off in a car of our own."

Then, as it all started coming back to him a little at a time, Claudie grinned and said, "Oh, yes; and we got the bottle of snake-bite cure to boot."

"All right," I went on, "what do you say we head for California? It's already hot weather here, and the summer in Texas will last until along about Thanksgiving anyway." Claudie nodded his head and said, "I always wanted to see Carlsbad's Cavern. It's in California, ain't it, Clint?"

"No," I said, looking at the road map, "it's in New Mexico, but that's on the way to California. You have to turn off the California road just this side of El Paso, Texas."

He wondered next whether we could afford such a long trip, so I told him I thought we could afford to go as well as we could afford to stay. "Remember," I pointed out, "we often do better in strange places than we do where people know us, and California is a hell of a long ways from Louisiana where the law is looking for us." Claudie nodded his head and chewed away on a sardine.

"We'll have to forage a little as we go along," I explained, and I could tell Claudie was ready, so we pulled out of the roadside park on our way to California. Claudie drove while I studied the road map.

At Fort Stockton the next afternoon we ran out of gasoline and money, and the oil in our car was getting pretty low, so I spoke to Claudie, as we drove into a trailer camp on the edge of town, and said: "Here is where we have to buckle down for a few days."

First thing the following morning we went into town looking for a post office building or a good hotel. The public washrooms in a few of the best hotels are as nice as they are in a federal building and we found a clean, new hotel right off. As soon as we'd shaved and washed up and put on clean shirts, we started to walk back down the little hall we'd followed when we went in. I'd have sworn that the door where we started to leave was the same one we had come in by from the lobby, but it wasn't.

When we went through the wrong door, we found ourselves in a big room with several people standing around a piano down at the far end. Just as we walked in, a lady at the piano started playing "The Last Roundup." She was very good, too; but just as I was beginning to enjoy it, she got to the *umpum-umpum, umpumpum* part, and I could see she was only going to accompany what was next. A tall, lanky fellow with shaggy hair the color of an old well rope and complexion like a brickbat got up and started singing. It was the worse thing I'd heard in all my life, and as a boy I'd heard singing back in Alabama that would curdle Grade A milk. It was so awful that I and Claudie just stood there, fascinated. The poor guy was trying, all right, but there was something in his voice like the noise you make scraping your fingernails across a stovepipe or a blackboard. Before he got through, I thought his high notes would peel the paint right off the rafters.

When the song was finished, another citizen who looked a lot like the first one got up and sang, but he was no better. "Must be his brother," I whispered to Claudie. "No two singers could be that bad in the same way by accident."

The third singer that did "The Last Roundup" was different. He was a soft little frying-size guy with watery blue eyes, thin, pinkish hair and a light tenor voice. He sang the song like a sweet old lady would sing "Bringing in the Sheaves" or "Brighten the Corner Where You Are," but it was the best singing we'd heard that morning by a damn sight.

When the little fellow had finished the song and the party started to break up, I went over to the lady who had been playing the piano. She was a well-filled-out brunette of thirty or so; she wore high-heeled boots, a slit whipcord skirt, and a leather-fringed jacket with two bucking horses embroidered on the front of it.

"Is the singing over?" I asked her.

"It's over," she said, frowning around her eyes, but smiling around her mouth. "Terrible, wasn't it?"

"It was pretty bad, all right, ma'am," I agreed. "I can't understand why such awful singers get together the first thing in the morning to sing 'The Last Roundup.' "

"It was an audition," the lady said. "We have a vacancy at the ranch."

"Excuse me, ma'am," I remarked. "I don't believe I understood you. You didn't say 'ranch,' did you?"

"Yes," she replied. "We are looking for a singing cowboy."

"You mean for a Dude Ranch?" I pounced on the idea like a duck on a June bug; I didn't even wait for her to answer me. "Turn right around, lady, and listen to a cowboy that can really sing."

As we walked over to the piano, I told her my name was Clint Hightower and that my associate, Claudie Hughes, was the man for the job. Claudie bowed and scraped the way he always does when I refer to him as my associate. The lady said she was Mrs. Lola Bender, the owner of the Lazy Day Guest Ranch, located forty miles away in the Davis Mountains. I told her we preferred to render "Home on the Range," if it was all the same to her, and she said that would be fine. I knew Claudie had never learned all the words to "The Last Roundup."

While Mrs. Bender struck off a few notes, Claudie took several deep breaths, cleared his throat a couple of times, and stood up his full six and a half feet; then, when she got to the *umpum-umpum, umpumpum* part, he swung into his "Oh, give me a home" in a voice that tumbled out like the deep bullfroggy notes that throb from the lower end of a church pipe organ. The big lug never had much sense, but he always could sing the finest bass I ever heard — country bass, that is. As he went on with the song, you could almost see clean, bright-eyed buffaloes roaming around on sunny prairies, with mountains in the rear as big and purple as the ones on calendars done by Maxfield Parrish. I told Mrs. Bender it would have been even better if Claudie had had any breakfast that morning; he wasn't ever his best on an empty stomach, I explained.

Next, I had Claudie sing "Bury Me Not on the Lone Prairie," just to show her that the first round was no fluke, and when he got through, there was a big tear in each one of Mrs. Bender's eyes.

Seeing those tears made me realize what a womanly person she was underneath all those ranch clothes. She was feminine, all right; not in the wispy, cobwebby way of women in toilet water advertisements; she had some meat on her bones, and she was shaped like the women that were chiseled out of marble by those old Greeks and Romans. She wiped her eyes and said she'd heard enough; she wanted to hire Claudie.

"What's the salary, ma'am?" I asked her.

"Twenty-five dollars a week if he can ride a horse."

"He can ride a horse," I told her, "but not as well as he can sing. Do room and board at the Lazy Day Ranch go with that salary?"

"Certainly," she said.

"How much did you pay the last one?" I asked her, and this threw her off balance.

She looked down and away, and finally said, "A little more than that, but he could yodel when he sang."

"But I'll bet he didn't sing bass," I argued.

"No," she answered, "he didn't. Anyhow, twenty-five dollars a week and board is all I can pay."

"You've filled your vacancy, Mrs. Bender," I told her,

"provided you'll make us a little advance — say twenty-five dollars."

She handed five five-dollar bills to Claudie and said the job would begin the next day when the first guests would start coming. Claudie passed me the money, and we left her.

2

That evening the orange-colored sun was hanging low above the blue mountain rim in the west when I and Claudie turned in at the Lazy Day sign. We were all macked out in tight Levi pants, big hats with the brims rolled, and high-heeled boots. Using the twenty-five dollars and the credit we got with flashing those fives around in the store in Fort Stockton, we had set ourselves up in the top of cowboy style. We'd even picked up a few things not strictly Western, in the splurge of our new charge account; things like a new razor for me and a nice silver signet ring with a fancy initial on it for Claudie. He'd always wanted a signet ring, he said.

Along the fence by the ranch gate there were bleached longhorn cow skulls and whitewashed wagon wheels, and over the gate there were several whiffletrees to put the customers in the mood of the West. At least that's what they did to us as soon as we drove in. We crossed a very old bridge over a little brook and parked our car right in front of the main ranch house, a big one-story affair with a dinner bell mounted on a stand by the front door. We saw several log cottages scattered around in the rear, and they were all named in signs burnt on wood, like WANDER INN, LINGER

Awhile, Where the West Begins, and other such names.

Mrs. Bender came out and spoke to Claudie. She said: "Your duties will be to take the guests on horseback trails into the mountains. You'll have to saddle up the horses for them in the morning. At noon we have picnic lunches on the trails. You serve them. At night you can build fires for them down there on the campground where you will sing them Western songs." She sounded like a woman with an awful lot of executive ability.

Claudie said, "Yas'm."

Then she turned to me and said: "Thank you for bringing him by. I know he'll like the work. Good-by." Very businesslike. So far she hadn't wasted a single word.

"But I'm not going anywhere," I said. "I like it here."

"What are you going to do?" she asked me.

"I'm his manager," I told her, and Claudie nodded.

"Oh, no you don't. I didn't hire you," Mrs. Bender told me and I could see that the time was due to be firm with her. In fact, it might have been overdue.

"What are you going to do for a guitar player?" I asked her. "You can't lug a piano down to the campgrounds, and you'd no more catch Claudie stealin' sheep than you would catch him singing without somebody to accompany him." This stumped Mrs. Bender, and before she could answer I went on: "You ought to've known that Claudie's union wouldn't let him sing without any accompaniment."

"You can stay here," she said, weakening fast, "but I can't pay you anything."

"That'll be all right with me," I told her. I was going to divide the twenty-five a week with Claudie anyhow. "Have you got a guitar I can use?"

She said there was an old one around somewhere and

walked back into the ranch house, the way a woman will walk when she is still a little put out. I explained to Claudie how you had to stop women from pushing you around in the very beginning; if you didn't, you'd have to backtrack all the way.

That night Mrs. Bender asked us both to have supper with her in the main dining room. When we went in, I noticed she had changed clothes. She was wearing a dress that certainly fitted her nicely here and there. I and Claudie wore our new cowboy clothes. She told us a number of things about herself, but the one I remembered best was that there had not been a Mr. Bender around for a long time. She said her husband had gone to the fiesta in Santa Fe, New Mexico, seven years before, and she didn't think he was coming back. At this Claudie made an awful stupid remark about how he didn't think Mr. Bender would ever come back either. Then I said: "Madam, I cannot understand how any man in his right senses could ever go that far away and stay away that long from — from all that he left." Mrs. Bender smiled and blushed, as she knew what I meant, although I wasn't sure Claudie did.

The next morning the first two guests of the season got there. They were Miss Prunie Stum and Miss Eunice Wooley, both from Lake Charles, Louisiana. They were dressed Western already, with tassels and leather fringe all over their jackets. Miss Prunie, a tall, pretty, limber-looking girl, had on tight riding pants and boots, and Miss Eunice, who was short and stocky, wore slick, satiny slacks.

While Claudie was putting their baggage in the LINGER AWHILE cabin, I opened up some conversation with them. I told them about myself and Claudie, and they said that they were both stenographers who worked for some branch of the government that dealt with agriculture of one sort or another.

Later on I and Claudie went down to the corral where we sat on the fence and talked the new guests over. Claudie said, "There's a pair that I don't understand."

"Why?" I inquired.

"Well," he went on, "that Prunie is sure an eyecatcher; big blue eyes, yellow curly hair — and built! Eunice is fat and stringy-haired; she's ugly as a bear trap. I can see how the ugly one likes to be part of that pair, but what can Prunie see in her?"

"Claudie," I said, "you don't know much about women. The pretty one likes the contrast, and maybe Eunice, the ugly one, has personality. Why don't you look into that?"

After supper that night we built a big fire down on the campgrounds, and Claudie sang some songs. I sat by that pretty Prunie, since I could tell we were supposed to make the guests happy, but I couldn't seem to keep my eyes off of Mrs. Lola Bender. The campfire gave a nice glow to her dark eyes and tan cheeks, and I was getting sold fast on the shape of the shadow she cast. Of course, Prunie went plumb soft-eyed over Claudie when he sang "Little Gray Home in the West," and Mrs. Bender showed in her look that she had a real love for good music when Claudie sang that classical number, "Long, Long Trail a-Winding."

As the singing broke up for the night, I realized that nobody had paid much attention to Eunice Wooley; she was so ugly and fat. We almost forgot she was there until the very end when she said "Yippee."

A couple of days later Claudie and Mrs. Bender took the Lake Charles pair for a horseback ride while I drove over to Alpine to pick up some guitar strings and meet four guests who were coming on the train from Houston. The reservation had been made for Mr. Norfleet Riggs, his wife, and her two sisters, Hester and Lula Belle Flint.

They were the only passengers to get off the train, so I went right up and took them over. Mr. Riggs was a spare little man of about fifty, and he was very timid and nervous in the way he handled himself. His eyes had a sort of scared, uncertain look, like a rabbit's, and he had a way of jerking his hand up to his face every time anybody said anything to him. Mrs. Riggs was a black-haired woman with a big nose and an alto voice. Her black eyebrows were thick and grew almost together. She had eyes like eagles' eyes, and she wore glasses that pinched onto her nose between her eyes.

While Mr. Riggs was lining up the bags on the station platform and getting himself out of debt to the Pullman porter, Mrs. Riggs stood there with the same posture I saw once in a picture of the Commandant of the Command and General Staff School at Leavenworth, Kansas. The sisters stood behind her. They both looked a great deal like her, but they were both somewhat older, and one of them had a mole on her jaw with black hair bristling out of it.

I loaded the luggage into the rear of the station wagon, and we started for the ranch. Mrs. Riggs stated that she did not like the color of the mountains; she noticed that a lot of dust was in the air, she said; she thought the road was rough; she had not enjoyed the breakfast on the train a little bit; she had wanted to go to New Mexico, anyhow; there would probably be nothing to do at the Lazy Day except ride horses, and she despised horses; so did Hester and Lula Belle. All the way to the ranch Mr. Riggs's sisters-in-law never spoke directly to him at all. They would speak sort of "to whom it may concern," and then Mrs. Riggs would take the matter up with Mr. Riggs.

After a while Mrs. Riggs spoke to me and said: "Driver, I guess there is plenty of starch in the food at the Lazy Day."

"Starch galore," I yelled back from the driver's seat.

"I knew it," she said. "What did I tell you, Norfleet? You can't stand starchy food, and you know it."

As we drove in the ranch gate, she said: "This is not it, is it?" I didn't say anything because there was an outside chance that she was not speaking to me. I was wrong.

"Well, is it?" Her voice was louder, and as I got out of the car and opened the door, I said: "Yes'm, this is it."

"I am not going to like it," Mrs. Riggs announced.

That night we softened them all up a little by the campfire. I had begun to get the hang of the guitar, and as Claudie sang the last song, "The Dying Cowboy," his voice would have melted the heart of a New Orleans madam. The Lake Charles pair said such nice things about Claudie's singing that it was enough to turn a vain man's head, but though Claudie had heard this sort of thing before, I had never let him get spoiled. Mrs. Riggs did not say that she liked it, but she didn't say she did not, and I figured that was about the nicest way she could have handled it.

As we walked back to the ranch house, I edged over to Mrs. Bender and said, when nobody else could hear, "Lola, couldn't I and you go for a little drive tonight?" Well, you should have seen how happy that made her. She giggled a little, and in the clear, cool night air she did not look like a woman who was overburdened with executive ability at all.

Then she said, "No — not tonight," but her tone of voice sounded to me a lot like "Pretty soon, though." From now on it's Lola to me, I thought; Claudie can call her Mrs. Bender.

I and Claudie went on back to the trailer house to turn in, and just before I went to sleep I had the biggest idea I'd turned up in weeks. "Claudie," I said, "we'd be in solid here if you could yodel a little with your singing. A singing cowboy should be able to yodel."

"I can yodel a little," Claudie answered, "but when I do, it upsets me. Once it made my nose bleed."

"Well," I told him, "I wouldn't try it then. I guess we're doing all right as it is."

"I'm doin' my best," he said.

3

Next morning I and Claudie were sitting at our table over on the side of the main dining room nearest the kitchen when we noticed a brand-new car parked in front of the WANDER INN cabin. It was a two-tone Cadillac convertible with white sidewall tires, and it had everything on it — bumpers front and back, bumper guards and bumper guard guards, all polished and shiny.

The guests had all noticed it, too, and during breakfast there was a hum and a buzz in the conversation about the millionaires that clearly meant everybody wanted to see what these new customers looked like. "They must have real class," Claudie remarked.

It was not until they were ringing the last chuck call on the big bell that the Cadillac guests came to breakfast; a very elegant couple, I thought. Lola Bender brought them into the dining room and assigned napkins and napkin rings to them. Then she took us over to introduce us and tell them what we did around the place.

"These are our wranglers," Lola said to the new couple. "They'll help you with your horses and arrange picnic lunches." Then she turned to us and said: "Men, these are our new guests — Mr. and Mrs. John Smith from Beaumont."

Mr. Smith said, "Pleased to meet you," in a terribly broken accent; Mrs. Smith said, "Hello there, fellas," but her accent was strictly that of a Southern girl. We made a little conversation there with them about the altitude and the weather, and I noticed Mr. Smith had a way of just shrugging his shoulders when spoken to; then he'd sit there with the look on his face of a man who had said something.

We went back to our table for a second cup of coffee, and Claudie remarked to me that he thought Mr. Smith sure was lucky to have such a pretty young wife. I agreed, because there was Mr. Smith, fifty years of age or more, and not a very handsome man at all. Mrs. Smith didn't seem to be over twenty-five or thirty, at most. She was as fancy a redhead as I'd seen in many and many a moon. Claudie said he'd bet Mr. Smith measured twice as many inches in the waist as Mrs. Smith did.

"Claudie," I said, "how'd you like it if you got to be Mr. Smith's age and looked like he does, and all you had done was make a million dollars? You wouldn't trade places with him, would you?"

"Depends on whether you allow for the redhead," Claudie answered.

By the time the guests got to the corral about ten, I and Claudie had the horses all ready. Everybody had signed up for the ride except Mr. Norfleet Riggs, who was staying at the lodge to pitch horseshoes by himself. Lola was there tending to the lunch pack and telling everybody about the Columbine Trail we would follow.

When Mrs. Smith came for the old roan horse we had saddled up for her, the poor old nag shied as if he'd been shot at, and I didn't blame the horse one whit. Until that morning Prunie Stum, the blonde from Lake Charles, had been our best-dressed guest, but Mrs. Smith made Prunie look like a warmed-over Topsy. Her hat was a big, milk-white Stetson, crushed deep, cowboy style; her shirt was fire engine red with green and blue rodeo figures embroidered all over it; she had a silk bandana held together in front with a polished cow horn; her pearl-colored whipcord trousers were as tight as the skin on a Dallas Fair hot dog, and they were buttoned in close around her knees. Her belt was made of rattlesnake skin, and her boots were stitched all over with fancy little patterns. Mr. Smith wore a sport shirt open at the neck, showing a heavy growth of bristly gray and black hair on his chest. It looked like the end of a gray fox tail.

We rode up the mountain single file, with Lola's horse in the lead. She knew the trail, so I and Claudie brought up the rear. The higher we got, the more there was to see behind us. The view opened and spread out across the gray foothills and green prairies beyond, but it was no nicer view than the one of Lola sloping along up there on the lead horse.

We had picnic lunch at a shady spot in a nice green canyon; then everybody lay on the grass a little while to rest up before we started back. Lola's horse kept pawing the ground and neighing, and finally I said I thought he was thirsty. "Claudie," I told him, "you ought to take that horse down the canyon a way and give him a drink of water." When Claudie started to leave, Lola said she'd better go too; she knew the horse better than anybody, and he could be pretty fractious with strangers. They went off with Claudie leading the horse and Lola walking along beside him. The sight would have almost made me jealous if it hadn't been for the talk I'd had with Lola the night before.

Mr. Smith propped his head against a log and went right off to sleep. He looked to me like a man that would snore, but he didn't. Mrs. Smith sat on a saddle blanket and smoked cigarettes in a long, keen gold holder while she talked with the Lake Charles girls. It turned out that Mrs. Smith had worked for the government once herself, and she got a lot of experience that way, she told them.

Mrs. Riggs spoke to me about the horses we'd given her and her sisters to ride. She didn't like them. I'd never heard such mean things said about dumb brutes anywhere, and after a while I figured it was time for somebody to mention one of their good points, so I said: "Madam, they sure are gentle horses, don't you think?" She gave me a stony stare, and I went on, "Mrs. Bender took the fractious one so everybody else could have the nice, gentle horses."

"Speaking of Mrs. Bender," she said, "she's been gone with that horse and that man for over half an hour."

Mrs. Riggs was right, and it was nearly half an hour longer before we saw them coming back up the trail. Mr. Smith had waked up, Mrs. Smith and the government girls had about talked themselves out, and Mrs. Riggs had got around to picking some little mountain flowers that grew in the shade of a broken log. She didn't think they were very pretty, though, she said.

Lola's horse was acting a whole lot better when Claudie

led him up to the campsite, but Lola said they had had an awful hard time making him drink.

That night, after the campfire singing was over, I got Claudie off to one side and said, "It took you a hell of a long time to water that horse."

"I was gonna tell you about that," Claudie said, and I knew he would because Claudie always tells me everything. "We purty nigh lost that horse," he went on. "He grazed off up a little gully, and I thought we'd never find him."

"Claudie," I said, "you've got to learn more about horses, or you're going to get us fired. We can't hold this job by music alone, you know."

"I know it," Claudie answered. "I'm doin' my best, but I'll try to do better."

"Well, please see that you do," I said. "Pay close attention to the horses, specially a fractious one like Lola's."

The next day we had a thundershower around ten o'clock, and we were about to call off the horseback ride when Mrs. Smith came down to the corral alone. She had on a transparent raincoat over her cowboy outfit; she even had a little cellophane cover for her big hat. She said she was a rain-or-shine rider, and Claudie was ready to take her off up the trail when Lola showed up and stopped him. She said she couldn't allow Claudie and Mrs. Smith to go off up the mountain in such weather. She went on to tell us something I'd never known before about mountain weather. She said: "A trip in the hills during a thundershower is very dangerous. We must keep an eye on our guests, you know." As she said it, I thought she put a mighty peculiar look on Mrs. Smith.

After the weather faired off that morning I pitched horseshoes with Prunie Stum and Mr. Riggs until Mrs.

Riggs came out and summoned him to come play bridge; but before he left the game, Mr. Riggs threw one more horseshoe, and he threw it twice as far as the peg. Must have slipped out of his hand.

That afternoon I had to go into Alpine to get some groceries, and when that pretty Prunie Stum said she wanted to go along, I took her. She bought herself the loudest bandana handkerchief she could find and a polished piece of cow horn to hold it around her neck, and I got Lola a nice shiny box of candy, but I got it wrapped up so Prunie wouldn't know what it was.

On the way back to the ranch, Prunie put her head on the back of the seat and sort of edged over toward my shoulder and said, "Clint, what has Mrs. Bender got that I haven't got?"

I could tell she was going for me in a hurry, so I said, "Prunie, how'd you know about Lola and me?" I figured I'd better shy away, because with so many women around I knew better than to be playing any two of them at one time. It wouldn't do. Prunie only giggled and changed the subject. She started telling me then how unfair the government had been to her about promotions, and by the time we got back to the ranch she had me pretty down on the government, too.

The sky was clear that night — clearer in fact than it had been, as sometimes happens after a mountain shower. The stars were bright and close-up, since the moon hadn't risen when it came time for the singing. I tuned up the guitar while Claudie built the campfire, and as the guests gathered around, I played a little while and Claudie hummed. Then he sang all the old favorites and finished off with "The Last Roundup." I'd always thought Claudie's bass was good, but he never sang so well before as he did that night. His voice rang out on the still air like bells in old missions; on the low notes it rolled and rumbled in tune with the rocks and ridges and the ravines that led down from the mountains. Then, without any warning at all, Claudie yodeled. I never heard such good yodeling anywhere before, and it didn't seem to upset him at all. He threw his head back like a coyote and almost bayed. It put us in solid with everybody.

After we got back to the trailer house I said, "Claudie, your voice is sure improving, and you can yodel, too. It must be the altitude." He grinned and said the yodel just popped out before he knew it. He went on to say he believed he could do everything better in the mountains than anywhere else that he'd ever been.

After Claudie went on to sleep, I thought a long time about Lola and the way she looked with the shadows from the campfire flickering across her face and lighting up her eyes.

I wasn't sleepy for some reason that I couldn't quite figure out, so I walked up toward the ranch house and watched the full moon as it eased up over the hills. I wasn't exactly looking for Lola, that I knew of, but as I came to the bridge in front of the ranch house, I saw her standing there, leaning on the rail and looking down at the water. The clean moon in the clear sky made her hair look soft and silky.

"Hello, Lola," I said. "What are you doing, still up? It's nearly ten o'clock."

"I wasn't sleepy," she said. "What are you doing, still up?"

"I wasn't either," I told her. Then I went ahead with some things that had been gathering in my mind. "You know, Lola, I am very glad you didn't go riding with me the other night. I think a lot more of you than I would if you had gone with me the first time I asked you." She smiled and looked down. I could feel my heart beating like one of those trip hammers that break up pavement, and I felt all over the way that citizen looks in the picture where he holds a fiddle in one hand and hugs a lady right off of a piano stool with the other.

"Clint," she said — this was the first time she had called me Clint — "I am sure glad that you and Claudie came along."

I said, "So am I, Lola, and so is Claudie. He ain't so smart, Claudie ain't. I hope you don't mind that."

"No Clint," she answered, "I don't mind it at all." Then everything was very quiet except for the soft gurgling noises made by the water on the rocks in the little stream there under the bridge.

I reached for her hand — I couldn't help it — but she slipped away, just a second ahead of me, and went toward the ranch house. As she did, she said, "I'm not sure of your motives," and there was something in her voice that rang bells inside of me. I stood there in the bright moonlight for a while before I realized that my motives had not been pure. I had been guilty of thinking more about Lola's flesh than I had her future. I'm a man who has battered his conscience around a lot, but I've still got one, and as I walked away from the bridge that night, it was acting up a lot and punishing me every step of the way. When I started to turn in, I discovered that Claudie was gone. I worried some about that, too, because I knew he'd gone off looking for me, but I was worn out from the fit my conscience had been giving me, so I went on to sleep.

4

A couple of days later Lola came over to our table at supper and told us to be ready to take the guests to Carlsbad Caverns the next day. "Everyone must see Carlsbad Caverns," she said.

"That's fine," I said. "Are you going along too?"

"Oh yes," she said. "I always do. We'll take the ranch station wagon, and Mr. Smith has offered to use the Cadillac."

Claudie perked right up, he looked as excited as he used to when he was driving that eight-horse team of Clydesdales on the Budweiser wagon back in Mississippi.

"We'll go," I said.

Claudie was already on his feet. "I've allus wanted to see Carlsbad's Cave," he remarked.

We left very early the next morning in the two cars, with Claudie driving the station wagon. The Lake Charles pair and the Flint ladies rode with him, and so did Lola. I drove the Smiths in their Cadillac, and Mr. and Mrs. Riggs rode with us.

Mrs. Riggs found every flaw in the country between the ranch and Pecos. She spoke of them in a loud, firm voice, but her remarks were put mostly to Mr. Riggs. She spoke in such a way as to make it seem that Mr. Riggs must have had some hand in creating these flaws — not an important part, but a small position on the Lord's staff, like "Agent in Charge of Minor Defects in West Texas Scenery."

Forty or fifty miles north of Pecos we pulled into a roadside filling station, and while the cars were being serviced our passengers stretched their legs and drank cold drinks.

Mr. Smith came back first and climbed into the Cadillac with me. As we were waiting for the others to come back, I saw a very strange look come over his face. He couldn't have looked worse if he had seen a striped ghost.

"What is that sign up ahead say?" he asked in his very strange brogue. "I haven't got on my glasses."

"New Mexico state line," I told him.

"Lorda'mighty," Mr. Smith said. "I don't know Carlsbad is in New Mexico."

"Sure," I answered. "Look on the map here; it's just across the line." He shrugged his shoulders, then they froze up high, even with his ears, so that he looked like a man without a neck.

When the others came back to the cars, Mr. Smith was a sickly green around the mouth, and his eyes were glazed over like the eyes of a calf caught in a gate.

"It's my gallstones," Mr. Smith said in a loud voice to the others. "Never can tell if I get bad attack. This is the worst one yet."

I and Claudie took him into the filling station, and while Mrs. Smith went for some water, Mr. Smith said: "Confidentially, boys, I'm in an awful jam. Man to man, I've got to tell you. Mrs. Smith is not Mrs. Smith."

"Gosh," Claudie said.

"Also," Mr. Smith added, "My name is not Mr. Smith."

"Claudie," I said, "it looks like we're among strangers."

"You fellers ever hear of the Mann Act? I learned about it the hard way in Providence, Rhode Island, where a man can hardly turn around without crossing a state line."

"What does the law say?" Claudie wanted to know.

"The law, it is very tough," Mr. Smith said. "It says I

cannot go from Texas into New Mexico with the girl who is not Mrs. Smith."

"Why?" Claudie wanted to know, and Mr. Smith only shrugged his shoulders. I had to call Claudie off to one side and explain it to him.

Mrs. Smith came back with a wet towel, and after she had bathed Mr. Smith's head, he looked some better. "It's the car ride that makes the gall bladder act up," Mr. Smith said. "You go ahead, Peaches, and see the Cavern with the others. I'll be okay here until you come back by."

We waited until everybody could see that Mr. Smith was all right so long as he stayed out of a car, then the Flint ladies and the Lake Charles pair got back in the station wagon. I got Mrs. Smith and the Riggs women in the big Cadillac and went back to tell Claudie to go ahead with the station wagon since Lola knew the way. Claudie and Lola were sitting in the front seat. Lola gave me a nice big warm smile, and I looked at Claudie, sitting there at the wheel.

"O.K., Claudie, let's go," I said, but Claudie just sat there. Something bad was wrong. He was as green around the gills as Mr. Smith had been. His eyes had that same glaze.

"You don't look so good yourself, now, Claudie," I told him, but Claudie didn't say a word. After a minute or so he got out of the car, went over to the bench on the shady side of the filling station, and sat down by Mr. Smith.

"I don't think I'd better leave Mr. Smith, here," he said as his color came back a little. Lola tried her luck with him, but it was no go for Claudie. He wouldn't budge. He said if he went he'd worry every minute about Mr. Smith. Mr. Smith said he wished Claudie would go ahead; all he wanted was to sit there alone until we came back.

"See, Claudie," I told him. "Mr. Smith don't need you. Remember; you've always wanted to see Carlsbad Caverns." Then he looked at Lola and looked at me with a very stubborn look on his face and said, "Clint, I ain't gonna go. My gall bladder hurts. What's wrong with Mr. Smith must be catching."

I was never so put out with Claudie in all my life. I said: "Who ever heard of gall bladder trouble being contagious?" But it didn't do a bit of good. Claudie wouldn't go.

So Lola drove the station wagon from there on, and while Claudie and Mr. Smith sat in the shade of the filling station, we went on to Carlsbad Caverns. Biggest dad-gummed cave I ever saw.

IX

Horace Q. Ball for Governor

I ALWAYS SAY pure chance has a lot to do with the turn a man's career will take. Like that time Claudie lost the list of groceries for the Lazy Day Guest Ranch. It was in the early part of August, and Mrs. Lola Bender had sent Claudie to Fort Stockton to get a broken bridle fixed and bring back some groceries. I'd gone along for the ride in the ranch car.

Claudie, who never could keep but one thing at a time on his mind, got the bridle fixed, but lost the grocery list. He bought everything he could remember and charged it to Mrs. Bender; then, along about dusk, we went down to the city park so Claudie could sit on a bench and try to think up the other things on the list. But before he thought of anything, a big voice blared out, "Come on over, folks." We looked and saw that a crowd was gathering around the bandstand in the middle of the park, and beside it we saw the sound truck that kept telling people to come on over. It had four big horns on top and a red sign on the side that said HORACE Q. BALL FOR GOVERNOR. I and Claudie went right over.

A slick-faced citizen with long sideburns and a sharp mustache was standing there on the bandstand in front of a microphone. He had a big diamond stickpin in his tie that sparkled in the lights as they came on. He told us to move in closer, and by this time people were coming across the park from every direction — men, women, and children, all craning their necks to see what was going on.

I sidled up to a tall fellow wearing duckins and a big hat and asked him if the man up there talking was the Horace Q. Ball that was running for governor. He said, "Nope. That's the magician drumming up the crowd. Horace Q. Ball don't speak till after the show."

Claudie, who is very slow at times, looked as if he didn't get it, so I asked the man, "What show?"

"The magician's gonna put on a show," he told me. "A speakin' don't draw much of a crowd around here if they ain't a good show first."

This was when I saw the magician's assistant, standing there on the bandstand beside a little square table that had a blue velvet cover with yellow tassels and fringe hanging down all around. On the front part of the velvet cover it said THE GREAT VAN AND HIS ASSISTANT, FLOSSIE, in gold letters. It was a mighty classy table, but I barely noticed it with Flossie herself there beside it. She was some shucks. On her head she wore a bright green scarf, pinned at the side with a gold clasp, and her lips were very red. Her little nose tilted up, and her eyes were cast down a mite, the way any lady's eyes would be in front of a strange crowd, but she had everything in every way that a magician's assistant or the Queen of Sheba ought to have, and she was well enough dressed for either part.

The yellow and blue striped jacket Flossie had on was a neat fit if I ever saw one, but it missed by several inches joining up with her skirt, which came in tight at the waist and then flounced out long and wide in a colored pattern of stars and moons and comets. At first I thought the lily-white strip around her waist was a satin sash, but when she turned around, I saw it was not silk or satin at all; it was the magician's assistant plumb bare in the middle, and for a girl so well filled out everywhere else, she had the smallest waist you ever saw.

I glanced at Claudie to see what effect Flossie was having on him. His mouth sagged, and his eyes bugged out until you could have knocked them off with a stick. Jacob couldn't have been more admiring of any angel on Jacob's ladder.

As soon as the Great Van started to do his tricks, it was plain that he was good all right — as country magicians go, that is. He pulled rabbits, playing cards, quarters, silk handkerchiefs, and finally a big pearl-handled six-shooter right out of Flossie's ear. All of this time Flossie never batted an eye; she only stood there, while a shy sweet smile flickered across her face from time to time, the way a light breeze will ripple across a still pond. When the Great Van did the trick of sawing Flossie in two in a big box, Claudie about halfway believed it, and he stood there twitching and fidgeting all over like a horse mule with the heaves.

Then the act was over, and the crowd cheered. The Great Van and Flossie went over to one side of the bandstand and sat there while the speaking got under way. Horace Q. Ball got up and walked to the microphone. He was a short, barrel-chested citizen of around forty with a shiny bald head, a square face, and a big mouth full of uneven teeth. He had on regular black politician's clothes, and high-heeled, square-toed boots to go with West Texas.

Horace Q. Ball pushed the microphone aside and said he didn't need any newfangled contraptions to talk to his old friends. I didn't try to pay him much mind as I stood there, stealing a look now and then at Flossie, but I couldn't help listening. He had a voice that cut through the night air the way a sawmill whistle does. He said his trip to Fort Stockton was like coming back home — not because he had ever lived there, but because he had always wanted to. He told us he had been born very poor and had to grow up in the mosquito swamps of deep East Texas, but he loved West Texas people just as much as if he had been privileged to live in that great sun-kissed climate all of his life. He said there were some of the finest open faces in the crowd he'd ever seen anywhere, and at this Claudie stood up real straight, took a deep breath, and swallowed.

Then Horace Q. Ball told us what he was in favor of, and he covered a lot of ground, too. He was for good roads — state highways, county roads, rural roads, and farm-to-market roads; he was for big ditches beside them all that could carry off the water when it rained. He was for higher prices for cattle and all kinds of farm produce and lower prices on plows, hay balers, and other farm implements. "Why," he asked, "haven't you good people got all of these things you so richly deserve? I'll tell you why. There is waste and extravagance yonder in Austin! That's why. It will be stamped out, fellow Texans, if you will go to the polls on August 27 and elect Horace Q. Ball your governor."

He then told us about some things he was against, and from the way he put it, nobody in Texas was actually for these things except one person — Tornado Timpson.

"Who's Tornado Timpson?" Claudie whispered.

"He's the other guy running for governor, Claudie; he's the one that's got the hillbilly band," I stated, while Horace Q. Ball went on reeling off the things he was against.

He was against Wall Street; he was against liquor and

gambling; he was against cattle stealing and the foot-and-mouth disease; he was against monopolies, and on this subject he bellowed like a Brahma bull. He hated monopolies, he said, worse than the devil hated holy water. Everybody cheered, and some men back in the crowd yelled, "Pour it on 'em, Q. Ball! Pour it on 'em!" Then he got to trusts. He was fierce about trusts. Fact was, he said, he believed he hated them more than he did monopolies, and he was in a steamy lather about them both. From the way he was going on up there, I figured he would like to drop everything else right then and there so that he could go out and fight a trust or a monopoly all the rest of his born days, without even as much as stopping for a drink of water. I was about ready to go out and help him, too.

Horace Q. Ball then took up the subject of Tornado Timpson. He said he despised to bring personal abuse into a race he had tried to run on a very high plane, but he had been driven to it by the treacherous tactics of his worthy opponent. "It is not true," he said, with his right hand on his left chest and his left fist in the air, "that the trusts and the monopolies are supporting me; they are supporting that snake in sheep's clothing, Tornado Timpson, and he knows it! Ask him, when he speaks here tomorrow night, if he's not their stooge. He won't admit it, but make him deny it."

"Too bad," I told Claudie, "we can't be here tomorrow night to hear him deny it." I was pretty mad at Tornado Timpson by then — as mad, that is, as I could be at anybody so long as I had that pretty Flossie up there to look at.

2

I am a man with more than a little romance in my nature, and that night after I turned in I could hardly get Flossie out of my mind. The red of her cheeks and lips against the green of the scarf kept flashing up in front of my eyes, and so did the milk-white waist that was not satin after all. I thought a lot about the odds on ever seeing Flossie again, and the more I thought, the longer they looked, but since I am used to outside chances, I finally went on to sleep.

The next morning it turned out that Claudie had forgotten more groceries from the list than he had remembered; also he had brought back a lot of stuff that had never been on Mrs. Bender's list in the first place. This all meant just one thing — Claudie had to go back to Fort Stockton, and after stalling around all day we went late in the afternoon so we could make the Tornado Timpson rally that night.

When we got to the park in Fort Stockton about sundown, the rally was just about to start. First some cowboys with guitars and some cowgirls with mandolins sang up a crowd with about an hour of good sound mountain music. It was loud and sweet. Then Tornado Timpson made his speech. He spoke in a high-pitched voice that had a snarl in it, and when he got to the part about trusts and monopolies, he was rough; in fact, he seemed to begin about where Horace Q. Ball had left off. With Tornado standing up there on the platform in his shirt sleeves, yelling bloody murder about trusts while the sweat poured down his face, I and Claudie got stirred up all over again.

On the way back to the ranch that night, I told Claudie

that I was afraid the Tornado was going to beat Horace Q. Ball. "Notice the size of that crowd?" I asked. "Twice as big as the one last night."

"Horace Q. Ball didn't have no mountain music," he said.

"You can say that again, Claudie," I told him. "Flossie and the Great Van ain't holding their own with Tornado's mountain music."

"I reckon Flossie is about the purtiest girl I ever seen," Claudie said.

"She's pretty around the waist too," I told him; then we had the wreck. With that part of Flossie on his mind, Claudie hadn't noticed a detour sign in the road ahead, even though it was as big as the side of a barn. The sign said HIGHWAY UNDER REPAIR — BRANIGAN AND SCHWARTZ, ROAD CONTRACTORS, and we hit it. We bashed in the front of the car and knocked out the lights, so we didn't make it back to the ranch until late that night.

Along about daylight the next morning the whole thing dawned on me. It was an enormous idea, and my mind froze on it like an old coon dog on a new trail. I was wide awake, sitting up in my bunk with this thought boiling around in my head: Horace Q. Ball needed music, and there wasn't a bigger, sweeter bass voice than Claudie's between the Pecos River and the Sabine. If I could borrow the guitar from the Lazy Day Ranch, we could go out and lick Tornado Timpson before August 27. We had just three weeks. I knew we didn't have to depend on pure chance any more. Lady Luck had dealt us a career on a silver platter.

I got up and dressed and went down to the mailbox and waited for the newspaper. When it came, I found that Horace Q. Ball was going to speak that night at Pecos, and as I walked back to the ranch house, I could just see that sweet, shy Flossie up there being sawed in two again for a cause that could never win without our help.

At breakfast I and Claudie both had an extra helping of eggs, and I told him about my idea. He didn't much want to leave, but when I told him his country ought to come first, his patriotism started getting the better of him. I pointed out that the State of Texas was a very large part of his country and that Mrs. Bender was apt to fire us anyhow when she saw what we had done to the ranch car.

When Mrs. Bender came around, she gave us the gate all right; she said she didn't see how anybody that wasn't blind could hit one of those big Branigan and Schwartz signs. She wouldn't pay us for the part of the week we'd worked, but she did let us take the guitar, and we left for Pecos in our own car about noon.

We waited until nearly six o'clock that afternoon for the Ball sound truck to reach Pecos. When it came, the Great Van was driving it, and he told us Horace Q. Ball and Flossie were coming along behind in the campaign car. I told the Great Van that we had a very important message for the candidate; then I put some questions to him, and from a lot of his talk that didn't count for much, I sifted out a few things that I really wanted to know.

For one thing, Flossie's name was Flossie Widgeon, and she had once been the Sweet Potato Queen of East Texas. She came from Beaumont, Texas, he said, and she was not married at the present time. I told the Great Van she was as pretty a magician's assistant as I had ever seen.

"She is right pretty in a drab way," he admitted. Then he went on, "But she don't add a great deal to my act. We ain't getting the crowds."

Such remarks about Flossie made me and Claudie both a little sore, but I figured that it was no time to be getting into an argument with the Great Van.

"Why do you keep her, then?" I asked him.

"She's Horace Q. Ball's stenographer, and he used his influence with Branigan and Schwartz to get her this job," he answered.

"What's Branigan and Schwartz got to do with it?" I asked.

"They're big road contractors. They are financing the entertainment for Horace Q. Ball."

"Who's paying for Tornado Timpson's mountain music?" I asked him.

"Branigan and Schwartz," he said.

3

When Horace Q. Ball came along with Flossie, he parked his car by the Courthouse. The car had campaign signs and slogans written all over it in white paint. One I remember said TEXAS CAN'T STALL WITH HORACE Q. BALL. The people flocked out of the Courthouse and crowded around.

Flossie wasn't wearing the scarf or anything on her head, and her light brown hair, combed back from her high forehead, looked soft and fluffy; but seeing her for the first time in broad daylight, I noticed that she looked a little older than she had on the bandstand. There was a trace of sadness around Flossie's eyes that made me wonder if she hadn't had some troubles that she didn't deserve.

There wasn't much of a crowd that night at the picnic grounds where the rally took place, and about half of them left when the Great Van got through sawing Flossie Widgeon in two. I could just feel it in my bones that they were losing to Tornado Timpson every day that the campaign went along on such an unsound basis.

After the speaking we followed them to the hotel. When we found what Horace Q. Ball's room number was, we went up, and I started to knock on the door, but since we couldn't help hearing the Great Van and Horace Q. Ball talking in there, we waited a minute on the outside.

Horace Q. Ball was saying, "Now that Flossie's gone on to bed, there is something I want to talk to you about, Van. We had another lousy crowd tonight. I'm afraid no magician is going to be able to hold his own with Tornado Timpson's hillbilly band."

"Listen, Q. Ball," the Great Van told him, "you can't run me down any more. Everybody knows why my act don't draw. Flossie hasn't got no appeal. Did I pick Flossie? No. Did Branigan and Schwartz pick Flossie? No. Who did? You did."

"That's a mighty lame excuse for the poor showing you've made," Horace said, and his voice quivered the way it had when he talked about trusts and monopolies. "That's a mean, cowardly thing, to lay it on Flossie. I guess I lost this race anyway when I let Branigan and Schwartz palm off a cheap magician on me."

I knocked on the door, loud. Horace Q. Ball said, "Who is it?" and I said, "Clint Hightower. I've got some important business to talk over with you."

He opened the door, and I and Claudie went in as the Great Van went out. Horace Q. Ball seemed a little agitated. I saw I had to get him sort of cooled off and used to us, so I said, "Are you one of the Balls from East Texas?"

"Yes," he answered. "Why?"

"They're mighty good folks," I told him. "Stanch people."

"Thank you," he said. Then I went on: "Mr. Ball, there is just one thing I want to know."

"Go ahead; what is it?" he said. "I'm tired, and I want to go to bed."

"Can Flossie Widgeon carry a tune?"

"She has a real nice soprano voice," he told me. "Now, good night, men."

"Horace," I went on, "when I heard you speak in Fort Stockton the other night, you sounded to me just like a man that wanted to be Governor of Texas. If you are ever going to be elected, you need some good music, and you need it bad."

"I need mountain music," he said.

"Exactly!" I told him. "My associate, Claudie Hughes, who is standing right before you, sings the finest country bass in this state, and I can play a guitar. What's more, I have already got the guitar. We can do mountain music, and we can teach it to Flossie. We'll work up an act with Flossie that will put you in the governor's chair. Just think of it: Governor Horace Q. Ball!"

I could see from the better look that came in his eyes that we had him. He put in a call for Branigan and Schwartz in Galveston, and in ten minutes he had us on their payroll in the Great Van's place. He told us they would pay us each a hundred dollars for the rest of the campaign, with room and board thrown in.

"Now that we're hired," I said, "that reminds me. We haven't had any supper yet, and the sign on the coffee shop downstairs says it's open all night."

Horace Q. Ball said that could be arranged.

4

We woke Flossie up at six o'clock the next morning, and after we'd had a bite of breakfast we rehearsed until nearly ten, when we had to leave for Big Spring. Sure enough, she had a light, sweet voice and could carry a tune. I figured we would put her close to the microphone and move Claudie a little way back, and it would about make up for the difference. You see, Claudie has a very loud bass voice.

We picked a theme song first — one I had heard some Austin people sing at the Lazy Day Ranch — and I taught it to Flossie and Claudie. The tune didn't amount to much, but the words were all about Texas. I don't remember them all now; the general idea was Texas first and last, and to hell with everywhere else.

Then we worked up a program from other popular songs about river valleys, homes in the West, Blue Bonnets, blue mountains, blue skies, true love on the plains, and rivers that flow. From the way the crowd took on over us that night in Big Springs, I knew we were on the right track.

We got billed as Horace Q. Ball and the Texas Sweethearts — Claudie and Flossie being the sweethearts — and we got famous. I stayed out of the billing on purpose, but behind the scenes it was plain from the first that Flossie was meant for me.

"Claudie," I stated after the rally in Lubbock the next night, "I don't mind it if Flossie is your stage sweetheart, but leave her to me off the stage, if you will be so kindly. I saw her first, you know."

"I thought we both seen her about the same time," he argued.

"You ought to know better than that," I told him. "I always see things before you do."

He didn't answer me right off, but before we went to bed that night he said, "Flossie shore is a purty girl, Clint."

As the campaign went on, we moved toward the big towns in the east part of the state, and the news of the Texas Sweethearts always beat us there. They were ready for us, and they called for more and more music until Horace had to cut down on his speeches. In Waco he didn't even get around to the part of his speech on trusts and monopolies before the crowd started yelling for the Texas Sweethearts. He spent all the time we gave him there talking about good roads.

The crowds got bigger and bigger, and the newspapers started saying that we might win if we could ever get over the puny start of the campaign with the Great Van. We figured out a way to hold the crowds by having the Texas Sweethearts begin and end the program, and we put Horace Q. Ball in the middle like a sandwich.

Wherever the Great Van was by this time, he must have been fairly ready to bite himself when he read about the way Flossie was packing them in. He had plumb overlooked Flossie's drawing power when he left her standing still in his show. I taught Flossie to swing and sway in the middle and roll her eyes at Claudie when they stood up there and sang mountain music. This made the difference, and we could see every night how it was going to pay off in votes.

We had less than a week to go when we got our pay from Branigan and Schwartz, so I and Claudie went into a store in Austin and macked ourselves out in some good clothes. I figured we had to finish up the campaign in style.

We didn't have to leave Austin until three o'clock to make the rally in San Antonio that night, so I put on my new clothes and took Flossie for a walk around the State Capitol grounds. We sauntered about under the big live oaks and their limbs with elbows in them. We looked at the old cannons and statues there, until we came to a little waterfall by a pond that had cress and lilies growing in it. It was some cooler there, so we sat down on a stone bench and watched the minnows swimming around in schools.

"Flossie," I said in a nice soft voice, "I don't think I ever felt about any girl the way I already feel about you."

She blushed and smiled, and a little dimple showed up in her cheek from nowhere at all. Her brown eyes, as she looked up at me, were wide open and very friendly.

"I like you too, Clint," she said, and it stirred up something inside of me that felt like cobwebs look in the morning when dew is on them.

"Flossie," I went on, "when I see you up there singing that mountain music with Claudie, and everybody calling you the Texas Sweethearts, it almost makes me jealous of that big lug. There's nothing between you two, is there?"

"Of course not, Clint," she said. "Me and Claudie is only chums." This was the first time she'd said it right out, and it made me feel so good that I wanted to go out somewhere and pull up a fence post and beat some big wild animal to death with it.

I said: "Flossie, you are about the prettiest thing I've seen in the whole State of Texas. Did you ever think any about getting married?"

"I've been married some," she said, as she blushed and looked down, "but I never did marry the right one."

"When we win," I told her, "I've got some plans. Want to hear them?"

"Sure I do, Clint," Flossie said.

"I want to settle down for good right here in Texas. Horace has already halfway promised me a job in the State Highway Department when he gets elected."

She sat there watching the minnows swim around the lily stems in the pond for a long time; then she asked me a funny question. It was: "What will Claudie do?"

"Probably go back to Alabama," I said. "I doubt that he could hold a state job, unless it's in the Department of Agriculture. Claudie's nothing but a farmer that can sing bass."

"He sure is a fine bass singer," Flossie allowed; then, before I could ask her anything more, she looked at the clock down on Congress Avenue and said wasn't it about time for us to leave for San Antonio? I had to admit that it was.

The rally that night was by far the biggest one we'd had, and the San Antonio people were crazy about us. While Claudie stood up straight with his head thrown back and rolled out the bass, Flossie sang and swayed and rolled her pretty eyes. The crowd ate it up. They cheered and whistled for more music until we almost crowded Horace Q. Ball plumb off the program. The next morning the *San Antonio Light* said the gamblers in Galveston were giving better odds on us, but it didn't say how much better.

Our next rally was in Dallas, and I noticed something that bothered me a lot; it was the way that Claudie was getting to look at Flossie while they were singing. It was disgusting. That big Oscar had such a soft, mushy look on his face that it made me want to brush it off with a dirty, stubby broom. Later on I got him off to one side and said: "Listen, Claudie. I know that singing sweethearts are supposed to put a friendly look on each other when they sing, but ain't you overdoing it a little?"

"I may be," Claudie said; then he walked away whistling.

5

We closed the campaign the next night at Hermann Park in Houston. It was a warm, clear night, and a bright full moon was shining through the oak trees. There must have been several acres of people sitting and standing in the park — the men in shirt sleeves and the women fanning themselves. The children were out, too; some little ones in arms and others chasing each other around.

When Flossie and Claudie had sung all the songs they knew, the crowd wanted more music, so they sang some of the same ones again. It was nearly nine o'clock when Horace finally got to go on.

After the speech, Flossie and Claudie sang "The Eyes of Texas Are upon You," and from out in the crowd the whistles and cheers rose up at us. Horace Q. Ball came over and said some awful nice things to us. He even stated that if he got elected, he believed some of the credit belonged to his musicians. I looked at Flossie, and her face was all lit up with excitement; so much so that tears brimmed up in her eyes and told of special tender ways she must have been feeling inside. She was lovely, and I couldn't figure when I'd been so all-fired happy before in my whole life.

A long line of people stood waiting to shake hands with

Horace Q. Ball; so he asked me to take the sound truck and drive Flossie to her room at the Rice Hotel. He wanted Claudie to stay and bring him along later in the campaign car.

As we drove toward town on Main Street, I glanced down at Flossie, and her face looked as soft and sweet as a ripe Alberta peach. I said, "Flossie, you look so pretty tonight it makes me want to go climb a big, steep mountain somewhere to find a little blue flower for you to put in your hair. You know I love you, Flossie."

Then we pulled up to a stop sign, the street light fell full on her face, and I could see the tears had spilled over and were streaming down her cheeks. Now I am strictly no good around any woman that is crying, and that goes double for one as pretty as Flossie was. While the cars lined up and honked behind us I tried to talk to her, but it was no use. All she would say was, "Oh, Clint, I'll never be married now," and she kept on saying it as she broke out in heavy sobs.

"What in the world are you talking about, Flossie?" I asked. "I want to marry you."

"It ain't no use, Clint," she went on. "You and Claudie are sweet fellows, but it's Horace Q. Ball that I love. Me and Horace has been keeping company for a year or more. He loved me when he was only the sheriff of Jasper County and I was the Sweet Potato Queen. He was just about to marry me when them politicians talked him into running for governor. Now it looks like we've put Horace in with our mountain music. I'm a loving woman, but I ain't up to being a governor's wife. Oh, I wish I'd never seen you and Claudie." Then she put her face in her hands and started sobbing all over again.

I felt all over like a man that is about to come unglued, and all I could think to say was: "Why did you sing so sweet then, Flossie?"

Flossie looked up, rubbed her eyes and said, "I didn't want him to lose, and I didn't want him to win."

There's a woman for you, I thought to myself; then I looked out of the sound truck, and there stood a cop. He said: "I don't care what you are running for, bub; you can't block this here traffic. Also, what have you been doing to the little lady there?"

"He hasn't done nothing to me," Flossie said.

"She's right about that, officer," I added, and we drove off.

I took Flossie on down to the Rice Hotel and sent her up to her room. Then I went up to bed, but I didn't go to sleep.

Next morning I found that Claudie had gone to Galveston to deliver the sound truck to Branigan and Schwartz, so I waited around the hotel for him to come back. Late afternoon came, and still I hadn't seen hide nor hair of Claudie, Horace Q. Ball or Flossie; but there was plenty happening in the election by then. The newspapers were full of headlines. It was a landslide for Tornado Timpson.

I ran into Flossie and Horace Q. Ball in the Rice lobby along about six o'clock — just in time, as it turned out, to tell them both good-by. Flossie's eyes were shining, and Horace looked about as well as anybody could that wasn't carrying a single precinct in the whole State of Texas. Flossie told me they were leaving for Beaumont to get a marriage license, and I told them I didn't blame them one bit. I even told them I hoped they'd be happy together, but it took about everything I had to say it.

A little later Claudie got back from Galveston, and he was low. He'd already heard the bad news about the election; he knew what had happened to Horace Q. Ball in the governor's race, but he wanted to know what had happened to Flossie.

"She had to go to Beaumont to see some of her folks," I told him. "She's got an aunt over there that is pretty sick."

"I'm surprised you didn't go with her, Clint," he said, "seeing as how you got so sweet on Flossie during the governor's race."

"No, Claudie," I said, "Flossie wasn't exactly my type, so I told her good-by for us both. Another thing —ain't it about time I and you got the hell out of here? I've bought some gasoline for the car, and I expect we'd better go down about Rockport for a little vacation. I feel the need for some rest."

We left Houston about dark, and after we got out on the Angleton road, Claudie said he'd be dad-burned if he could figure how I could go off and leave Flossie that way. "I thought you was in love," he argued.

"Love?" I said. "Love is a high and elegant thing, I am sure. Love is a feeling that can be stout and sweet — but it comes and it goes, Claudie. It comes and it goes."

X

The Weather Prophet

"LISTEN, CLAUDIE," I said, "I'd about as soon be plumb out of money as to have only five dollars."

"I druther have this here five dollars, Clint," he answered.

"But what I'm trying to tell you is this," I went on — "we've got to get our car fixed, and that five dollars won't do it. You know what the man at the garage said; he won't touch the burnt-out bearing for less than twenty dollars."

Claudie just stood there on the docks looking at a battered-up old shrimper nudging its way into the pier. It was late in the afternoon, the hot Texas sun was beginning to ease up on us a little, and the mosquitoes were moving in. We'd been watching the fishing boats for an hour or so as they came in from the Gulf of Mexico to unload their catch at the Rockport wharf.

"Remember, Claudie," I said, "we've been here on the waterfront for three days now, and nobody has offered us any kind of a job at all. You know that. The only thing we've been asked to since we broke down here is the crap game on that big yacht tonight. Who worked up that invitation? Me or you?"

"You did," Claudie admitted, "but you didn't have to tell the man on the yatch that you was a friend of the Governor of Texas. He'd have asked you anyhow."

"Well," I said, "I can't figure how I'm going to get even one roll with the dice if I haven't got any money."

"You shoulda thought of that last night before you tried to break all them pin-ball machines," he answered.

"Listen, Claudie," I went on, "do you know what happened to the man in the Bible with five talents?"

"No. What?"

"I'll tell you," I said. "He put the talents to work, that's what; and in the long run he turned out better than the fellow that just sat on what he had."

Claudie's stubborn look was softening up around the edges.

"Another thing, Claudie," I went on, "you might have noticed how I've been watching the birds in the sky all day."

"What have they got to do with it?" Claudie wanted to know as he kicked against a rotten pile on the docks and watched the splinters fall among some jellyfish that were squooching around there in the water.

"Plenty," I told him. "It's in the sky that changes in a man's luck first begin to show up. You can tell it first in the flight of the birds — the gulls mainly, but now I can feel it in my bones too. This is my lucky day with the dice."

"Trouble is," Claudie fussed, "you've felt it before and been wrong."

"Tell you what I'll do, Claudie," I said. "You keep four dollars and let me have one. If I'm wrong, the whole five wouldn't last long; but if I'm right, that'll be enough to get me started. I'll give you exactly half of what I win, and your dollar back to boot."

That got him; he fished out an old dollar bill and turned it over to me, and I said: "Thank you, Claudie. Now I want you to come along to the crap game with me. You might bring me even more luck."

When we got down to the private docks about dusk we found the yacht we were looking for. The name was printed in gold letters on the rear end: *The Pride of Texas, III.* It was the biggest of eight nice long shiny boats tied up there. The lights were already burning inside, and we could see how fine it was fixed up in there; big comfortable chairs and sofas, a radio and pretty rugs on the floor.

The man that had asked me to the crap game stuck his head through a window and said, "Come aboard, men," and we climbed on the boat's rear end, where it was like a porch with a big awning over it.

I said to the man, "I didn't get your name this morning, Captain."

"Hinder," he said, "but they call me Squatty," and I could see why. He wasn't much over five feet tall, and he was nearly square. His jaw set out a little like a bulldog's, but he had nice, friendly little eyes. He was wearing a blue cap with some gold palms on the front.

"Clint Hightower is the name," I told him, "and this big guy here is my associate, Claudie Hughes. He came to bring me luck." Claudie grinned, and we went inside.

While we waited for the other crap shooters to come along, Squatty told us the *Pride of Texas, III,* belonged to a rich oil man named Easley who lived in Fort Worth. Squatty said he was pretty sure that Mr. Easley was still in Canada on a vacation, and that, he explained, was why the crap game was going on in the owner's cabin that night.

Squatty told us he lived on the boat and kept it shipshape all the time. He was real proud of the way it looked, too, and he should have been. All the brass was shining, the windows were clean, and you couldn't see a speck of dust anywhere.

It wasn't long before the other crap shooters came along. I remember one was a San Antonio plumber with one eye; there was a fat shrimp boat captain that they called Fishmouth; there was a Mexican, too, and a Bible salesman with a peculiar motto tattooed on his arm. It said, "Oh hell, what's the use?" There was another one, too; a very grubby-looking character that came late, lost his money and left early. His name was "Bird Dog" something. I noticed they all called Squatty "Captain Squatty."

That owner's cabin was something! There were two big bunks, wide almost as beds, a dresser with real drawers and a mirror above it, and bright lights all around. A nice, smooth rug covered the floor — perfect for dice — and there was plenty of room to move around on it.

We all got right down on the rug and went to work with the dice. The first time I rolled I shot a half and ran it up to five dollars before I fell off. It looked like my lucky day, but Claudie just sat there on one of the bunks with a droopy look on his face. Then I faded some of the others, as the dice went around, and when it came my turn again, I was down to about where I had started. But I put down a dollar and made four passes before I fell off again. I almost didn't drag in time, but I came out with three dollars.

It went along like this for three or four hours; several times I was up, but not much; other times I got down to nearly even. Along about midnight people started to gape and stretch, and it began to look like the game was about over. The luck had been pretty even all around, except I could tell from the ugly looks they were giving Fishmouth that he had been stashing some money away.

I figured it was time for me to hit a big lick if I had one in my system, so when I got the dice I counted out and put down all I had — eight dollars and a half. They covered it, and I rolled two big, ugly sixes — boxcars. They gathered up my money and yelled, "Go ahead, Clint; you've still got the dice."

I looked at Claudie, and he was sound asleep there on the bunk. "Wake up, Claudie," I said. "I need another dollar." Claudie woke up, but he did not give me another dollar. I whispered to him that I still had the dice and told him it was the unluckiest thing in the world for a man to pass a roll he had coming to him, but Claudie just sat there blinking. Everybody was looking at me, and I had to do something right away. It is at such times as this that a man may have his best ideas. The best one I had was to say, "Gents, my associate here, Claudie, will shoot for me. I've got a little cramp in my right arm." Nobody said no, so I said, "Go ahead, Claudie, and shoot a dollar."

He was still too drowsy to argue, so he put a dollar down. Somebody covered it, and Claudie rolled the dicc out on the rug. He made a neat seven.

"Fade it, men," I said. "We shoot the two dollars." The two got to be four, the four got to be eight, and when it was sixteen, Claudie said he wanted to drag it and quit.

"Are you crazy?" I asked him. "I knew I'd seen luck for somebody in the sky today. It wasn't me. It was you. Let it all ride!"

Claudie let it ride and passed again. Next he made two hard points: a nine and then a ten. We had sixty-four dollars won, and they had to dig deep to cover it, but they did. Claudie came out with eight for a point, and on the very next roll he made it the hard way — two fours. His luck was in the light of the moon.

"Eighter," I yelled, "from Decatur, the county seat of Wise," and all I got was some black looks. Then I said, "We let it all ride. A hundred and twenty-eight dollars is begging."

Captain Squatty went through a little door in the front of the owner's cabin and came back with a roll of bills you could have wadded a cannon with. He counted them out, and with what Fishmouth dug out of his jeans they finally got our pile of money covered. There on the cabin floor was two hundred and fifty-six dollars — half ours and half theirs — and one more pass was all we needed to break up the game. I looked at Claudie, and I could see he was ready. He was lightning ready to strike, and he did! He rolled a great big sparkling eleven, and it got so quiet we could hear the oysters clapping their shells together on the bottom of Rockport Bay.

Captain Squatty spoke up first; he said he was out of cash, but he had a government bond in the bank at Port Lavaca; he wondered if he could put in his I.O.U. to cover the two hundred and fifty-six dollars.

"Sure. Let's have it," I told him, so he wrote it out on the back of an envelope and put it on top of the pile of bills there on the cabin floor. By this time Claudie had a wild, rich look in his eyes, like a trapeze artist taking a bow. He was blowing on the dice and whispering soft words to them. Captain Squatty was pale as a ghost, and little beads of sweat were cropping out all over his face, but he said, "Go ahead, Claudie, and shoot; but you'd better roll them hard against the bulkhead."

"Against the what?" Claudie asked.

"The door to the head, right there in front of you," the Captain told him. He was almost fussy with Claudie, I thought.

Claudie snorted like a mule colt as he came out with the dice. "Come seven," he said in a hoarse voice. The bones bounced against the door and settled back on the soft rug — a six and an ace.

"Seven it is," I said as I picked up the pile of bills and Captain Squatty's I.O.U. "You can't beat a shooter that is in tune with the sky."

After all the others left, I and Claudie stayed on the boat a little while to speak with Captain Squatty alone about the I.O.U.; but before we could, he went to the icebox and got out three bottles of cold beer. A little color came back to Captain Squatty's face as he swigged the beer, and he licked his lips where they'd been drying up after Claudie's last roll; then he said, "Gents, I am worried about that I.O.U. you've got there."

"We're not, Captain Squatty," I told him. "You can get your I.O.U. back in the morning when you cash the bond."

He swallowed, and his face got the color of the underside of a raw oyster. "Trouble is," he said, "the bond ain't enough to do it. It's only a twenty-five-dollar bond."

Claudie began to count on his fingers, and I said, "Captain, I wouldn't worry a minute about the difference. It ain't but two hundred and thirty-one dollars."

He lit a cigarette and took a drag that burnt it about halfway down before he said, "That's what I figure it, but I haven't got the money."

"Think nothing of it, Captain," I said. "I and Claudie can take it out in board and room on this yacht. We'll use this room right here and credit you with ten dollars every day we stay. Before long it'll all be paid out."

Captain Squatty said, "But this is the owner's cabin — "

Then I cut in, "And now I wonder if you could pass us another couple of bottles of that nice cold beer. We're going to like it here fine."

2

The next morning it was cloudy and a little cooler, so I and Claudie slept late. As I was waking up, I thought what a shame and a waste it was for those lovely mattresses not to be used every night of the world. When Captain Squatty came from the little room in the front of the boat where he had his bunk, I told him that I and Claudie had one weakness we hoped he could get used to.

"What's that?" he asked.

"We like our breakfast in bed. The other meals we get up and dress for."

Without a word, Captain Squatty went into the kitchen and started pumping away on the alcohol stove.

"Claudie," I said, "would you like a little coffee first, or with your breakfast?"

"I like coffee first thing, Clint," Claudie answered.

"Hear that, Captain Squatty?" I yelled. "I and Claudie like coffee first; one lump for me and two for him. No cream please; we like it hot and black."

After breakfast we got dressed, and I sent Claudie up to the garage to get the burnt-out bearing on our car fixed. "See about a new battery too, Claudie," I told him as he left. "I like for a battery to turn the starter over fast, and you might want a coon or fox tail for the radiator cap. Get it if you like."

While Captain Squatty cleaned up the kitchen and washed the dishes, I went out on the rear end of the boat and stood under the awning to study the sky. Higher up it was solid gray, and dark clouds were rolling in low from the gulf. The gusty air had the feel of worse weather coming, and I called Captain Squatty out to speak with him about it.

"Tell me, Captain," I said, "what do you make of this weather?"

"The glass is low, Clint," he answered.

"The what?" I asked.

"The barometer," he said. "It's below twenty-nine. There's a hurricane somewhere out there in the gulf."

"Don't tell Claudie," I said. "He's always been afraid of storms."

But when Claudie came back to the yacht around noon, he had already heard about it. In fact, he said, the town was pretty full of hurricane talk. The storm was still way down in the Gulf of Mexico, close to Yucatán, they were saying, but it could blow in anywhere along the gulf coast.

The next day the sky looked a lot better, and there was almost no wind at all. The talk along the waterfront was that the hurricane was about to peter out down around Mexico somewhere. Captain Squatty said the glass was higher, and told me he liked the feel of the weather. I said, "Couldn't we fire up this here yacht, Captain, and go out there in the bay and catch ourselves a nice mess of fish?"

"I can't do it," he answered.

"I don't know why," I said. "We'll credit you ten dollars on the I.O.U. for every fishing trip we make."

"Mr. Easley's orders are not to move the *Pride of Texas* from this dock except for a hurricane."

"What?" I asked him. "You mean you would go right out in a hurricane?"

"Sure," he said. "In case of a big blow, the *Pride of Texas* would be bashed all to hell against this dock here if I left it tied up. Out in the bay you can anchor a boat and ride it out. That's part of my job; to pull out in the bay if there's a hurricane coming."

The next morning our car was ready to run again, so we left Claudie to watch the boat and the weather while I drove Captain Squatty over to Port Lavaca to get our bond. We cashed it for twenty-five dollars, and I marked up the Captain's payment on the I.O.U. I gave him credit for another twenty dollars to cover the two days we had lived on the boat and another five dollars on account of the Captain's fine cooking. That cut it down to two hundred and six dollars.

On the way back from Port Lavaca, the sun broke through the clouds, and Captain Squatty said he believed that old hurricane must have blown itself out somewhere.

"Don't be too sure," I answered; "the sky don't look too good, and the air don't feel right to me yet."

The Captain grunted and said, "I just think you want to go fishing, Clint, but you wouldn't get me in any more trouble with Mr. Easley than I'm already in, would you?"

"The last thing I'd want to do," I told him, "would be to get you in trouble with Mr. Easley."

The next morning there wasn't a cloud in the sky, the water was clear and blue, and the air felt fresh and clean. A lot of fishing boats shoved off early. I and Claudie got up, and dressed for breakfast. Captain Squatty served it to us on the rear end of the boat under the awning. While he was bringing us toothpicks, I credited him with ten more dollars for another day; then, while I was at it, I credited him with another ten dollars for the next day and said, "Captain, from here on we're going to pay in advance every day. See here, this I.O.U. is down now to a hundred and eighty-six dollars."

Captain Squatty only nodded his head and chewed a while on one of his thumb nails.

After breakfast Claudie went to get us some cards and cigars and bring Captain Squatty's mail back from the post office. We smoked and played pitch all morning on the deck while the Captain freshened up the boat. He wiped all the windows with a chamois skin; he swept the boat out from one end to the other and waxed the floors and the wood inside; then he hosed and mopped the outside of the boat and polished all the brass on it. By noon there wasn't anything about the boat that wasn't shining, except our cigarette trays, and Captain Squatty emptied them and wiped the ashes out inside. Then he went to the store where Mr. Easley had a charge account and bought provisions for the day.

When Captain Squatty came back with a big basket full of groceries and things, I asked him how the glass was, and he said, "Rising; the hurricane must be gone."

"That's what I want to speak to you about, Captain," I told him. "I have a feeling about the weather."

"The glass is good enough for me," he answered as he went down to the kitchen with the food. I followed him down there and left Claudie at the card table.

"Captain Hinder," I spoke very serious and firm, "suppose you got warned that a hurricane was coming and you didn't take the *Pride of Texas, III,* out in the bay to ride it out. Then if a hurricane did come, you'd really be in trouble with Mr. Easley, wouldn't you?"

"I'll say I would," he answered.

"Well," I said, "I'm warning you, Captain; there may be a hurricane. Don't tell Claudie; he's afraid of storms, but I figure we'd better get this yacht out in the bay."

The Captain's jaw tightened up, and his eyes seemed to get smaller, but he didn't say a word.

"Of course," I went on, "we can fish until it comes up. We'll give you an extra sixteen dollars' credit for the trip. That'll cut the I.O.U. down to a hundred and seventy dollars. I'll bet you never thought you'd work it off so fast!"

"I'll do it if you credit me with twenty-six dollars for the trip," he answered, and I took him up in a hurry.

I pulled out the I.O.U., wrote the credit on the back and showed it to him. "See?" I said. "Paid in advance."

Captain Squatty fired up the motors while Claudie untied us from the docks, and we took off. As we hummed along through the water with the motors singing together, I and Claudie sat back in the deck chairs on the rear end smoking cigars and feeding bread crumbs to the gulls.

"Claudie," I said, "this is the way a man should live every day of his life. A lot of people get themselves so tangled up in work that they never take time to pleasure themselves; they get old before they learn to enjoy the finer things in this great big world. Take Mr. Easley; I'll bet he's up there in Canada bothering himself about taxes and expenses the way the government is spending money all the time."

"I shore feel sorry for Mr. Easley," Claudie said.

When we got out in the middle of Copano Bay, we saw a

big bunch of gulls working above the water, close to a little green island, and the Captain said that was a very good sign; the gulls were eating mullet that had been driven to the top of the water by a school of bigger fish. We circled the island and found that the gulls were working above a long narrow reef where the water was light green and so shallow that the waves broke and splashed in a line along the surface. Captain Hinder said it was an oyster reef where the fishing was sometimes good. He eased the boat across the blue channel that lay betwixt the island and the reef and backed us up to the edge of the green water. He showed Claudie how to throw the anchor over, and we settled down to fish from the rear end of the boat.

Mr. Easley had the fanciest hooks and lines and winding reels I ever saw anywhere. Captain Squatty rigged our tackle and baited our hooks with shrimp, and from the first the fishing was fine. We caught speckled trout, gaff-top catfish, croakers, whiting and a few little sharks that we threw back. Claudie caught a sting ray about the size of a catcher's mitt, and that long stinger whipping around scared Claudie aplenty. I stepped inside the boat and watched Claudie dodge and dance away from the sting ray until Captain Squatty got it back in the water.

The sun was slipping behind a big blue cloud bank in the west, and we had the fish box half full when Captain Squatty pointed out that the other fishing boats were leaving.

"We better get back to Rockport, Clint," he said. "It'll take us an hour or more."

"You must be forgetting my warning, Captain Hinder," I said, looking him straight in the eye. He looked down.

"What warning?" Claudie wanted to know.

"Never mind, Claudie," I said. "We'll be on the reef at daylight, and that's when fishing is always best."

The Captain moved the boat away from the edge of the reef into the deeper water, and Claudie threw the anchor in the water. He was getting very handy with it. Captain Squatty fried us a mess of fresh fish in corn meal, and we had a big supper on the yacht. We washed it down with cold beer. The slap, slap of the water against the sides and the easy sway of the boat back and forth made us sleepy on top of all that food and beer, so we turned in early.

3

When a man has got himself used to the finer things in life, it jolts him to be roused in the middle of a deep sleep. This thought bruised my mind way in the middle of the night when I felt the boat take a big sway that batted my face up against the magazine rack next to my bunk. I wondered why they couldn't put shock absorbers around the owner's cabin to save him from such rough movements of the boat. Then Claudie said, "What the hell was that we hit?"

Captain Squatty came in and turned on the lights. He said that a big wave had hit the boat.

"It ain't gonna sink, is it?" Claudie wanted to know as he got up and started buttoning his shirt.

"No, Claudie," I told him, "it ain't gonna sink," but I wasn't too sure, since by this time the yacht was rolling and swaying around more than ever. Then another wave hit us, and a lot of water flew in the porthole by my bunk and sprinkled me all over. It tasted salty.

"Captain Hinder," I said, "take a look at the glass." He did and said it was low and falling.

"Here's your hurricane," I told him. "I'm glad your dad-gummed glass has found out about it."

Then another wave hit and slammed us all down on one side of the owner's cabin. It broke loose the pots and pans below, and you couldn't have matched the racket they made if you'd beaten a tow sack full of tin cans against the bottom of a washtub.

We went out on the rear end and, sure enough, it was blowing hard, and the rain was coming down in sheets. The awning was flapping around back there, popping in the wind like a buggy whip, until Captain Squatty finally got it down and brought it inside. Then the hurricane really got into high gear.

I've seen the wind blow the wash right off a clothesline, and I've seen it blow knotholes out of pine fences, but that was on dry land. It's worse on the water. The wind was coming in gusts; hard, howling gusts, each one stronger and longer and louder, until I had a feeling deep in my insides that something had to give somewhere; then it would ease up a little before it came again, harder each time than the time before, until the *Pride of Texas, III,* was bobbing around like a dead fly in a churn.

I told Claudie how the yacht was better off where we were, and he tried to believe me, but all he could say was, "I've allus been scared of storms." He began to gulp and swallow like an old tomcat with a fish bone in his throat, and a light skim came over his eyes. He turned green around his mouth and chin like the sticky, gummy green of scums that form on stagnant water. He said he might be a little sick if the wind didn't die down pretty soon. It didn't, but as it went on and on, howling and screaming and whining out there, we got down on the floor of the boat and tried to get used to it — as used to it, that is, as a man can get to that much wind. For a long time nothing happened except a whole lot more of the same thing, and Captain Squatty told us that was about all there'd be to riding out the hurricane. Claudie said he figured that was enough.

When daylight came it made us feel better to see that we were still where we'd been the night before and not away off somewhere in the middle of a stormy ocean. The little island was right where it had been, and on the other side the waves were still piling up and breaking over the reef, but the water wasn't green any more; it was muddy gray. The gusts were getting easier by the time it was broad-open day, and the rain was pouring almost straight down in between them. In an hour it was dead calm, and Claudie was looking more like himself. He said his liver was still bothering him some, though, and he believed he'd go back to bed.

"I wouldn't," Captain Squatty told him. "It's only half over. The center is passing us now. In a little while we'll have the other half."

He was a man who knew his hurricanes all right, and pretty soon the wind started to blow again — but from the other direction. The yacht swung around on the anchor rope so that the rear end was pointed toward the reef, and the island was up ahead. We drank some coffee while we could, and by the time we were through, the hurricane was up to full steam again — and then some. It was raining harder again, and it was raining plumb sideways — that's how hard the wind was blowing.

"Two halves of a hurricane is all they is, ain't they?" Claudie asked once between gusts.

"Certainly, Claudie," I told him. "You got that far in arithmetic, I know."

I don't know what made me glance out in front of the boat as it swung back and forth against the anchor and rolled in the wind, but when I did I saw that something awful had happened to the island. It was a long way off. First I thought it had moved, and then I knew it must have been the yacht moving. Captain Squatty saw it at almost the same time that I did; then we looked back of us, and there were the waves piling up on the reef not fifty feet away. The Captain's little eyes got big, and he said, "Good God, we're dragging anchor!"

"How's that?" Claudie asked.

"We're dragging anchor," he said. "If we pile up on that oyster reef, there won't be a piece of this here yacht big enough to pick your teeth with. Get up on the bow and get ready to raise the anchor. I'll start the motors."

I said, "Who? Me?" as Squatty ran to start the motors and yelled, "Both of you, or it'll be too late."

I looked at Claudie, and Claudie looked ready. We went through Captain Squatty's cubbyhole to the lid that opened on the front of the boat where the anchor rope was tied.

"Go on, Claudie," I said. "I'm coming behind you." He opened the lid, and when he did a gust of wet wind swept through it and slapped us down on the floor.

"Go ahead," I urged him, "we haven't got much time," and somehow Claudie got his six and a half foot bulk through the hatch. Then I got out, and we both held on to the little stob on the front of the boat where the anchor rope was tied. We were in a long, high gust that got harder and stronger until I felt like it would buckle-in my eardrums if it got any worse.

Finally we both got a good hold on the anchor rope. It was tight, and I could feel a quiver in it as the anchor would give and drag a little. I knew that anchor was plowing a furrow there on the bottom of the bay. I looked back once and saw that on one of our long swings against the anchor the rear end of the yacht was nearly even with the breakers on the reef. I figured we might clear it once more, but I figured if we did, it would be the last time. When the wind slacked between gusts, I knew it was our last time to get her away before all hell broke loose on the rear end. By this time the motors were whining and groaning, and we could feel the whole boat throb as they fought against the wind. We eased forward a little, and I and Claudie pulled the rope in and kept it tight, coiling up the slack behind us. Finally, we were right over the anchor, and the rope went straight down from the front of the boat.

"It's now or never, Claudie," I yelled, and we heisted hard on it, but the anchor wouldn't budge.

Claudie reached down and got another hold on the rope; I got one just behind him, and we pulled with everything we had. I could see the big veins standing out on his neck like chicken guts, and it seemed that new muscles rose up around his eyes and ears as he strained to lift it. But the anchor was stuck solid in the bottom of Copano Bay. Captain Squatty was yelling something at us, but it wasn't any use. You couldn't hear anything above the roar of another gust that was building up, and by that time we were pulling as hard as we knew how, just to hold our own. Then we weren't holding our own; we had to pay out some rope or go over with it, and I yelled, "Latch it onto the stob, Claudie, or we'll be back where we started."

Claudie wrapped the anchor rope several times around

the stob there, as the gust blew out, and then the boat was pitching and rolling hard against the tight rope. That was what broke the anchor out, and as soon as it gave way, we pulled the rope in until the anchor was out of the water. I could see we were moving forward, away from the reef, with both motors screaming and straining down in the heart of the *Pride of Texas, III.*

In a few minutes we were clear out in the deep water, a hundred yards or more away from the reef, and Captain Squatty was yelling and motioning for us to drop the anchor again. We did, and this time it held. We got back down into the boat and closed the lid as another gust came and grew into full flow. Then Claudie was sick — very sick — but Captain Squatty said it was all right, since he'd cleaned up after seasick people before.

The hurricane petered out almost as fast as it had come. In an hour or so the yacht settled down to an easy roll, and the rain slacked up, but none of this cured Claudie. He was stretched out on the floor of the owner's cabin, blinking his eyes and swallowing.

Around noon we pulled up the anchor and started back. As we left Copano Bay and headed south for Rockport, the water was plumb smooth again. I got out Captain Squatty's I.O.U., and gave him credit for another day's room and board, and showed him how this cut it down to a hundred and fifty dollars.

Then I went down to the owner's cabin to check up on Claudie. He was still on the floor, and he had laid beside him some things out of his pockets — wet matches, cigars, a deck of cards, and a letter. When I saw the letter was addressed to Captain Earl Hinder and postmarked Fort

Worth, I said, "Where the hell did you get that, Claudie?"

"At the post office, whenever it was I went to get the mail," he answered and rolled over on his stomach. "I must have forgot to give it to Captain Squatty."

I took it up to the Captain, and as he read it, the muscles started working and quivering around his jawbones. He said, "It's from Mr. Easley. He will be here Tuesday night with two guests."

"Tuesday night was last night," I reminded him.

"Oh, my God!" he yelled. "I'm ruined."

"Ruined?" I said. "What do you mean ruined? Suppose you hadn't taken the *Pride of Texas, III,* out on Tuesday?"

By this time we were getting close to Rockport, and we could see what an awful mess the hurricane had made there. Tree limbs and chunks of wood were floating all around in the water. Four of the other yachts were partly sunk, and the back end of another one was battered and busted plumb out. There wasn't a one of them that wasn't bashed in one way or the other. One yacht, a blue one nearly as big as ours, was turned over and half sunk. There was a hole in the bottom a horse could have walked through.

A crowd of people stood there on the docks looking at all the damage, and as we eased up to the place where the *Pride of Texas, III,* belonged, they all came over toward us. They grabbed our ropes and helped us tie up, and we climbed back onto dry land.

Mr. Easley was there to meet us. He was a nice little gray-haired man, all macked out in sport clothes. He shook hands with Captain Squatty and shook hands with us.

"Any damage to the *Pride of Texas, III?*" he asked.

"None, sir," Captain Squatty said, standing straight and looking Mr. Easley in the eye.

"Hinder," he said, "you are a real skipper. I knew you could smell out a blow if anybody could."

Squatty said, "Mr. Easley, I couldn't have done it without the help of these two fine seamen here, Clint and Claudie."

Mr. Easley beamed on us and took out a big green roll. He peeled off a hundred-dollar bill and handed it to me. He gave Claudie one, too, and said he wondered if it was a big enough tip at that.

"Mr. Easley," I stated, "this is your change," and I gave him fifty dollars out of the roll we'd won in the crap game.

"I don't get it, fellows," he said.

"I and my associate, Claudie, are professional men," I said. "We do not work for tips. A hundred and fifty is all we are due, and that is all we will take. If you feel like it, you might want to give that extra fifty to Captain Squatty, though. He's a fine skipper."

X I

A Town in Very Fine Print

THE HOT SUN was still an hour or so high, and we could already see the tall buildings in San Antonio when we had the blowout. There was a sharp pop, followed by a sour, sickly whistle; and we went weaving back and forth on the pavement until Claudie managed to get the car slowed down and stopped on the dusty shoulder of the road. Then there was nothing to break the dry quiet except the husky buzz of a bull bat that dived in the still air above us. I put a stony look on Claudie, and he sat there gazing down at the steering wheel as he admitted that the tire was in bad shape that morning before we left Rockport.

Now Claudie had money in his pocket from the crap game at Rockport, and so did I; but do you suppose he got the tire fixed before we left for San Antonio? Not Claudie; he only got the tire extra full at the filling station where the air was free. He said it was a slow leak, and he figured he got enough air to last all the way to San Antonio.

"Claudie," I said, "did you ever stop to think that a bad tire is a lot like one of your sins that has not found you out? It's only waiting for the time that it will bust right out in the open and put a real crimp in your life."

About that time an old Model T Ford came along, headed toward San Antonio, and I waved it down. The fellow that got out of the car was about the countriestlooking citizen I'd seen in Texas, or anywhere else, except maybe in that part of Alabama where nothing but wire grass grows. He was tall and skinny, and his lean jaw looked hard and sharp under about a two-day growth of sandy beard. His straw hat was frayed out all around the edges. He had a lot of gold teeth, and on the little finger of his left hand he wore a gold ring with a big green stone in it. His yellow horn-toed shoes were buttoned about halfway up, and his overalls were way too short. An odd thing, though — as he produced cold patches for the inner tube and a pump, I noticed that his overalls were new, and the price tag was still sewed on the suspender part.

While Claudie went to work on the flat tire, our country friend told us he was Jonas Lord, and he was on his way to Boerne where he was going to take in the Kendall County Fair. He said there wasn't a better fair in Texas, except maybe the State Fair at Dallas.

"Where's Boerne?" I asked him.

"About thirty miles beyond San Antonio," he answered.

"We may see you there; we're about due for a fair," I told him, as I peeled a dollar bill off of my money and handed it to him. "Buy yourself a nice treat at the fair, Jonas." He allowed he didn't want to take the money, but he didn't try quite hard enough to give it back before Claudie had our tire fixed; then Jonas went on.

That night in San Antonio, I and Claudie didn't find anything that we were not ready to leave the next morning, so we drove on to Boerne. We got there about noon and went straight to the fairgrounds.

It was September and the weather still hot and dry, but we didn't notice the heat and dust much since we found the place was fairly alive with cold watermelons, pink lemonade, cotton candy and shaved ice that had red cherry flavoring poured over it. We also found Jonas Lord, and, since he seemed so glad to see us, we asked him to help us take in the Kendall County Fair. Jonas said he sure would like to, but he wanted to be certain we'd let him pay his own way; he didn't want to impose on us.

So with Jonas going along paying his part we looked over the fat-stock show and fine poultry exhibits, the award of the pickled fruit prizes, the rodeo, the tug of war and the three-legged race. We watched the boys under fourteen chasing a greased pig, and we threw baseballs at a target which, when you hit it, sprung a trap and dropped a Negro boy into a tank full of cold water. Then there was a long band concert, followed by a good, loud patriotic speaking. Afterwards we saw a dead calf with two heads and watched a weight-lifting contest that I'd have put Claudie in if we hadn't had plenty of money from that crap game in Rockport. Late that afternoon we saw a quarter-horse race; then we sat twice through a dancing girl show and stayed on for the concert. We really had ourselves a fine time; we were all three eating high on the hog at the Kendall County Fair.

That night Jonas Lord was still with us, and we moved in on the part of the fair that was left. Claudie just about cut the management to pieces on the one where you pay a nickel and swing the sledgehammer to make a little gadget fly up a pole with a bell on the top. Every time Claudie rang the bell, the fat man there gave him a ten-cent cigar. Pretty soon the fat man started whining. "Come on over, folks," he said, "I can't stand this. I'm going broke. Nobody else ever rang the bell eleven times out of twelve." But he let Claudie keep on swinging at a nickel a swing while the crowd moved in, and right away I had a hatful of cigars that I was holding for Claudie.

Jonas Lord just stood there with his eyes and mouth hanging open, watching Claudie go. I knew by this time that Jonas admired us both very much but here it was plain that Claudie was making a real hit with him. Jonas finally spoke up and said to me that he had never seen anybody that could swing a sledgehammer the way Claudie could. I agreed that Claudie was fairly good for a man that did it only as a sideline, but Jonas wouldn't believe at first that Claudie didn't swing some big heavy implement like that for a living.

"No, Jonas," I told him, "we are just having a little fun here at the fair. We probably won't even smoke up all these here cigars. Have one."

Jonas took it, and as he fired it up I could see he wasn't used to smoking cigars. He had only taken a couple of puffs when it started shucking out like an ear of corn with weevils in it. "Here, Jonas," I said, "have another one; that one's about to burn you."

All this time Claudie was passing the cigars over to me while our crowd got bigger and bigger. Claudie was buying tickets twenty at a time and peeling dollar bills off his roll of Rockport money, when Jonas pulled me off a little to one side. He said he really could use some help from a man like Claudie; not swinging a sledgehammer, he explained; swinging a pick.

"No, Jonas," I said, "Claudie works for me, and besides, he only does this sort of thing to pleasure himself."

"I need some help from a man that can read maps, too," Jonas said.

"Well," I told him, "I don't believe Claudie would be

worth a damn at that; he even has a lot of trouble with road maps."

"Do you understand maps?" Jonas asked, and as he did, I noticed that he had a very earnest look in his eyes. Just about this time Claudie brought me another handful of cigars, and I thanked Jonas; I told him I understood maps all right, but explained that I didn't care much about them as a general thing.

"I am sorry, mister," he said. "I'd hoped to get an expert to help me with a map. You see, the one I have is a very old one — a treasure map."

"Buried treasure?" I asked him.

"Yes, it is buried," Jonas answered as he turned to walk away. "That's why I was looking for a man that can handle a pick."

Claudie rang the bell again, and I yelled at him, "Come on, Claudie; follow me. The hell with those cigars."

2

I worked my way through the crowd until I found Jonas standing out there on the edge. He looked like a man that had just buried his last friend, and I couldn't remember when I ever felt so sorry for anyone in my whole life or wanted so much to do somebody a good turn. I went straight over to Jonas and told him I had been thinking it over and decided to take a look at his map. That seemed to help his feelings a lot.

I and Claudie went with Jonas to the close-by tourist court where he had a room, and he showed us the map, but not until he had pulled down all of the shades and cautioned us both against talking too loud. It was an awful old map, brown and yellow stained. Jonas showed us where it was about to give way altogether at the places where it had been folded a long time ago. All the words on it were written in Spanish, and the ink looked weak and about faded out, but beneath the Spanish, the English words were written in new green ink. Jonas said he'd had that done by a translator in Laredo. Right down at the bottom of the map two forks of the Devil's River came together, and about halfway up the one called Dry Fork was an X that marked a cave.

"It's out in West Texas," Jonas told us. Then he showed us where the cave was tied in on the map at eighty-eight varas north of a round red rock; the red rock was located on a dotted line drawn straight between a notch in a limestone outcrop on the west of the Dry Fork and a blazed mesquite tree on a big mesa east of it. The only town on the map, written in with green ink, was Chorro Perdido, Texas.

"I've already got this map figured out, Jonas," I said.

"What's a vara?" Claudie asked.

"A Mexican yard," Jonas said; "about 33⅓ inches."

"Where did you get that map, Jonas?" I asked him.

"Sssh, not so loud; these walls are like paper," he said. "I got it off a dead Mexican in Monclova, Mexico. Now here's the key: the treasure is buried in the cave eighteen varas from the mouth. It is buried at a depth of one vara."

"How do you know that?" I asked him.

"That's what the murdered Mexican's sweetheart told me before I left Monclova," Jonas answered. "After her

Mexican got killed, she was the only living person that knew where the treasure was."

Since I am the one that always had to take up the business arrangements, I asked, "What's our part, Jonas, if we help you find the treasure and dig it up?" I was all set to argue with Jonas, but I didn't have to. He was a very fair man, and we settled on one third for Jonas, one third for me and one third for Claudie. We all shook hands on it, then I and Claudie got us a room in the same tourist court and went to bed for the night.

I slept so hard after the busy day we'd had at the fair that when I woke up next morning I had been thinking quite a little while about Claudie and the way he had rung up all those cigars before the treasure deal popped into my mind. When it did, I jumped out of bed and woke Claudie up. We put on our shoes, buttoned our shirts and stepped outside. There was Jonas sitting on the running board of his old Model T parked by his cabin. He was holding his head in his hands and shaking it. We went over to him, and when we spoke, he looked up, all red-eyed and miserable in the face.

"What's the trouble, Jonas?" I asked him.

"This," he said and showed me a telegram, which I read out loud to Claudie. It was from Kansas City and it went: MOTHER VERY LOW. SHE MUST GO TO A HOSPITAL FOR EXPENSIVE OPERATION. COME AT ONCE. PLEASE HURRY. SISTER LULA.

"I don't know what in the world I am to do," Jonas went on as I gave him back the telegram. He was in the dumps for sure.

"That's tough, Jonas," I told him. "It's really too bad."

"The worst part of it is," Jonas went on, "I haven't got any money, and I've got to go to Kansas City right away to help Mamma."

All this time I had been ransacking my mind for an idea, and finally I got it. "Jonas," I said with my eyes right on him, "how much money do you need?"

"Several hundred dollars, anyway," Jonas answered. "I can't spare any expense where Mamma's health is in danger."

"Maybe you could sell us the map, Jonas," I said in a most sympathetic way. "We've got some money."

Jonas gave me a very hurt, helpless look; almost like that of some small animal caught in a trap. Then he stiffened up all over and said: "Oh, no, you don't; not the map. Not the treasure map. It almost cost me my life. I could never give it up. I wouldn't take a thousand dollars for it."

"Well, Jonas," I told him, "that is too much money. We only had about two hundred dollars yesterday, and we have spent a part of it at the fair; but we might give you what we've got left."

Jonas was crying by this time and talking about his mother way up yonder in the north going to die and all if she didn't get the money to have an operation. It was enough to get next to a man with any Samaritan at all in him, and I was feeling so sorry for Jonas I didn't know what to do, when he said, "Just how much money have you got left? I might have to let the map go after all."

I told Jonas to wait right there while I and Claudie could go back to our cabin and talk things over. Inside, we counted up our money, and found we had $181.50 in all, but Claudie had over half of it, and at first he didn't want to give Jonas any of his part for the map. He said he didn't understand maps anyway. He argued that maybe we couldn't find the cave; maybe there wasn't any treasure in the cave anyway; he even said Jonas might have already tried to find it himself, or that the map might be bogus, and a lot of other puny reasons for not giving Jonas the money.

"What about Jonas's mother, Claudie?" I reasoned with him. "Haven't you got any heart at all?"

That got Claudie to thinking, and we worked out a proposition we could make Jonas. Claudie kept $31.50, and I agreed that that would be all his. We offered Jonas $150 in cash, and Jonas took it. He said there wasn't anything else he could do, and as he left in his car, I told him it was Claudie's fault, not mine, that we'd had to beat him out of the rest of the money.

3

It was a pretty good thing, after all, that Claudie had held out some money on Jonas, since we had to buy a pick to do the digging with. Claudie bought a lantern, too, and a jug that would hold a gallon of water in case we got dry, as he allowed we might before we found the treasure. I got us a free yardstick for use in measuring off the varas on the map and had Claudie saw it off at 33⅓ inches to make it exactly a vara long.

It took us an hour to find Chorro Perdido on the road map, a town in very fine print west from El Dorado, but there wasn't a road that led to it except the one through San Angelo. We pulled out of Boerne about noon, headed west, and drove until we got into San Angelo late that night.

Next day, before we left San Angelo, we loaded up with water and some provisions — crackers, canned sardines and apples. We already had plenty of cigars from the Kendall County Fair.

We drove west, out the San Angelo–El Paso road, until we came to a side road leading south. It was marked by a sign that said Chorro Perdido and we took it. It was a warm day and very still, except for the dry whine of the single-strand telephone wire along the road. The only clouds in the sky were some cottony wisps away off to the south of us, and as the sun got higher, it singed them all away.

There wasn't anything in Chorro Perdido but a general merchandise store, a filling station and an adobe church. The man at the filling station told us the flat-topped hill we could see out northwest of town was known as the Gold Mesa. It was the only one in sight, so we took out for it on an awful road covered with briers and goat weeds. We went as far as we could go in the car, parked it under a huisache bush and took out on foot toward the mesa.

We were in rough country; hot, rocky and scorched. Between us and the mesa we could see a dozen or so whirlwinds — long columns of dust that swayed back and forth in the heat waves. We walked an hour or so through the mesquite, tumbleweeds, bull nettles and prickly pears without seeing a sign of life except several chaparral and one big rattlesnake skin.

As the day kept warming up, we took several long swigs from the water jug to keep from drying plumb out; then, after we'd stopped and eaten some sardines and crackers about noon, we found that the jug was empty. We walked up a long rise that led toward the mesa, and by the time we got there I was spitting cotton, and Claudie had the hiccups.

On top of the mesa I sent Claudie to look for the mesquite tree with the blaze while I studied the map. There weren't but five trees there, and on the oldest one Claudie found a big gash where the bark had been knocked off. We stood under the tree and looked west across the valley. We could see the dry white bed of the creek below us, and beyond the ground rose to a rocky ledge a mile or so away that was nearly as high as the mesa. On the north end of the ledge a big notch stood out as plain as day.

"That must be the Dry Fork of the Devil's River," I told Claudie. "Over there is the limestone notch that's on the map. This is almost too good to be true; it's too easy."

Claudie was sitting on the ground picking some sand burrs out of his socks. I noticed the sweat was drying up on him, leaving little white streaks of salt on his face. He said he wished to God we'd never had the blowout; then we'd never have met Jonas Lord, and we wouldn't be so all-fired dry. "Claudie," I said, "aren't you about to forget the treasure?" and he admitted that he was. He claimed it must have been because he wanted a drink of water so bad.

"Of course you do," I said, "and so do I, but it's water we're out of. Maybe we can find some in that little branch down there."

"You mean in the Dry Fork of the Devil's River?" Claudie asked. It was about the most sarcastic thing I'd ever heard him say, and it stung me some to hear it.

"Come on," I told him, "let's take another look at the treasure map. I want to see which side of the bed of the stream the round red rock is on."

We studied it and found that it was on the west — the

far side, on a straight line between the blazed tree and the limestone notch. I figured out the map some more and said to Claudie: "We can't miss that rock if we walk direct from here to the notch over there. We can walk on a line if we head straight from here to the notch. Let's keep our eyes on that notch. Let's go straight toward it as we walk down the slope and up on the other side, and we are bound to find that red rock."

Claudie didn't begin to have any better idea than that, so he gathered up the pick, the empty water jug, the lantern and the groceries we had left, while I took the map and the sawed-off yardstick. We started out with our eyes glued on the limestone notch across the valley. The way ahead was very steep and rocky, and about everything that grew out of the ground had thorns on it. We soon found that we couldn't get through the nettles and briers or around the cactus without looking down at where we were going. What made us sure of this was that Claudie slipped on a loose rock and rolled down the side of the hill until he came to a stop in a clump of prickly pears. After he'd picked the needles out of himself and I'd dusted him off, we made a better plan and started again. This time Claudie walked ahead, and his job was to look at the ground in front of us. I walked along behind, holding onto one of his shoulders and sighting over the other one at the limestone notch across the valley. This way we made it all the distance down on a fairly straight line.

When we got to the old bed of the stream, the notch was not in sight any more; it had slid behind some trees as we walked, and I had to hold my eye on the place in the trees where I'd seen the notch last. As we went along, Claudie hiccuped every step or so — enough to throw a less steady man than I am off his course. I was afraid to bat my eyes for fear of losing the line we were on, but by this time I was so parched out that it wouldn't have done me much good to bat my eyes anyhow.

We were working our way across the gravel in the dusty bed of the stream, and I was holding a tight bead on the trees that the notch was beyond, when Claudie pulled up and stopped like a balky old mule. I figured he must have seen a tarantula or a centipede or something, because he couldn't walk or talk. It was hard for me not to look to see what had stopped him.

"What the hell's the matter, Claudie?" I asked. "Let's go on before my eyes peter out on me."

"There's a low place down the stream a little ways, and I think I can see some water."

"All right," I said, since I could tell it wasn't any use to waste any more time arguing with him, "go get yourself a drink and hurry up about it unless you want my eyes to crack out like two grains of popcorn."

It must not have been as long as it seemed that I stood there with both eyes nailed on the trees that the notch was beyond, but long before Claudie came back I felt a hot misery that began around my ankles and started working up my legs. Those trees were weaving and swaying before my eyes like pussy willows in a high wind, and my legs felt like they must have been on fire when I heard Claudie coming back. He stated that the water tasted like stump water and only made his hiccups worse.

"Come on, Claudie," I said. "My eyes are plumb tuckered out, and my legs are going bad on me."

"I can see why," said Claudie, who could look; "you're standing on a big red anthill."

He got the ants off after the longest, and we went on. It was uphill now as we climbed the west bank of the Dry Fork, and I was looking for the limestone notch to come back into view any time, when Claudie stopped again; and this time he said, "We can't go no further, Clint."

"What's the matter now?" I asked him — a little fussy too, I guess, since by now my ankles were swelling from the ant stings, and my eyes felt like broken blisters in salty water.

"There's an old rock in the way here," he said. "It's too big to go over. Can't we go around it?"

"Is it round?" I asked him, still holding on with my eyes to the trees ahead.

"It's round, all right," he answered.

"Is it red?"

"Sorta rusty red," Claudie said, and I looked at it.

"This is the rock on the map, Claudie," I said. "Don't you see? Right north of here eighty-eight varas is the treasure cave. We're in the money, Claudie. I can just see that treasure now. Old Spanish coins made out of pure-D 14-carat gold; maybe some diamonds and rubies set in rings and bracelets. Everything is turning out just like the map says."

All Claudie did was hiccup, and I went on: "We've got that yardstick sawed off to a vara. All we've got to do is measure it off eighty-eight times due north and we're there. That sun that's getting a little low over there is bound to be in the west, so while you measure on the ground, I'll run us north by keeping the sun on our left. Also, I will count."

Going north took us through the dusty bitterweed and needlegrass on the west bank of the rocky river bed until we recrossed it at thirty varas. The east bank from there on was steep and covered with loose gravel. Claudie complained some of shooting pains in his back from laying the stick down on the rough ground as he measured. At fifty varas we were in a little baygall, and by the time we reached sixty-five, the way ahead of us was clear again. Around a little bend in the east bank we could see a herd of scrawny goats as they nibbled in the scraggly brown horseweeds that grew in the dry river bed. On the seventy-sixth vara we saw the mouth of a cave, and on the eighty-third we saw the Mexican. He was sitting on the ground with his back propped up against a little thistly bush right beside the mouth of the cave, and across his knees was a double-barreled shotgun. We could tell from the tilt of his hat over his eyes and the slack look around his mouth that he was sound asleep. His chest rose and fell in slow, regular motion.

I shushed Claudie, and we started to ease by the Mexican to get into the cave when he spoke, without moving at all. What the Mexican said was, "*Buenas tardes, señores.*" Claudie stopped and threw up both hands. I guess I must have too, because the Mexican spoke again. "No, *señores.* I am no robber. These gun is for the coyotes." As he spoke he straightened up and pushed his big hat back on his head.

Claudie was too scared to talk, so I took over. "Hightower is the name," I said; "Clint Hightower. I and my partner, Claudie, here, have been a little lost, I am afraid." Then I gave the Mexican a couple of the cigars that Claudie had won at the fair and asked him what his name was.

"Pedro Arroyo," he answered as he got up, stretched, and leaned his gun against the tree. He was not over five feet tall, and in spite of his wrinkled, leathery skin, his big hat made his face look small and almost childish.

Claudie had got himself together by this time, so he asked Pedro for a drink of water. The little Mexican nodded, went into the cave and brought out a goatskin bucket that had a small amount of water in the bottom of it. I and Claudie drank it, but it tasted so bitter and weedy that Claudie made an awful face when he drank.

"I am sorry, *señores*. The water, she is not good. Not good water here. These year is very dry year, and the pool is very low."

"Whereabouts is the pool?" Claudie asked.

"In the dry bed of the Rio Diabolo, close by to my house. It is the only water on the Arroyo Rancho now. It is not far; just over the hill there," and Pedro pointed toward the clean red sun that hung low in the west.

"He says it ain't far," Claudie pointed out.

About that time I heard a very peculiar noise for such a place as that. It sounded sort of familiar, and I thought I'd heard it a time or two before after we found the Mexican, but we'd had our mind on other things. This time it was louder and closer — a long groaning roar that rose and faded away, a lot like the noise of automobile tires traveling at high speed on concrete pavement.

"What's that noise, Pedro?" I asked him.

"Big truck on highway. Main road from San Angelo to El Paso runs in front of my house. I go now to take goats to pen. Will you go with me and have more water?"

"No, Pedro," I told him. "We ain't so thirsty, I don't expect. We are going to sit around this here cave for a little while and talk things over. We may see you a little later."

Pedro left with his goats as the sun slipped behind the ridge. Then the bats started coming out of the cave. They came by the hundreds and thousands, it seemed; they wheeled and whirred by our heads and disappeared into the dusk. It was dark before they quit coming, so we fired up the lantern and started into the cave. Claudie did the measuring, and I went along behind to count the varas and hold the light.

At the mouth the cave was about wide enough for two people to walk, and the top of it was eight or ten feet high, but it got smaller as we went along. It was pretty rough going, though; there were holes and piles of rocks and dirt all around. Claudie said it looked to him like it had been all dug up by somebody else before we got there. "Claudie," I said, "you have a very suspicious turn of mind. I'm afraid you never did believe in the treasure very much. Jonas Lord would be very hurt if he knew you didn't trust him any more than this."

Claudie only mumbled something about the blowout. We had not gone far into the pitch dark of the cave when we saw a light ahead of us. First, it was dim, bobbing up and down, then it got brighter, and pretty soon we saw several others clustered around it. They were bobbing too, and it was enough to give a man goose pimples across the back of his shoulders and down his sides. Even in the dark I could tell that Claudie was scared from the hoarse way he said, "Look at them lights, Clint. What the hell's that?"

I had not figured out what the lights were either, so we stopped and moved over to one side, where we found what looked like a little passage branching off of the cave. We squatted down and backed into it. Then I told Claudie to blow out the lantern and be quiet. It almost upset me personally to see how bothered Claudie was over the lights.

In a few minutes we heard a heavy voice that said, "Straight ahead, men. Straight ahead." It sounded like a big, strong guy that was going straight ahead unless he ran into something like a stone wall trimmed with barbed wire. Up to this time Claudie had been breathing pretty heavy, but when he heard the voice, he seemed to quit altogether. Finally, we began to see from our hiding place where the lights had come from. First, there was a stocky figure of a man in khaki clothes with a stick in one hand and a lantern in the other. He walked right on by without looking toward us. Behind him traipsed a dozen or so little guys, all dressed in the same kind of clothes. As they passed on by, we heard the big one say, "I'm afraid we overstayed our time in the cave, fellas; it's already dark outside." It wasn't until he said, "But 'a scout is brave,' " that I realized Claudie had been scared by nothing but a Boy Scout troop. "Right, sir," the kids said as they marched on out.

I and Claudie could not remember how many varas we had measured, and we could not find the place where he had measured the last vara anyhow, so we had to go back to the mouth of the cave and start all over again. At eighteen varas from the start we made a mark on the floor of the cave, where Claudie started to dig away into the *caliche* rocks and hard clay while I held the lantern and studied the map. The roof was not over about five feet high at this point, and it was hard digging for Claudie until he dug down to where he could take a full swing with the pick. He said he was too thirsty to dig very hard, but I had told him the harder he dug, the sooner he would reach a vara deep, where the treasure was buried; also I explained, the air seemed a little more moist in the cave than it had been outside.

It was pretty slow digging. We had not brought along a shovel, so Claudie had to use his hands to throw the dirt out. After he'd dug about an hour, I measured the hole and found that it was nearly a vara deep.

"Now's the time to dig harder, Claudie," I told him. "From now on it's the most important part of all." He hit a few more licks in the bottom of the hole and threw out the chunks of clay and rocks. Then he swung hard, and the pick went in all of the way to the handle.

"Wup," he said. "There's a soft place." I held the lantern up to see, while Claudie pulled the pick out; and as he did a little stream of clear water spurted up at him. He dug a little more around this place, and then it gushed up so fast that before he could get out of the hole, Claudie was waist-deep in water. He said it was cold.

We stood beside the hole and watched it fill up and start, first in a trickle, and then in a full stream, down toward the mouth of the cave. Soon it started boiling up more and more, until it was ankle deep on us, and we hurried to get out of the cave before we got any wetter. We stood in front of the cave and watched the stream in the lantern light until it got good and clear; then we got down on our bellies and drank the cool, sweet water. It was the best water I had ever tasted, and nobody who wasn't there would believe the amount of it that Claudie drank. He put his head down in it like a horse and drank and snorted.

We ran over the hill where the Mexican had gone until we saw the lights of his house. We yelled as we went up to the place, and Pedro came out while his wife and half a dozen little Mexicans stood in the doorway looking out.

We told Pedro what had happened, but he wouldn't believe a word of it. "No water close by except sour pool in Rio Diabolo," Pedro said. "Americanos make cruel jokes."

I and Claudie took Pedro right back to the cave with us, and when we got there, we found that the flow of water had built up until a wide, clear stream ran out over the rock and down a gully toward the Dry Fork of Devil's River. I noticed Pedro was making a funny, choking noise; and when I turned to see what the trouble was, I saw that he was down on his knees. The look on his face was a match for what you see in the colored Bible pictures of prophets who have been sprung from dungeons or delivered from plagues and pestilence. Pedro was praying in soft musical Mexican as he looked up toward all the stars in the sky and made the sign of the cross over and over. Tears were streaming down his cheeks and sparkling in the lantern light.

Claudie's face was wet too, from drinking some more of that good water, horse-fashion. We both took off our hats at the same time, and it was like standing in a church somewhere with sacred candles burning all around.

As Pedro prayed, I noticed that he spoke the name of the town, Chorro Perdido, from time to time, and when he'd finished and stood up, I asked him what that had to do with the water.

"It is old legend," Pedro said, and in the dim glow of the lantern light his face still had on it the look of a man praying. "The old legend of the Chorro Perdido — the lost springs. Always my father said that big springs, covered and hidden by Navajos when Spanish came, would flow again to give water for Rancho Arroyo. Father of my father one time had map showing hidden springs. He buried it in churchyard in Monclova before he went to fight under Santa Anna. He was killed at San Jacinto in 1836. The map of the Chorro Perdido was never afterwards found by my people." Then Pedro made the sign of the cross again, and I gave Claudie a very stinging look.

The next morning Pedro gave us a framed picture of the Virgin of Guadalupe with mother of pearl set in all around her head. He said it was the only one he had, but he wanted us to take the image of the Blessed Virgin along with us. Then I and Claudie left and struck out toward the gold mesa to find our car.

As we worked our way through the cactus and briers Claudie was not having anything at all to say. This gave me a good chance to think, and after a while I told him what I'd thought up. "Claudie," I said, "we learned a lot about treasure at the Rancho Arroyo. Treasure depends. It depends a good deal on what you haven't got. Like the water, I mean."

"That's fine for Pedro Arroyo," Claudie allowed.

"Also," I said, "until today we did not have a single solitary sacred picture, did we?"

Claudie grinned as he admitted that that was true.

XII
The Revival

A MAN THAT KNOWS the law is after him is never going to get it plumb out of his mind, even if he knows good and well that he doesn't done anything very wrong; and I expect it's harder on him still if he don't know just what it is the law wants him for. And you never get altogether away from that or anything else that has made you unhappy, because the thing is there inside of you, and it goes along with you wherever you go. And sooner or later you will go back, or at least you will start back.

If I had to put my finger on the reason why I and Claudie drove east from Chorro Perdido, Texas, that fall, I'd say it was because east was toward Louisiana where Jules Rabinowitz had told us the law was after us. East was toward the French Quarter, too, in New Orleans, Louisiana, where Aunty Blossom had taken after Claudie with a butcher knife when he went to see Evangeline; but of course it was never Claudie that decided which way we would drive, and I myself had not decided how far east we were going.

We were back in the deep piny woods of East Texas, though, and not very far from the Louisiana border, when we had our car trouble. The engine began to knock on every little grade, and then steam started boiling out around the radiator. We just barely made it to the big white house by the sawmill, and when we pulled up in front of the gate, our old Ford was heaving and steaming like a worn-out teakettle. We had to have water.

I got out and went right in, while Claudie sat in the car. First, I had to win over the brindle dogs that came out, barking and growling, from behind the crepe myrtle bushes by the front gate. Then I and the dogs went up to the wide veranda of the big house where a fat man was sitting in a wicker rocker. He was fanning himself in the muggy October heat and I thought he looked mighty worried about something.

"Stranger," I said, "I need some water for my car, and my man out there is thirsty. My name is Hightower; what's yours?"

"Bass," he said. "There's the well," and he never looked toward me but once. He called the dogs, and they tucked their tails between their legs and slunk under the house.

"Pretty warm," I told him, as I drew the water; but his only answer was to take the handkerchief from around the back of his collar and wipe his forehead with it. I noticed he was pulling away at a cob pipe too fast and too hard to be enjoying it.

I drew the water, filled the radiator, and gave Claudie a drink, all the time watching Mr. Bass out of the corner of my eye. He never looked my way again until I went back to the veranda to return the bucket and see what was bothering him. By that time I knew that he needed help. Whatever it was, I knew I could do it — or have Claudie do it. I put the bucket back on the well casing, made the well rope up into a nice, smooth, even coil; then I went over to where Mr. Bass was sitting.

"That's a mighty nice bunch of dogs you've got there, Mr. Bass — mighty nice," I opened up.

"I like 'em pretty fair," he said; but I could see his heart was not in it. Still, I thought, he was getting a lot friendlier for a man that was paying me almost no mind at all.

About this time the hinge on the front gate gave out its complaining whine, and through the gate strode a great big, rawboned young guy, who came up the walk between the crepe myrtle bushes. He was wearing boots, a big shiny sheriff's star, and two pistols. One of the pistols was pearl-handled.

If I had any thoughts about getting away, they didn't last long. He was there between me and the car, and he was the man with the guns. I couldn't figure any way but to give up if it was I and Claudie he was after, so I just stood there by Mr. Bass. Up to that time nobody had told me to sit down.

As the sheriff came up the steps, I looked beyond the gate, and there alongside our Ford was the sheriff's car. In the front seat there was a bareheaded girl, and in the bright sunshine I could see that her hair was the color of cornsilk. Claudie was still sitting in our car, looking straight at her, and she was looking the other way. Something very familiar about the way she looks, I thought to myself. It was vague, but it was there.

"Come on in, Sid," Mr. Bass called out to the sheriff. "Come up and have this extra chair."

The sheriff said, "Howdy, Mr. Bass," and sat down. Nobody said anything to me, so I went to the well and drew another bucket of water. All the time, though, I could see the big sheriff eying me around the corner of his red mustache. I sat down at the far end of the veranda by the well and listened.

"The timber thieves are out of hand again, Sid," Mr. Bass was saying. "That's why I sent for you."

"I know it, Mr. Bass," the sheriff answered. "There ain't even enough dogwood left in the forest to bring them Garden Club ladies up any more. They are stealing dogwood to make ax handles."

"The timber thieves are in the white oak now," Mr. Bass went on. "They cut several thousand feet this past month and sold it in Beaumont. For barrel staves. And now they're cutting some pine. They burn the stumps so the evidence will be gone. What are you going to do about it?"

"Hit's mighty, mighty hard to get a conviction any more since the Legislature made timber stealin' a felony, Mr. Bass. You know we used to keep old Hooks Butler in jail about half the time when it was only a misdemeanor. Juries will send a man to jail for thirty days for timber stealin', but it hain't serious enough a crime to send a man to the penitentiary; they just won't do it."

Mr. Bass looked glum for a while; then his face began to get redder and redder. "Sid Cotton," he said to the sheriff, "I spent a thousand dollars to get that law passed. I knew that Hooks Butler and his sorry kin were causing all the trouble, and I thought we could keep them all in jail for a long time. I pay you $50 a month and get you deputized, and still things get worse and worse. If you don't go do something to stop that stealin', I'm going to fire you. Good-by!"

The sheriff left without even looking my way again. He and the bareheaded girl were driving off in front of a cloud of red dust when Mr. Bass turned around my way and said, "You still here?"

That's when I made my move, and with the sheriff gone, my mind was working like greased lightning. "Mr. Bass," I said, looking him straight in the eye, "what you need is a first-class evangelist. Yes, sir," I said, taking the chair that the sheriff had vacated, "these timber thieves need a good, old-time, knock-down, drag-out revival; they need to be 'saved.' "

I'll bet Mr. Bass hadn't looked any better in weeks than he did when this idea started to percolate. He just sat there and watched a swarm of gnats that hung in the air there by the cistern until his face brightened up like a coal-oil lantern when the wick is high. That sour, bilious look went away; and he turned to me and said, "What faith is hardest on stealin'?"

"The Apostolic," I told him, and now he was listening. "You see, Mr. Bass," I went on, "a very kind fate must have brought me here. I go about in this world just helping people. You might be too close to the forest to see the thieves. I can cure this stealing."

"You might be right. What did you say your name was?"

"Hightower, *Reverend* Clint C. Hightower," I said, speaking from a point far down below my collarbone.

"You mean you can handle a revival?"

"That, sir, is my specialty," I said, standing and folding my hands firmly behind my back end. "When do I start?"

We haggled over the price for an hour. I reminded him how much money he had spent for no results at all, and he argued that he did not know how much better I could do than the sheriff had done. I agreed that it might take a little time. We both decided that nothing would do the job short of a two weeks' revival in the Turkey Trot neighborhood; it was right down in the middle of the whole nest of Butlers, the worst timber thieves of the lot. Mr. Bass let it out that there had not been a revival down there in eleven years, so I got the price up a little more to pay for the backsliding I would have to undo. He finally agreed to pay me $100 a week for the work, in addition to the collection plate, and a bonus of $100 more if we could convert old Hooks Butler himself. Claudie was to do the singing, which I agreed would be bass or better. Then it took me the last hour to talk our new boss into a $25 advance.

I and Claudie drove down to Houston that night. It was about dark when we got there, and we went to a little café down on Congress Avenue to get ourselves a beer or so and a bite to eat.

"Claudie," I said, after a couple of beers, "Mr. Bass has got a real place for us up there."

"How?"

"His community is steeped in sin."

Claudie put his glass down and looked at me like an old pig looks at a new gate.

"Clint," he said, "I ain't agonna do it; when it comes to sin, I draw the line."

I explained to him that we were not going to promote any sin; we were going to stop one of the worst sins of all — stealing. Then I told him how, and it almost seemed to scare him. He hummed and hawed some about singing in a revival, but he agreed to it when I told him I would give him a full half of all the collections. Naturally, I didn't mention Mr. Bass's bonus. Claudie was suspicious at first about getting this full half cut of the collection plate. You don't have to be smart to be suspicious, you know. But I told Claudie the beer had just made me overly generous, and I agreed to handle all the preaching.

"You can still sing, can't you, Claudie?" I asked. Claudie answered by singing off a few bars of a song he had learned in the wrong part of Fort Worth. His voice seemed fuller and stronger than usual with all that beer foaming up in it, and pretty soon all the customers in the place were staring at us. You, would hardly think so, but there was a very good side even to this. One of the customers was our old friend Jules Rabinowitz, the Persian Prophet from New Orleans. It was the first time we'd seen Jules since he'd told us a couple of years before about the Louisiana law being after us. Jules came over to our table and stated that we were going about things in such a way as to get booted out in the street if we didn't quiet down. Claudie quit singing, and I asked Jules to sit down and have a beer with us.

First, I asked him how business was with him; then, before I heard his answer, I put the question to him that had been bothering me ever since we'd left Louisiana in such a hurry. Had he ever heard what it was the law wanted us for in New Orleans? Claudie chimed in and said he wanted to know too.

"Sure, fellows," Jules said. "It came up right after I seen you all the last time. The trial, I mean. They got me, and so they didn't need you two any more. Those cops were looking for character witnesses for a character called Aunty Blossom. She was tried for vagrancy or something like that — you know, no visible means of support, they said. She had all her friends subpoenaed to testify about her good reputation. Came clear, too."

"You mean that's all they wanted with us?" I heard myself ask.

"That's all," Jules said; then, to me — and, I could tell, to Claudie too — the whole world looked level again.

2

We spent nearly a week and most of the twenty-five dollars in Houston. We had a fine time. I got a Gideon Bible and a black frock coat for myself and bought Claudie a haircut. Then we went to the Turkey Trot job.

Our revival got away to a mighty slow start. In fact, it was nearly left at the post when the weather faired off the day the services began, and the catfish got to biting at night on Big Sandy Creek, which runs right through the Turkey Trot neighborhood. We didn't have enough congregation that first Sunday night to make a ring in a boardinghouse bathtub. There were a few of the womenfolks, sitting here and there and fanning themselves with palm-leaf fans, while the children fussed or slept under the pews. All but three of the men stayed outside the tabernacle; they stood around in little groups smoking and talking in low tones. We found out after the services that not one of Hooks Butler's tribe was there.

The next day it rained a gully washer, and the creek got up half-bank full and too muddy for even catfishing. There was a good deal of lightning and thunder — sharp, gashy streaks of zigzag flashes and rough, rumbling thunder, clapping close up and bouncing away over the piny hills until it played out in a threatening mutter far away.

There is nothing like an electrical storm to stir up a revival meeting. We had a fine attendance the next night, with the tabernacle over half filled, nearly all the men inside, and three Butlers in the congregation — but not old Hooks.

Sid Cotton, the sheriff, was there with his wife; and she was certainly a beautiful thing, with big blue eyes, peachy complexion, and honey-colored hair. There was something striking about the way her hair grew away from her high forehead that seemed almost familiar, like a picture that just fills the molds of your fancy and so gives you a feeling of dim recognition. It hit me the same way it had when I saw her in front of Mr. Bass's house.

The singing was better than I had hoped for. Claudie stood up there, with his hair parted way over on one side and his shoes laced all the way up, and sang loud and sweet. You know, there is something about good, loud, full-voiced country singing of religious songs, such as "Rock of Ages" and "Faith of Our Fathers," that makes feelings rise up in you like yeast in a churn by the fire, and sends tingles out to the ends of your fingers. I knew we were getting somewhere.

It must have been Wednesday or Thursday of the first week that we had our first flurry of trouble. About nine o'clock or ten in the morning, I was on my way to the tabernacle to get a song book when I met that lovely girl, the sheriff's wife. I stopped, and she stopped, and we looked at each other for a minute or so before either of us spoke.

"Sister Cotton," I said, not wishing to lose any more time, "what's your first name?"

"Lurline." She almost smiled as she said it.

"Lurline," I said, "you look so beautiful to me that it is almost like recognizing a fond old dream of beauty."

Then Lurline's smile froze, and she said, "You ought to recognize me, Mr. Hightower; you're the fellow that took Pappy's order for a lightning rod in Mississippi about two years ago, but the lightning rod never came. I was the oldest daughter, and you made a pass at me only ten minutes after you came to our house."

"Oh, Claudie!" I yelled. Claudie was in the car. "Come here, quick." Then I remembered it all from that hard winter we'd spent in Mississippi after Claudie lost his job on the Budweiser wagon. I was glad too that the lightning rod orders had all been C.O.D.

Claudie came quick and said, "How d'ya do, Sister Cotton."

She said, "How d'ya do." It was frigid.

"Claudie," I went on, "don't you remember Sister Cotton? Her father's lightning rod order is the one you lost over in Mississippi, Remember?"

Claudie just looked dumb and said, "Did I?" Sometimes I could kill him, and this was strictly another one of those times.

"Of course you did. The thing has been worrying me these two long years. Now we can clear everything up." I turned to Lurline and said with all the dignity I could work up at the time, "Kindly hand me your father's address, Lurline, and I'll have the lightning rod sent to him. It must still be in New Orleans, ready to be shipped."

"You can't," she said, looking me straight in the eyes, and not batting hers at all. "He's dead."

"I'm awful sorry," I told her. "What did he die of?"

"He got struck by lightning." Then she turned and walked away without another word. But she looked back once as she left.

Claudie wanted to leave Texas right then. He said he'd had enough, and I figured I'd had too much to know what

I wanted to do. We went over to the blacksmith's house where we were boarding, and Claudie started putting our clothes in the suitcase. Right in the middle of it I told him to quit. "Claudie," I said, "I know women pretty well. If she just suspected us, she'd talk about it, and these people would tar and feather us both and ride us out of Turkey Trot on a rail. But Lurline has got us both dead to rights, and she knows it. I'll bet she doesn't squeal on us. I'm going to stay, and I can't stay without a singer."

I must have sounded a lot surer about things than I really was, because Claudie said, "Well, you're gonna bet a lot," and started unpacking our things. He had us unpacked by the time he'd said it.

That night at the services, Sid Cotton, wearing his sheriff's star, and the lovely Lurline sat on the front row. It was plain that she had said nothing to anyone, and I want to put it down right here and now that she looked so sweet and pretty to me that it made me wish all over that I had not gone to some of the places I'd been to or done some of the things I'd done in my time. She might have been just the farmer's daughter a few years before, and a bareheaded blonde a few days ago, and a neighbor's wife to covet until that morning, but she was the angel Lurline to me that night. I wanted to go out and fight a dozen wildcats with my bare hands, just to keep her from having to hear their ugly mewing. I couldn't have preached a sermon that night if hell had been next door, so we sang an extra number of songs and gave over the rest of the time to calling on members of the congregation to volunteer and testify about what the Lord had done for them. It began to sound like a liquid asset to hear those old nesters get up and talk right out in a crowd like that about the Lord's blessings. I knew that timber stealing would not mix much with this sort of religion.

One of the Butlers spoke of the running sores he'd had all one spring, and he had been cured by faith. One dear old lady had had fits, chills and fever, for "nigh onto a year." She was cured too. Next, her husband got up to testify after she had nudged him. He had had the liquor taste, and when he got full he had delirium tremens, and the Old Scratch used to come and poke him in the rear with a pitchfork. He couldn't get rid of the habit or the Old Scratch until he joined the church. Right after that, five shoats he had lost had come back. The schoolmarm got up and cried and said that once when she was in Chicago in summer school, she had gone astray with a man who ran a billiard hall. She was pretty complete about it, and she went into so many details that I was afraid for a while that she was not making anyone want to go to heaven; she was only making the menfolks want to go to Chicago. She vowed and declared that after she joined the church she had not been astray a single time. What a pity, I thought; then I found myself plumb jolted by what I'd been thinking. "Clint," I said to myself, "you damned, dirty, hypocritical dog, you do this for money that you can do nothing with but spend; still these people believe you. Where the hell are you headed?"

But I had to get on. I had taught Claudie a little speech and rehearsed him in it. This seemed to be a good time for it.

"Dearly beloveds," I said, "my colleague, Brother Claudie Hughes, has not spoken to you of his struggles in the clutches of sin. He is a shy man, and he does not like to talk about it, but I will ask him to tell you of the long, thorny path he followed back to grace. Once he was steeped in sin." I turned and pointed to Claudie, like the referee points toward the champion at a prize fight. I could feel the drama of it all tingling its way right up my backbone and out through the end of the finger I was pointing. Claudie looked scared.

"Brother Claudie was once a common thief," I told them. I shuddered, and Claudie shuddered, and people in the congregation all shuddered and looked at each other. I looked at all the Butlers there, and they shuddered too.

"Yes," I said, "a common thief. The blackest sin in the catalogue. Taking that which belonged to others, and depriving them of it against the peace and dignity of the state. Tell them, Claudie," I said, "tell them all about what happened to your awful stealing ways when you gave your heart to God."

"I quit," Claudie said. Then he looked at me the way a man in quicksand might, forgot the rest and sat down.

"Let us pray," I said.

Saturday night after the meeting broke up, I and Claudie counted up the first week's collection and divided it fifty-fifty, just as we had agreed. It amounted to $18.80 each. Then, after Claudie went on to bed, I drove up to Mr. Bass's house, collected my hundred dollars for the first week, and asked Mr. Bass what effect the revival was having on the timber stealing.

"It's dried up down around Turkey Trot," he said, "but there is trouble up north of here a few miles."

"Too bad; I'm sorry," I said, but I was thinking all the time about making this thing into a job that might last all winter.

"Yes," he went on, "I just sent Sheriff Sid Cotton up

there to lay out in the woods all night for 'em and try to catch one red-handed."

"I see," I said. "Good night, Mr. Bass."

3

It was around ten o'clock, or maybe a little later, when I got to the sheriff's house, but the light was on and Lurline was still awake. Somehow she didn't seem surprised as she came out, and we sat in the old Ford and talked. It was a prime fall night with a thin sliver of a new moon lying back of the pine trees and just a few soft, fluffy clouds like uneven bolls of open cotton floating by on the south wind. Somewhere in the distance a mockingbird sang in the night, and I said to Lurline, "Nobody but God could set up a night like this." Lurline just sat there and looked sweet and very sad. After a while I went on. "Lurline," I said, "do you mind if I call you Lurline?"

"No," she replied, softly, but I knew something was eating on her inside. She was so beautiful and her hair looked so fine and silky in the pale light of the moon that I felt myself stinging all inside the way you do when you work one of those electric shocking machines for a nickel.

"Lurline," I said, "how would you value the love of an honest man?"

Lurline looked at me for a moment or so, with a speck of a kindly gleam in her eye, and then she seemed to stiffen as she said, "An honest man? What difference could that possibly make to you? What were you doing up at Mr. Bass's house tonight?"

"Why, I wasn't — " I started, and then I knew that she

knew how I found out that Sid was away and was not coming back that night. I knew, too, that I'd have to do some tall talking before she figured the rest of it out — my deal with Mr. Bass and all. . . . Then, somehow, I knew at once that there wasn't any use; that wouldn't do. So I said, "Lurline, there's no point in pretending to you any more. You know I'm no good. I'm bogus. I'll leave. Thanks for keeping mum about me and Claudie and the lightning rod. You're the finest, sweetest woman I ever saw, and I love you. Good-by."

By this time I was hanging my head and feeling much worse than a sheep-killing dog looks. Usually, when I look down, and then look up, I have a pretty good idea of what I'll see, but this time I was dead wrong. When I looked up, there was Lurline putting her arms around me, and there was Lurline in my arms and a tear glistening on her cheek in the light of the new moon.

You can take all the fresh sweetness of the new green buds in the springtime, and the soft purple peace of twilight in the woods in winter; you can take the relief that it is to drink cold buttermilk of a hot summer evening when you're tired, or the rising beauty that hums and buzzes in you when you hear sung the old songs you heard in childhood. You can roll all these into one and smother it in the sweet scents kissed from a million hyacinths, and that's the way I felt that moment with Lurline in my arms. I kissed her and held her and my heart went sailing up into my throat like a tightrope walker in pink silk tights is lifted to the top of the circus tent while the drums roll. Then Lurline pulled herself away and ran back to the house.

4

The next day was Sunday, and I preached a stem-winding sermon to them that made the woods ring. Lurline was there on the front row again, with Sid, the sheriff.

That was the night that Hooks Butler came for the first time. He got there late and sat way back, but I knew who he was before anybody told me. He was one-eyed, and he carried his head a little to one side so that it gave him the same look of alert slyness you see in certain dumb animals. His face had a sharp, thin hardness about it that I figured you could almost chop wood with. He never took any part in the singing.

All of a sudden I decided on a double header; two texts and all. "Be sure your sins will find you out" and "Thou shalt not steal." It seemed to be the only fair way to give Mr. Bass his money's worth — and mine, because this might be my one and only shot at the Butler bonus.

Two hours and fifteen minutes later I finished with the best descriptions I could give them of the sharp, crackly tongues of hell's fire, blazing blue and licking away at a bunch of thieves and Judas Iscariot. When I sat down I was in a lather.

There was a fair sprinkling of "Amens" in the congregation, and Claudie led the singing off, while I panted and shooed the gnats away. As we all sang, I could see by the lights of the coal-oil lamps that there were tears on the cheeks of some of the ladies. Then I looked at Lurline, and right away I wanted her bad. The thing that happens to people in songs and poems and storybooks had already happened to me — but she was married to the sheriff.

Then I looked at old Hooks Butler, and he was actually singing. "Clint," I said to myself, "strike while the iron is hot; extend the invitation to that old buzzard out there. There's a hundred dollars in it." So I spoke up between songs and asked them to come and be saved. I let them have it with all the stops out, and eight more people hit the sawdust trail and got themselves saved, bringing the total to seventeen for the duration of the meeting. Three were Butlers too, but not old Hooks.

After they were all gone that night, I and Claudie sat on the front pew and talked awhile. Claudie said he'd heard me talk myself into places where I didn't belong and out of places I ought to have kept in, he'd heard me argue politics in Tennessee, he said he'd heard me outtalk Ferd Schultz when he wanted to shoot us and Mr. Wigginbotham when he wanted to run us off the place, but he'd never before heard me so good as I was in my sermon that night. I told him his singing was first-rate, and think I must have meant it, too.

"Clint," he said, "you know what I almost done tonight?"

"No, Claudie," I said, "what's that?"

"Well," he said, "I near about got saved. I damn near hit the sawdust trail myself."

"You fool," I said. "You dope, that would have really ruined things!" But I thought about what Claudie had said until I went to sleep.

The next week the weather got fair again, and the creek cleared up, but the Turkey Trot folks kept coming to the revival anyhow. Hooks Butler never missed another meeting. Tuesday night he came up to the rostrum to shake my hand after the services, but I could see he wouldn't have done so if he hadn't been convoyed up by his old lady. She told me how much good they had got out of my sermon on "Love thy neighbor as thyself." Hooks just fidgeted and hurried away, looking down.

The following morning I and Claudie were working over the pump on the organ that had sprung a leak when I saw Lurline coming toward the tabernacle. She held her head high and her walk was quick and firm, so I could see that this was no ordinary call.

"Go ahead with the organ, Claudie," I told him. "I'm going out to speak to Sister Cotton."

"Clint," she said, in a scared, trembly voice, "somebody saw us Saturday night."

"Who?" I asked.

"Old Granny Strickland. She lives about a mile down the road, and she was out looking for her cat."

"Did she tell anybody?"

"Yes, Clint; she told Sid this morning, but I told him she was crazy. She has awful spells, anyhow, and Sid ain't sure yet. I knew I'd better find you before Sid did."

"Lurline," I said, and my heart that was pounding in my chest took over, "we had better get in that Ford and see how quick we can get how far. I love you, and you know it. You love me too. There's going to be trouble here, and I'll take you somewhere where nothing can hurt us because we will be together."

She looked at me for a long time, and I knew I was seeing exactly what I wanted to see in her eyes; then she said, "No, Clint, it wouldn't be right."

5

Saturday night was the last night, and up to that time we had a total of fifty-four dollars and twenty-nine converts. All we needed to shoot the moon was to save Hooks Butler, and he was on hand early. Mr. Bass came, too, and sat way over at the right, a little away from all the others. Sid and Lurline came later and sat over by him.

Claudie led them in the songs we had picked out from the way our customers had sung them before. My text was one I had saved for this last chance — my last chance with Hooks, and Hooks's last chance with God. It was "The wages of sin is death." Before I started, I thought, Hooks, you damned old thief, tonight you're my meat.

I began by telling them how God and man despised all hypocrites — people who would sit in church on Sunday and steal during the week. I told them how sin and deception ate away at the soul, like the boll weevil eats the cotton boll. I gave them some Beatitudes I had learned from my grandmother, the Twenty-third Psalm, and a whole passel of proverbs. I worked in a passage or two that I'd once memorized from *Black Beauty* and then some of the things Little Eva said before she passed out in *Uncle Tom's Cabin.* The words crowded and flowed like a spring branch after a quick shower when I told them about the awful death of the spirit that is steeped in sin and hypocrisy. I told them stealing was the worse sin of all, and then I asked all sinners to come and repent and be saved. Claudie led them in singing "Almost Persuaded," and Hooks Butler pulled out from his pew and started down the aisle.

"There comes one hundred dollars," I said to myself,

and looked at Mr. Bass, who was looking at Hooks. When Hooks came up to shake my hand, the tears were streaming down his face — even from his bad eye. Someone shouted, and the others took it up, and then the music stopped. Seeing Hooks Butler converted was no mere incident in the Turkey Trot community. You wouldn't do it right by calling it an event. It was an epoch.

"Brother Hightower," he said to me, "you are a man of God. I want to be like you." He cried some more and scratched himself about the back of the neck; then he sat down on the mourner's bench with his head in his hands.

I had no words to reply to Hooks Butler. After a bit, things quieted down, and I wanted to say something, but still I could not for the life of me. So I looked at Claudie, and he started singing, in soft and mellow tones, "Shall We Gather at the River." The others joined, and the piny woods around the tabernacle were all in tune with the singing.

When the song was ended, Mr. Bass got up and told how proud he was that the revival was such a big success. Then he turned to the congregation and said that the tabernacle looked pretty old and worn-out to him. He said he certainly would like to see a new one built, and there was a lot of solemn nodding.

"Very well," Mr. Bass went on, "it can be done for six hundred dollars, and I will give half of it. I am ready to write my check for three hundred dollars." There was quite a stir in the congregation, a lot of whispering, and a quickening in the movement of the palm-leaf fans as another shouting humor came over the congregation.

As soon as the shouts died away, Hooks Butler rose to his feet and said, "I'll give a hundred dollars," and with this

Granny Strickland fainted dead away. We took up a collection that produced about a hundred more. Then I realized that the Hooks Butler bonus Mr. Bass owed me would put us over the top.

"Peace," I said, "dearly beloveds, we only need a hundred more, and that is the amount of my contribution." This really created a stir. Someone started singing, "Praise God from Whom All Blessings Flow." I looked at Lurline, and there was a glow in her face; her eyes were shining; in Lurline's look nothing was held back.

Claudie was stunned by what I'd said. He came over to the pulpit, grabbed me by the coattail and whispered, "Where in the hell are you going to get a hundred dollars?"

"Claudie," I replied, "trust in me and trust in the Lord." He went on back to his singing, but it sounded a little blurred from then on.

There was a heap of rejoicing and handshaking and everybody loved the Lord and everybody else that night as the meeting broke up. It was a good, sweet, weepy occasion all around; and everybody was very happy.

Among the last, Lurline came up to the rostrum to tell me good-by. When she shook my hand, she left a note in it, and the first chance I got, I went over to one side and read it. It was short:

> I'll go with you — anywhere. Be here at the tabernacle at daylight tomorrow if you want me.

"Clint," I said to myself as I read and reread the note in the dim coal-oil light, "you never did believe all of the Bible story of Joseph in Egypt. Remember how you choked on that part about Joseph when he was made a pass at by Potiphar's wife? Well, here is one that is happening to you in Texas, Clint, and you are not going to believe the way this one comes out either."

I and Claudie went back to our room, where he packed our things. We told the blacksmith and his wife good-by and drove down the road that leads from Houston to New Orleans. We drove along for an hour or more in the direction of New Orleans before I or Claudie said anything. Along about midnight Claudie said, "Clint, you are awful smart, but I think I might go back to Alabama next week and help Pappy gather the cotton crop."

I did not answer right off. We got a tank full of gasoline at a filling station in Lake Charles; and while Claudie checked the air in the tires I reckoned by the road map that by daylight we could be in New Orleans — or we could turn around and be back at the tabernacle in the Turkey Trot community. Lurline would be there, I knew.

"Claudie," I said, "drive us on to New Orleans tonight, will you? Close the cutout and don't go too fast; I want to meditate."

The End

DOUBLE MOUNTAIN BOOKS

Classic Reissues of the American West

Alkali Trails: Social and Economic Movements of the Texas Frontier, William Curry Holden

Texas Panhandle Frontier, Revised Edition, Frederick W. Rathjen

Big Ranch Country, J. W. Williams

www.ingramcontent.com/pod-product-compliance
Lightning Source LLC
Chambersburg PA
CBHW050502260626
47157CB00004B/1149

9780896724297